I0653261

Half of the Puzzle

by

Ann Worthington

aventine press

Copyright © 2022 Ann Worthington
First Edition

Without limiting the rights under copyright reserved above,
no part of this publication may be reproduced,
stored in or introduced into a retrieval system, or transmitted,
in any form or by any means (electronic, mechanical,
photocopying, recording, or otherwise),
without the prior written permission of both
the copyright owner and the publisher of this book.

Published by Aventine Press
55 East Emerson St.
Chula Vista CA 91911

www.aventinepress.com

ISBN: 978-1-955162-11-1

Printed in the United States of America
ALL RIGHTS RESERVED

Acknowledgements:

A heartfelt thank you to the ear y readers of this book: Amy Hanacek, Amy McCoy, and Lee Watson. I am grateful for your encouragement and support.

I also want to thank Laurie Viera Rigler, an outstanding book editor and writing coach. Your suggestions and critique helped shape this story. I appreciate your advice and wisdom.

Chapter

1

If I don't make the golf team, I'll never see my dad again. At least that's the way it feels. I've only seen him twice this summer. Without golf, I probably wouldn't see him at all.

My throat tightens as I swallow a sip of water. If I make the high school team, my dad will practice with me and come to my matches like he did last year. And if I don't? The bagel I ate for breakfast feels like an anchor in my stomach. I need to play well for the rest of the round or I'm history.

I approach the thirteenth tee, clearing the static from my brain. I relax my shoulders and focus on the dimples of the small white sphere near my feet. The stress squeezes my chest in a vise, forcing bile into my throat. When my club contacts the ball, it shoots to the right, slicing through the trees and flying out of bounds into the adjacent cemetery. Not again. What's wrong with me? Why can't I hit my driver today?

"I'm hitting a provisional," I say to the other girls, grabbing another ball from my bag and resetting the tee. I take a practice swing and remember my dad's instructions. Line up with your target and cradle the grip like a delicate bird. I push from my mind the image of him walking out the door with his laptop and bulging suitcases. Think about golf, not the divorce.

I steel myself and swing the club. This time, the ball soars high into the air, landing on the right side of the fairway.

"Nice shot, Penn," says Lynda, captain of the varsity team last year.

"Thanks," I say, wishing I had hit it like that the first time.

After the rest of the group hits their tee shots, we walk down the lush expanse of freshly cut grass. Lynda takes the lead, striding out ahead, pushing her new golf cart bag in front of her.

She's wearing a pink and white Lululemon skirt with a matching top. Leila and Emily follow, whispering and giggling to each other. But I can hear them.

"Did you see her hair?"

"What's up with that color?"

"It's so effing ugly."

"I wouldn't be caught dead looking like that."

They're talking about me. Last night, I dyed my hair midnight violet. I love it, and so does my best friend Tara, but my mom freaked out. Why can't she just smile or say something nice? I lag behind, bag strapped over my shoulders. Did my dad leave because Mom was hyper-critical of him, too? I know they argued, but after twenty years of marriage, isn't it easier to stay together?

I need to erase all thoughts of my parents and focus on the next shot, but my mind feels scattered. When I'm home later, I'll organize the clutter on top of my dresser. It's piled with trinkets like barrettes, earrings, bottle caps, bouncy balls, and coins. All items I pick up from the ground. It relaxes me to sort and group the treasure by category.

When I get to where my errant shot vanished out of bounds, I pull out my five-iron and drop my golf bag in the tall grass. I leave the other girls while I search for my ball. They're expensive, and I can't afford to lose another one. I poke around for a minute, visualizing the ball's height and trajectory before it disappeared between the trees into the cemetery.

I've hit into this area before, and sometimes it's lucky. Last week I found a twenty-dollar bill. The eerie silence and aging headstones don't bother me. When I peek around a blue spruce, its prickly needles grazing my arm, I spy a middle-aged man crouched near a grave. He's wearing blue jeans, a flannel shirt, and a baseball cap with the bill pointed backward. I grasp my club and stare as he sifts through the dirt with his bare hands.

When he spots me, he leaps to his feet. "What are you doing here?" he asks, jerking his head from left to right like he's afraid someone else is watching.

"Looking for my ball," I say, taking a small step backward. "Did you see it?"

He shakes his head and narrows his eyes. A tingling sensation moves up my spine to my neck. He has a crazy look in his eye, like a guy who talks to himself in a 7-Eleven parking lot. I plant my feet and grip the club with both hands, raising it like a baseball bat.

He shrieks and scurries away toward the road. I watch him disappear, then turn my gaze to the scattered dirt he left behind. Was he digging a hole? I take a few more steps in that direction, scanning for my ball. I'm ready to give up when I spot it a few yards to the left. As I bend down to grab it, something shiny catches my eye. It looks like a coin or a ring, and a burst of excitement floods my chest. More treasure for my dresser.

I creep closer and a glass vial rests in a small pile of soot. Although partially concealed by a knot of crabgrass, the silver top glimmers in a shaft of sunlight. I pick it up and peer over my shoulder toward the road where the guy disappeared. Dust clings to the bottle, but the label is clear: Lot C5402, Clinical Trials TR-97. My grandma was in a clinical trial, but why is this here in the cemetery? Is it a sign from the universe? I don't have time to figure it out. I need to get back to the group, so I shove the vial into my pocket and hurry back to the fairway, wiping my dirty fingers on my shorts.

For the rest of the round, finding the vial and seeing the guy digging in the dirt distract me. I wish I had found a ring or something valuable, but the vial is kind of cool. My fingers wander to the front of my shorts, touching the lump through the fabric. I've never found anything like it before.

I don't mention it to the other girls, not to Lynda. She would tell me to forget about it and focus on my game. She's right. I'm thirty over par. I won't make the team with a score like that. My dad will be pissed.

When I finish the round, I calculate my total and turn in my card.

Coach Moore frowns. "One-oh-two? Is that the best you could do today?"

"Sorry," I say, unable to meet his eyes. "I had a bad day."

"You've had several bad days in a row, Penn."

I nod. "I'm struggling a bit, especially off the tee, but I'll work on it with my dad this weekend." If he remembers to schedule a tee time and he actually shows up.

"You better. With only one more qualifying round before I choose the team, you'll need to shoot much closer to par to make varsity. I'm not taking any juniors on JV this year."

I bite my quivering lip and nod again. I'm a junior, so varsity is my only chance.

He rests his hand on my shoulder. "Practice more this weekend, and I'll see you Tuesday morning for the final tryout."

"I will," I say, trying to sound upbeat, but the familiar cloud of defeat surrounds me. Last year on JV, I only played in one match and finished last.

I hoist my bag and amble to the parking lot. The vacant bench near the clubhouse entrance welcomes me, and I sit before texting my dad. *I need a ride from the golf course.* My gut tells me he won't respond, at least not right away. I check Instagram and wait.

After several minutes, my phone remains mute. I really don't want to text my mom. After our argument this morning, she'll be annoyed to hear from me. I hesitate, chewing my thumbnail, then text her. *I need a ride.*

While I wait for her reply, I pull the vial from my pocket and examine the label. When my grandma had ovarian cancer, she took part in a clinical trial for a new drug. It didn't work, though. She died last summer.

As I ponder the meaning of TR-97, my mom responds. *I'm showing a house. Where's your dad?*

Idk. I reply. *He didn't respond*

U have 2 wait. Or call a friend.

K, I text. *I'll find someone else*

It may be hours if she has a motivated client. I didn't have to worry about a ride last year. My dad picked me up from every practice. We discussed my progress and made plans to play during the weekend. But those days are over. He and I haven't spoken to each other or played golf together in weeks.

I text Tara. *Can u pick me up?*

On kid duty, she replies. *Can't leave the brats alone*

Kk, I text.

I look up from my phone and watch a parade of girls march to the parking lot. Lynda drives a brand-new Mustang, of course. Grace and Brooklyn ride together in Grace's old Suburban. Anna doesn't even glance at me before lifting her clubs into the trunk of a Tesla. Madison waves to me, but doesn't ask if I need a ride, so I text Mel. *U around? Need a ride from the golf course*

We've been friends since fifth grade when he helped me create a project for the science fair. Maybe he'll rescue me again.

Yes, he replies. *I need a break! C u in 10*

I respond with a thumbs-up emoji.

These days, I depend on Tara and Mel more than either of my parents. When Mom dropped me off this morning, I told her I'd probably need a ride home, and she exploded like it's my fault Dad hasn't been around.

"How can he be busy?" she said. "He's not even working."

"But that's temporary, right?" I asked meekly. He told me he was taking a leave of absence. I hoped we would spend more time together, but not so far. I cradle my phone and try to forget my mom's rant, but it clings to my brain like a wet towel.

"And now the burden falls on me," she said. "I have to take care of the house, do all the parenting, and earn all the money, too."

I squeeze my eyes shut and bow my head, telling myself I'm not a burden. Mom was just angry with Dad. But the image of him emptying his closet and dresser drawers makes my stomach lurch. And why did he have to take the framed photographs from the end table in the living room? I loved the one of him and his friends from the fire academy after graduation. Their smiles radiated confidence, like they owned the world.

I shake my head and sigh, turning my attention to my phone. TikTok will cheer me up.

In a few minutes, the brakes on Mel's ancient car squeal as he pulls up beside me. I stand and open the hatch of the Volvo, hoisting my golf bag inside. Old sneakers, sweatshirts, an umbrella, a few books, boxes, and grocery sacks occupy the back of the wagon.

"You've got a ton of crap back here," I say. "I swear those shoes have been in here since Christmas."

"I know," says Mel. "I promise I'll clean it."

"It's not like you. Are you still moping because Tucker broke up with you?"

Mel leans his hip against the car and stares at the ground. "No."

"Are you sure?" I ask.

"It hasn't been that long."

I raise my eyebrows. "Two months."

"So?"

"That's all summer, Mel. You have to move on."

"I know."

"He wasn't good enough for you, anyway."

"That's true," he says with a slight nod.

I hop into the front passenger seat. "Thanks for getting me. My mom's showing a house."

"No problem. Your hair looks great, by the way. Better than in the selfie you sent last night."

"Thanks. My mom hates it, and the other girls think it's stupid, but I think it kicks ass."

Mel shifts the car into drive and pulls out of the parking lot. "Screw them. It's dope. You could be Leela from Futurama."

"Not what I was going for," I say, "but I'll take it. What've you been up to?"

"Practice exams. My head is spinning. They really try to trick you."

"SAT prep? Still?"

"I need a high score so I can apply to Chicago and Michigan, and maybe Princeton."

"But you have an entire year to take the test."

Mel keeps his hands on the steering wheel but turns his head to look at me. "I know, but I want a good score right away, so I don't have to worry about it. I'll have subject tests and a shit-load of essays to write."

"You're going to do great. You'll get into a bunch of good colleges."

"But I won't have a chance without a near-perfect score."

I fasten my seat belt to stop the annoying dinging, and the bulge in my front pocket draws my attention. "I saw something in the cemetery today," I say. "It creeped me out."

"What were you doing in the cemetery?" he asks. "I thought you were golfing."

"I was, but horribly. On the thirteenth tee, you know the one in back by the enormous elm trees? I hit it out of bounds again."

"Why didn't you let it go? It's just a ball."

I shake my head. "You know I can't afford to buy more balls."

"I'll get you some for your birthday."

"Thanks, smartass."

Mel shudders. "Cemeteries give me the creeps."

"Shocker. You're scared of trick-or-treaters on Halloween."

"Only the zombies and vampires, and anyone who carries an ax or a chainsaw."

I shift in my seat to face Mel. "I saw a guy in the cemetery. He was sifting through the dirt with his bare hands."

"That's messed up."

I nod. "I startled him and he took off."

"Was he homeless?" asks Mel.

"I don't think so."

"Definitely creepy."

"He left a hole near a grave with dirt scattered all over."

"How big was the hole?" asks Mel, stopping at a red light.

I shrug. "I didn't have time to get a decent look."

"Do you think the guy made the hole?"

"I don't know, but I want to go back and get a closer look."

"Why would you want to do that?"

"Because of what else I found." I reach into my pocket and pull out the glass vial.

Mel snickers. "Your long-lost golf ball, I hope."

"This," I say, holding it up for him to see. It's about the size of my thumb.

He squints, then returns his eyes to the road. "What does it say?" he asks.

"CLINICAL TRIALS, TR-97."

"Are those initials? The year nineteen ninety-seven?"

"That's what I want to find out. The vial looks new. It hasn't been sitting in the cemetery for twenty years."

Mel taps his fingers on the steering wheel. "This reminds me of that pendant you found last year."

"I was thinking the same thing. Remember how it was engraved with initials and a date?"

"It took us weeks to figure out who it belonged to."

I smile and nod. "The lady couldn't believe someone found it. And then she gave us a one hundred dollar reward."

"Do you think it's valuable?" he asks.

I hold up the vial again. "Beats me."

"It would be awesome to get another reward."

"I think the guy in the cemetery was looking for it," I say.

"Really?" Mel brakes to let a jogger cross the street.

"We need to go back and check it out. Maybe a gravestone has matching initials or dates."

"Wait a second. *We* need to go back?"

"Yeah, all of us together, like before."

Mel sighs. "Are we going to leave a note near the grave?"

"Should we?"

"It seems risky. Some weirdo could call."

I examine the vial again. "But you need to see the hole."

Mel glances at me and frowns.

"Tara too," I say.

He shakes his head. "Sometimes, I think you're a bit nuts."

I shrug as we turn onto South Hill Drive. "I can't help it if I find cool stuff. I get it from my grandma."

"What did she call you?"

"Her little Blue Jay."

"That's cute, but weird."

"No, it's not." I fake punch Mel in the arm. "She was the raccoon, and we loved to find shiny treasure."

"Okay, fine. When are we going to check out the hole?"

"Tonight after dinner."

"You know that's not really my thing, cemeteries at night."

"But we need you, Mel. You're the brains of the team."

"Thanks, coach."

When we arrive at my house on Marinette Trail, Tara stands outside hers next door. Her three younger brothers play tag and run through a lawn sprinkler in their front yard. Mel gets out to help me with my golf clubs, and Tara joins us near the curb.

"Are you free tonight?" I ask. "We've got a secret mission planned."

"Hell yeah, I'm free," she says. "For once, I don't have to babysit the monsters after dinner."

"Great," I say.

"What's the mission?" she asks. "Are we going to buy beer?"

Mel laughs. "Not unless you have a fake ID."

"This is more exciting," I say. "Besides, if we want beer, we can just take it from my house."

"Cool," says Tara. "Bring some beer tonight."

"Don't you want to know where we're going or what we're doing?" asks Mel.

Before Tara can reply, we're interrupted by shrieking and crying. Two of Tara's brothers hold the youngest one's face in front of the sprinkler.

"Tell me later," Tara shouts, sprinting across the yard to break up the battle.

Mel shakes his head. "I'm so glad I don't have any brothers. An older sister is enough."

"Me, too," I say, knowing that most of the time, I really wish I had a brother or sister.

"I suppose I'm the Uber," says Mel. "What time should I come back for you?"

"Eight o'clock," I say.

"See you at eight."

Chapter
2

I stash my golf bag in the garage and step into the house. The smell of roasting meat tickles my nostrils and I salivate. A bubbling crock pot occupies the kitchen counter. The sink contains a pile of dirty dishes, a cutting board, and several knives. A half-empty bottle of wine sits on the counter. And she thinks I'm a slob?

I ignore the mess and proceed to my bedroom, closing the door. My sweaty body deserves a shower, but I want to Google "TR-97." When I type it in, I get thousands of results, many with the initials and most with the year 1997. The list includes research papers, laboratory reports, and government publications. I add the words "clinical trial" to narrow the search. One result says "it's an interventional trial of a non-randomized group to treat post-traumatic stress disorder." Another says it's "a combination therapy utilized on trauma patients to compare qualitative and quantitative effects." My head spins. I've heard of post-traumatic stress disorder, but the rest sounds like gibberish. I retreat to the shower, letting the hot water and steam clear my thoughts.

Later, I text Tara. *Mel will b here at 8*
K. What should I bring?
Phone. Wear black
Got it

My mom arrives home in time to eat dinner with me. We sit across from each other at the table and when she looks up from her plate of pot roast and potatoes, she sighs.

"What's wrong?" I ask.

"I just wish you hadn't done that to your hair." she says. "It was so pretty."

"And now it's ugly?"

"That's not what I meant."

"What *did* you mean?"

She shakes some salt onto her meat. "People will notice."

"That's kind of the point."

"I'm concerned you'll get the wrong kind of attention."

"What are you talking about?"

"Some people find alternative hair color deviant or scary."

I stop eating and stare at her with my mouth open. "So, you're saying I look scary?"

"No, it's just different."

"Well, in my opinion, different is good."

She purses her lips. "What's done is done. Let's talk about something else. How was golf today?"

"Fine," I say, still stinging from her comment about my hair. "I didn't play very well." I'm not going to tell her about finding the vial.

She takes a sip of wine. "You'll do better next time."

I nod and take another bite. She always says that.

After dinner, I change into a black T-shirt and sweatpants, then study the vial again. Should I bring it with me? Instead, I snap a photo with my phone and tuck the bottle into a pair of white crew socks in the back of my drawer. I'll find a better hiding place tomorrow. I have fifteen minutes to kill, so I toss my dirty clothes into the hamper in my closet and organize the trinkets on my dresser, stacking the coins by size. I check Instagram again and watch a few TikToks.

Precisely at eight, I say goodbye to my mom. She's in her room watching television.

"Where are you going?" she asks.

The door to her room is open a crack, and I poke my head inside. "To Mel's house to watch a movie."

"Did you clean up the kitchen?"

"Yes."

"And your room?"

"Yes."

"Thank you. Be home before midnight," she says.

"I will," I say, backing my head out of the room.

"Nothing good ever happens after midnight."

I don't respond.

In the kitchen, I open the fridge and grab several cans from the twelve-pack on the bottom shelf. Mom mostly drinks wine, so she won't miss three beers. When Mel pulls up to the curb, I climb into the front seat next to him.

"You didn't wear black," I say, scrutinizing his khaki shorts and white t-shirt.

"How was I supposed to know?"

"I thought it would be obvious."

He looks over his shoulder. "I've got a black sweatshirt in the back."

Tara opens the rear door and slides onto the seat. "Did you bring the beer?" she asks. "I really need one."

"Of course," I say, and pass a Heineken back to her. We open the cans, then clink them together as Mel pulls away from the house.

"Keep those out of sight," he says. "It's not exactly legal to drink in the car."

"It's not exactly legal for us to drink at all," I say with a grin.

"And that's what makes it so fun," says Tara.

"Just try to be discreet," says Mel. "I'm only supposed to have one of you in the car."

"Don't worry, we'll be cool," says Tara.

"Where are we going?" asks Mel. "Cemetery or golf course?"

Tara smirks. "Are we hunting for the ghosts of dead golfers?"

"Funny," I say. "I think we should park in the cemetery to avoid the night sprinklers on the golf course."

"Not that I mind because anything's better than being at home," says Tara, "but why are we going to the cemetery?"

I show her the photo on my phone. "I found this today when I was looking for my golf ball."

"What does it mean?"

"It's a drug from an old clinical trial," I say.

"A drug? Like medication?"

I nod. "I looked it up on the internet. They used it to treat trauma patients or for post-traumatic stress. I'm not really sure yet."

"Is the bottle empty?" she asks.

I shake my head. "There's a clear liquid inside."

"Why are we going to the cemetery?" asks Mel. "We should just find more info on the internet."

"We're checking the graves for the year and initials," I say, taking a swig of beer. "Plus, you need to see the hole." I turn back toward Tara. "There was a strange guy in the cemetery today, digging in the dirt near the graves. Since I found the vial nearby, they could be related."

"Sounds like fun to me," says Tara, tipping her can back to receive the last drops of beer.

In a few minutes, we approach the cemetery entrance. The narrow road is deserted and Mel slows the car.

"Turn off the headlights," I say.

"How will I be able to see?" asks Mel.

"It's not that dark. Go slow and turn right up ahead. Follow the road until it T's. Then go right again."

"How will you know if we're in the right spot?" Tara asks. "Didn't you come from the golf course side?"

"Yeah, but this part borders the thirteenth hole."

Tara cracks open another beer. "Thirteenth? I love it. And it's Friday!"

"Don't remind me," says Mel. "I'm not thrilled to be here."

"It'll be fine. We'll stick together," I say, spying the grove of elm trees. "Stop up there. We're close."

We exit the car and Mel slips the black sweatshirt over his head. "Should I lock it?" he asks.

Tara and I look at each other. Nobody is around, but if somebody shows up, we don't want them getting into the car. But if we need to make a quick escape, having the car unlocked is the better option.

"Keep it unlocked," Tara and I say in unison. "Jinx," we say with a laugh, punching each other in the arm.

"Help me finish this," she says, handing me her beer.

I chug the rest and throw the can back inside the car.

Armed with our cell phones, we traipse toward the elms, careful not to trip over the flat headstones. We study the smooth, vertical marble on others. As we creep forward, I envision where I found my ball earlier today.

"It's over there," I say, pointing toward the blue spruce. In a few steps, we see the outlines of a jagged cut in the earth. "Shine your lights on it," I say.

Both Mel and Tara aim their phones in that direction, illuminating the scattered dirt and broken pieces of stone. "Try not to make any footprints."

"Wow," says Mel, tip-toeing around the area to take a photo. "It really is a hole. I thought you were kidding."

"And it's kind of deep," says Tara, approaching the edge and taking another photo. We inch closer and peer inside, aiming our lights into the gap.

"Is somebody going to be buried in that hole?" asks Mel.

"You could if they cremated you," says Tara.

"Or somebody *was* buried there," I say, pushing the tall grass away from the nearest headstone. Mel and Tara look at me.

"HERE LIES GWENDOLYN P. (HUGHES) OLIVER. LOVING WIFE, DEVOTED MOTHER, AND BLESSED DAUGHTER. *1961–1999.*"

"She's not in there anymore?" asks Mel, his voice cracking.

"No, stupid, the hole is empty," says Tara, leaning over and looking straight down. "It's just an open vault."

I take a photo of the gravestone and move closer. "A what?"

"You know, a burial vault."

"Let me see."

"They don't just put you in the ground without protection," says Tara. "They put the urn or box with the ashes into a concrete or stone box."

"And you're sure it's empty?" I ask.

"Absolutely," says Tara. "Someone dug up the dirt, crushed the top of the vault, and removed the urn. That's why these pieces of stone are all over the place."

"Should I stick my hand in there to be sure?" I ask.

Before Mel or Tara can reply, a flash of headlights sweeps through the trees and the low rumble of a motor hits our ears. We freeze like statues as the car stops and the doors open.

"Oh shit," says Mel. "Somebody's here."

"Quick, up toward the golf course," I say, and take off running. Tara and Mel follow, and we drop onto the grass behind the elms. On our knees, we slow our breathing while our eyes strain in the twilight.

"They're going to see my car," says Mel.

"Shhh," I say. "Be quiet."

We hear a female voice first. "Like I said, we need to keep looking."

"Around here?" asks a male.

"Over this way," she says. "I can't believe that fool dropped it."

"You're sure?" asks the man, stumbling in the half-light.

"Yes, you idiot, I know where it is."

They approach the hole, and the guy says, "I'm supposed to fill it?"

"Yes, but put this back in there first." We watch as she hands him a square object that looks like a small box. "We can't leave it empty," says the woman.

"Okay," he says, bending down toward the hole.

"And get rid of this stone." She nudges a few pieces with her foot. "Make it look like nobody was here."

"But the dirt will be obvious," he says. "I can't grow grass overnight."

"Just make it look like the others."

"That's not easy."

"Which is why I'm paying you," she says.

"Got it."

"But first, we need to find the other vial. She said there were two."

Tara, Mel, and I remain rooted behind the trees. We stare at the shadows and listen to the voices.

"How are we going to do that?" he asks. "It's dark."

"Crawl around and look for ashes in the grass."

"What if it's not here?"

"Like I said, we have to find it."

When the pop of the sprinkler heads catches my attention, I whisper, "Cover your phones, we're going to get wet."

Mel squirms and muffles a squeal while Tara curses under her breath. We stay flattened on the ground, getting drenched with water, unable to hear more of the conversation between the man and woman. After what seems like an eternity, the other car's engine starts and the lights move away.

"Oh my god, I'm frickin' soaked!" says Tara, jumping up and leaping around.

"Me, too," I say. "But who the heck was that?"

"Who cares," says Mel, shaking his wet hair. "Let's get out of here."

We wade through the darkness, making our way past the hole and the grave. It looks the same, so we scramble to the safety of the Volvo. For a moment we sit in stunned silence, then everyone talks at once.

"Do you think they saw us?"

"Was that the guy I saw earlier today?"

"Did he put the box back in the hole?"

"What's so important about the vial?"

"Did they take a photo of my car?"

None of us have any answers, and we spend the rest of the ride pondering the scene in silence. When we return to my house, we march to the basement to discuss the situation. My mom is in her bedroom, which is right next to mine. I can hear her talking on the phone.

"I'm not asking you to do everything. Dammit, you told me you'd pay this month's mortgage. But that's not good enough. Stop making excuses."

She's squabbling with my dad, and I debate whether to interrupt. After a long pause in the argument, I knock softly. "I'm home," I say.

She doesn't reply.

I linger outside the door for a moment, then get three towels, and join Tara and Mel downstairs. We sit on the shag carpet, our bodies forming a triangle.

"What should we do?" I ask, blotting my hair with a towel.

Mel peels off his sweatshirt. "Should we report it to the police?" he asks.

"Robbing a grave is a crime, right?" asks Tara.

"We're not sure they did anything," I say.

"Come on, you *know* they did something," says Mel.

I hold up my hands. "Let's think this through," I say. "The police would want to know why *we* were in the cemetery."

"They'll ask a ton of questions," says Mel.

"You'd probably have to tell them about the vial," says Tara.

I shake my head. "I don't want to do that yet."

"Unless they trace my car, nobody knows we were there," says Mel.

"My dad would ground me for life if found out the police wanted to question me," says Tara.

"Okay," I say, draping the towel over my shoulders. "No police for now. What do we know for sure?"

"That we saw an empty grave," says Tara.

"And they're going to put something back in the hole and cover it up," says Mel.

"And they were looking for a vial," I say. "It might be the one I found today."

We stare at each other and I shiver.

"What should we do?" asks Tara.

"We need more info on Gwendolyn Oliver and TR-97."

We grab our phones and start searching.

"Here's an obituary for Gwendolyn Oliver," says Mel. "She was only thirty-eight when she died from breast cancer. Survived by her husband, Doctor James B. Oliver, and their daughter, Sasha."

"Okay. I'll look up Doctor James Oliver," I say. "Tara, you look up Sasha."

"Do you think her last name is still Oliver? What if she's married?"

"Hard to say. Try Oliver first and see what you find."

"I found a ton of stuff on Doctor James Oliver," says Mel, sitting up straighter. "He was a professor at Wisconsin State University, Department of Psychiatry."

"I see that," I say, looking at my phone. "He also worked with patients at the V.A. Hospital. That's a connection to PTSD."

"Did you find an obituary for him?" asks Mel.

"No. You?" I ask.

Mel shakes his head. "Not yet, but it looks like the university fired him in 2013."

"Where are you seeing that?" I scoot closer to him.

He shows me his screen. "This newspaper article talks about the fall from grace of the university's top researcher."

"What happened?"

Mel skims the article. "Ethical problems, patients dying, lawsuits. A real shit-show, my dad would say."

"We need to look into all of that,' I say, turning my focus back to my phone. "What about you, Tara? Any luck on Sasha?"

"Not yet. There are some people named Sasha Oliver, but they don't live around here."

"Keep looking," I say.

"Maybe search by first name only," says Mel. "Sasha isn't a very common name."

"I'll try that in the local *White Pages*," says Tara, hunched over her phone. "Here's someone named Sasha Hughes."

"Hughes?" says Mel. "I recognize that name."

I look up from my phone. "You do?"

"It was on the gravestone."

I pull up the photo. "That was Gwendolyn's maiden name," I say. "Sasha could be Gwendolyn's sister."

Mel scratches his head. "Or it's just a coincidence."

"She lives right here in town," says Tara. "Actually, after putting in the address, someone named Sasha Hughes lives a few blocks away."

"Really?" I lean toward her and study her screen. "Do you think it's her?"

Tara shrugs. "Beats me."

"Send me the address."

"Then try James Oliver," says Mel, looking up from his phone. "See if he has a local address."

After a few minutes, Tara replies. "Nothing on James Oliver in Mendota, but that doesn't mean much. He could live anywhere."

"True," I say, stretching my legs out in front of me. "We've got a lot more research to do."

"But it's getting late," says Tara with a yawn. "I work a double shift at Rocky's tomorrow, so I have to get up really early."

I look at Mel.

"I gotta go, too. Tomorrow is my mom's birthday, and I have tutoring all morning."

"Okay," I say, nodding my head. "I'll carry the load tomorrow. I'm supposed to play golf with my dad, but he hasn't texted. Do we all agree that we do nothing, say nothing, to anyone, about any of this until we have more information?"

"Agreed," says Mel.

"Fine with me," says Tara.

Chapter
3

I wake up early on Saturday, expecting a text from my dad. Nothing. I roll onto my back and stare at the ceiling. He did this last week. What's wrong with him? He used to be so dependable. I'll probably have to go to the stupid driving range by myself.

When I make it to the kitchen, I pour cereal into a bowl and turn on the television. My mom breezes in wearing crisp white slacks and a floral print blouse.

"Another house showing?" I ask, my mouth full of Cheerios.

"Open house today," she says. "Two of them. I'm already late."

I put down my spoon. "But I need a ride to the golf course."

"Isn't your dad taking you today?"

"I haven't heard from him."

She grabs her purse, briefcase, and keys. "Keep trying. I need to go."

"He probably forgot again."

"Then you better remind him."

"Why can't he just remember?"

My mom kisses the top of my head. "If you're ready to go now, I can drop you off, but it has to be right now."

I look down at my rumpled sleep shirt and baggy boxer shorts. "Obviously, I'm not ready."

"Then I'll see you later."

She disappears into the garage, and I slump down in my chair, frowning at my soggy cereal. Last summer, my dad scheduled tee times every week so we could play. As I debate whether to call or text him, a breaking story pops up on the morning news. I reach for the remote and turn up the volume.

"Last night, vandals damaged several headstones here at Westmoreland Cemetery. As you can see behind me, spray paint covers several markers, and others are broken or cracked. There also appears to be digging near some graves. Police have cordoned off the area and are investigating. They will not reveal the names on any of the damaged headstones, but will notify the families of the deceased. If you have any information about this crime, or witnessed anything unusual in the area last night, please contact the Mendota police department."

I stare at the screen for a few moments, recognizing the area. Holy crap! That's where we were last night. Did the guy we heard talking go back and do that? Will he remember seeing Mel's car? What if he reports it to the police? I grab my phone to text Mel and Tara. *Just saw the news! Vandalism at cemetery!*

Mel replies immediately. *News?*

On TV, I text.

Can't check now. Online with my tutor

That's right. Sorry

And Tara's at work

Right

Talk later, texts Mel. He signs off with a puzzled-looking emoji.

I'll give them the details later. Somebody trashed the area after we left. But who? And why? I don't have any idea, so I text my dad. *Are we golfing today?*

I watch more of the news, hoping they'll repeat the story, but they don't. I turn off the television. Even if I want to go to the driving range, I don't have a ride. Everyone is busy.

I dump the mush from my bowl into the sink and flip the switch for the garbage disposal. The metal blades grind and clash, while my phone remains silent. I wish it would spring to life with a text or call from my dad, but no luck.

I stare out the kitchen window and sigh. Maybe it's for the best. A sign from the universe. I won't make the team anyway, so I might as well focus on something interesting. I retreat to my bedroom and close the door. I need more information on TR-97, Dr. Oliver, and Sasha.

After several hours, and no word from my dad, I'm going stir-crazy. School doesn't start for a couple of weeks and I'm already cooped up in my room. I hop on my mountain bike and ride several blocks to the address listed for Sasha Hughes. After Tara shared it with me, I found a few photos on the internet of Sasha Oliver as a teenager. Maybe she doesn't look that different.

I cruise by a tidy, ranch-style house with two large maple trees out front, and take a quick photo. The sunshine and light breeze caress my face as I continue riding to the end of the street, then around the block. When I make it back near the front of the house, a car pulls into the driveway. A woman occupies the driver's seat, and it looks like she has a large crate in the back. She waits patiently for the garage door to open before driving in. As I watch, the garage door descends before she exits the vehicle.

That's odd. It's a beautiful day. Why would you close the garage door before getting out of the car? It makes sense in January or February when it's freezing cold, but in August? Who does that? I take one more lap around the block, pedaling at a leisurely pace. I didn't get a good look at the woman in the car, so I need a plan to meet her face-to-face and see if Sasha Hughes is Sasha Oliver, daughter of Dr. Oliver.

Ten minutes later, I press the doorbell at her house and wait on the front porch, glancing from the door to what looks like a tiny video camera. As I shove my hands into my pockets to keep from fidgeting, a woman's voice crackles from the device. "Can I help you?"

I lean in toward the doorbell. "Hi, my name is Penn. I'm a high school student looking for work walking dogs."

"Hang on," she says.

I stand on the porch and listen to the chip, chip, cheer of a nearby cardinal and search the treetops for the bird. When I don't find it, I study the flowerpots and the new brass light fixture. Damn. She's going to ghost me. As I turn to leave, the door opens a crack. A young woman with freckles and curly auburn hair stands in the gap.

"Sorry," she says. "I was downstairs and couldn't hear you through that thing." She nods toward the doorbell.

"That's okay. I'm Penn. I'm looking for work walking dogs."

"I don't have a dog."

"Any other pets?"

"Nope."

"I also do yard work, housework, and babysitting." I sound desperate, but I need a few more seconds to study the woman's face.

"Thanks, but I don't need any help right now," she says.

"Okay, sorry to bother you."

As I turn to leave, she calls after me. "Hold on a minute."

She disappears for a moment, then returns with a business card. I take the card and read it: "Shorewood Veterinary Clinic."

"I need some help at the clinic, if you're interested."

"Yeah," I say, standing up straighter.

"Stop by this week with your resume."

"I'll do that."

"Okay," she says and walks back inside the house.

"See you later," I say, and give her a wave. I skip to my bicycle and smile. The universe is speaking to me. Based on the old photos, that's definitely Sasha Oliver, now Sasha Hughes.

Later that evening, I convince my mom to order pizza from Rocky's. "We'll get a discount, and Tara can deliver it on her way home from work."

"I guess we can do that," she says, staring at my hair again.

"Would you rather have me shave it off?" I ask, irritated by the look on her face and the tone of her voice.

"Heavens no!"

"Then stop staring at my hair. It's going to be purple for a while."

She frowns and shakes her head, then turns the corkscrew into a bottle of red wine.

When the doorbell rings, I dash to the entry and fling open the door, eager for a friendly face. But instead of Tara holding a large deep-dish pepperoni, it's my dad, standing alone on the front porch.

"Oh, hey," I say, looking around him to the street. "What're you doing here?"

"Hi, sweetie," he says. "What happened to your hair?"

"I ate too much eggplant," I say.

"You did what?"

I raise my eyebrows. "I dyed it."

"You're not turning punk rock on me, are you?"

"What?"

"You know, punk or Goth?"

"It's just hair. Why does it matter what color it is?"

"Sorry," he says. "It's shocking. You should have warned me."

I roll my eyes and glance over his shoulder, searching for Tara's car.

"How's my golfer?" he asks.

"Why are you here?" I ask, still holding the door open.

"It's nice to see you, too." He opens his arms for a hug, and I lean into his body for a moment, then step back.

"I was expecting someone else," I say.

"Not a boy."

"No."

"I came by to pick up the rest of my stuff, and see you, of course."

I frown. "How come you didn't come by earlier or respond to my text? We were supposed to play golf."

"Was that today?" he says, looking at his watch.

"Yeah, it's Saturday. You told me you were going to get a tee time."

"I got caught up with other things. How about next week?"

"You didn't even call." I cross my arms over my chest and scowl.

"You could've called me," he says. "Or scheduled a tee time yourself."

I clench my teeth and glare at him, feeling the heat rise to my face. "I texted you."

"I didn't see it."

"And I couldn't even go to the range to hit balls because I didn't have a ride. I should have my learner's permit by now and be driving like everyone else."

"Don't start with me, Penn. You're not ready to drive."

"I am ready. Everyone I know is ready."

"But you're not, and that's the only thing that matters."

The fever in my face expands to my chest. "What do you want from me? I'm responsible. I get good grades."

"But that's not enough," he says.

"It's so stupid. I'm sixteen. I should be driving."

"Trust me, you're not ready."

"That's so lame. If I don't make the golf team, it's going to be *your* fault."

"Why is it *my* fault?" he asks.

My voice rises in pitch. "Because you don't drive me to practice anymore."

"Driving is really dangerous. Teenagers are more likely to die in car accidents than any other age group."

"All my friends drive, and no one gets hurt. Even the losers who get D's in school can still pass the frickin' driving test."

"Don't argue with me, Penn. My decision is final. You'll learn to drive when you're eighteen."

"Whatever," I say, turning my back on him and stepping inside. "You never listen anyway." As I escape to my bedroom, my mom appears at the front door.

"What's going on?" she asks.

"She's mad at me," he says.

Even closing the door to my bedroom doesn't prevent their shrill words from reaching my ears.

"You could've called first instead of just showing up," says my mom.

"But this is still my house, and I should be able to see my daughter."

"You can see her anytime, but you need to communicate with her, and with me."

"I'm right here in front of you, ready to communicate."

"Don't be an ass. You didn't let us know."

"What's the big deal? I have to tell you everything?" he asks.

"A simple text goes a long way."

"I don't need to text before coming to my house."

"But you don't live here anymore,' she says. "You moved out."

I should go out there and beg them to stop, but I'm paralyzed by their squabbling.

My dad's voice rises. "But my name is on the deed, so it's still my house."

"If this is *your* house, when are you going to pay some bills?"

"Listen, Maggie, I've got bills of my own."

"And so do I," shrieks my mom. "Plus expenses for Penn. I'm working overtime to make ends meet."

"Forget it. I can't do this. Let the lawyers handle it."

"Jesus, Jason. Don't you see? Penn is really upset."

"She'll get over it. She's *not* ready to drive."

"I'm not talking about that."

"Then what's wrong with her?"

"You didn't call her about golf," she says.

"I was busy, okay?"

"It's not okay. Penn feels like she's not an important part of your life anymore."

"There you go again, doing what you do best. Piling on the drama. Making me feel guilty."

"I'm not making you feel anything, but if you feel guilty, it's probably because you screwed up."

I cringe as my dad shouts. "I did *not* screw up."

"No one's perfect, but you should apologize to her."

"Don't tell me what to do! I don't take orders from you."

"Fer chrissakes, Jason. Calm down. It's a suggestion about how to help the situation."

"Well, I don't need your help or your bullshit. I just came by to get my things."

"Then get your shit and get out."

I want to burst through my bedroom door and scream at both of them. How can they do this to each other? How can they do this to me? To calm myself, I think about my grandma and sort through the junk on top of my dresser. Along with my treasures, I keep a framed photograph of my dad and me when I was nine. We had just built the tree house in the backyard, and my sparkling eyes and wide smile say it all. I had the best dad in the world.

But now, tears well up in my eyes as I listen to him trudge up and down the basement stairs. His life no longer revolves around me. I go to the window and watch him carrying boxes, a rusty floor lamp, and the old card table and chairs to his truck. He cares about that crap, but not about me. I press my fists against my eyes so I won't cry. When the truck is loaded, my dad glances at my window and gives a half-hearted wave goodbye. I want to lift my arm and wave back, but my limbs have stiffened like concrete. After he backs down the driveway and drives away, I turn toward my bed and fall in a heap.

I smother my face with my pillow, unleashing a wounded howl into the lumpy folds of foam and cotton. Soon, my screams turn to sobs, and I surrender to the avalanche of tears. I'm tumbling down the mountain, being battered by the rocks. Broken into pieces. I'm barely able to breathe as I choke on my tears. When it's over, I lie motionless on the bed, wishing the pain in my chest would disappear. Please let me go back to when I was nine. I just want to laugh and play and have a dad who loves me.

My eyes are still closed when a gentle knock sounds on the door.

"Penn? Honey? Are you okay?"

"Yeah," I say.

"The pizza is here. Tara brought it by."

"I'm not hungry."

"Can I come in?"

"Why?"

"I want to talk to you for a moment and give you a hug."

I get up and open the door for her. My mom changed out of her work clothes and wears jean shorts and her old college sweatshirt. She pulled her hair back into a loose ponytail. We gaze at each other through red puffy eyes, then wrap our arms around each other. We linger, savoring the warmth of mother and daughter. I can smell the wine on her breath when she speaks.

"It's going to be okay. We'll get through this together."

I embrace her again, sniffling and wiping my nose on my sleeve.

"I don't get it," I say, swallowing the ache in my chest. "Why is he that way?"

"I don't know."

"He never calls, but when he shows up, he's angry, like it's my fault."

"It's not your fault."

"I never know what to expect."

She strokes my hair, pushing it behind my ears. "I understand, honey. It's tough right now."

"We used to be a family."

"We're still a family."

"We used to do things together, go camping and biking and building the tree fort."

She glances at the photo. "I remember that day. He was so excited when the trap door worked."

"Thanks to me," I say.

"Yes, you like to solve problems."

"Remember how Dad created those scavenger hunts for me?"

"He was very creative."

"I couldn't wait to figure out another riddle."

She manages a feeble smile. "You were determined to find the answer."

"And how he thought it was important that I learn to play golf? We played all the time. And now, it's all gone to crap."

"It's complicated, honey," says my mom, picking up my eighth-place trophy from the city junior golf tournament last summer. "But he still loves you."

"It's so unfair."

"Lots of things in life aren't fair."

"But why is he like that?" I ask.

"I don't know."

"He's two different people. Normal and friendly one moment, then moody and angry the next."

She hands me a tissue. "I know."

"Is it because of the accident?" I ask.

"I think so."

I dab my eyes and blow my nose. "Why won't he get help? Can't he see a doctor?"

"I've suggested it, but he doesn't listen to me."

"It's like he's given up."

"Well, I'm not giving up. I'm here for you, Penn. I'll never give up on you or me."

"Thanks, Mom."

I extend my arms for another hug, and my mom holds me for a few moments.

"We'll get through this together," she says.

I nod.

"Are you hungry now?" she asks.

"Starving."

"The pepperoni pizza in the kitchen has your name on it."

Chapter
4

On Sunday morning, I move the TR-97 from my dresser drawer to the basement. I don't want to leave it where my mom might accidentally find it. I consider stashing the vial in a bin with her old *Nancy Drew* books, but select a box labeled CHRISTMAS ORNAMENTS instead. I tuck the socks and serum in with an array of gold and silver decorations.

Around noon, I ride my bike to Mel's house. On my way, I stop briefly to pick up a shiny quarter in the gutter. Tara is at a family picnic, and I need to get out of the house. I also want to talk with someone about all the dirt I dug up on Dr. Oliver. When I get to the Castlemans', the front door stands open, but I wait outside and knock on the screen, texting Mel. *I'm here*

Bebe, a fluffy white Bichon Frise, rushes to the door barking. Mrs. Castleman follows the dog and lets me inside.

"Hi, Penn. How are you? I haven't seen you in a while." Her eyeballs dart from my hair to my face before settling on the dog at our feet.

"Good, Mrs. Castleman. How are you?" I bend down to pet Bebe, who runs around my legs wagging her tail.

"I'm doing well, thanks, just grading papers for the summer school class I'm teaching."

"That doesn't sound fun."

"It's not so bad. All part of the job when you're a professor."

"Hey Penn, how's it going?" says Mel, looking down at me from the top of the interior staircase. His phone dings, and he looks at the screen as he descends the stairs toward the entry hall.

"Watch where you're going, Melvin. You don't want to fall," says Mrs. Castleman, shaking her head.

"Come up to my room," he says, giving me a wave when he's halfway down. I follow him up the carpeted steps, then turn left toward his bedroom. Bebe follows us.

"I haven't been up here in a while," I say. "Something's different."

"Fresh paint." He wrinkles his nose and makes a funny face. "They thought it would be more serene in green."

"It's nice."

"Good one. It's ugly, but who cares, right?"

"Did you ever see the story on the news about the cemetery vandalism?" I ask.

"No, but people posted about it online."

"You didn't post anything, did you?"

"No way."

"Okay, good. When I talked to Tara last night, she didn't think it was going to be a problem."

"Of course not. It wasn't her car at the scene." Mel moves his books aside and sits on the bed. Bebe stands on her hind legs, front paws resting near him, and barks. Mel picks her up and holds her in his lap.

"What are the odds those people will go to the police?" I ask. "With the vandalism, they might have more to hide than we do."

He nods. "Why would someone do that?"

I sit down on the bed. "I've been thinking. Remember how the woman told the guy to make it look like the others?"

"Yeah."

"I think he went back, and since he couldn't clean up the area completely, he messed up other graves to throw people off."

"Like a diversion?"

"To make it seem random, not targeted."

"That's good detective work."

I grin and pat myself on the shoulder. "Thanks."

"I think it's safe to assume that's what happened," he says.

"I agree."

"I'm changing the subject," says Mel. "Have you seen the movie *Knives Out*?"

I shake my head. "But I've heard it's pretty good."

"We should make that this week's mystery."

"Great idea," I say. "What's the goal?"

"We have to write our guesses about 'who did it,' within the first twenty minutes."

"I'll take that challenge."

"So, what else is going on?" asks Mel, setting Bebe back down on the floor.

"I found a ton of information on the web about Doctor Oliver. Did you know they committed him to the Monona Mental Institution in 2017?"

"No way. He's insane?"

I sit down on the bed. "I guess."

"A modern day mad scientist. Is he still alive?"

"I think so. I haven't found an obituary, and a prominent scientist would have one if he died."

"Good point," says Mel.

"I plan to learn more about Doctor Oliver from his daughter Sasha."

"How are you going to do that?"

"I stopped by her house yesterday."

Mel snickers. "You stopped by? What did you do? Just walk up and ring the doorbell?"

"Yeah, kind of. She gave me her business card." I pull it out of my pocket and hand it to him.

"She's a vet."

"And she needs help at the clinic," I say.

"You're going to work there?"

I shrug. "Or volunteer. I don't know yet."

"You're certain that Sasha Hughes, who lives in the neighborhood, is actually Sasha Oliver?" he asks.

"Absolutely."

He hands the card back to me. "She might have a lot of information."

"I'm going to stop by tomorrow, but I need a resume. Can you help me?"

"Sure, let's work on that first, then you can tell me all about Doctor Oliver."

An hour later, Mel, Bebe, and I go downstairs for a snack. Mr. and Mrs. Castleman sit across from each other at the kitchen table.

"Hey, kids. Do you need some lunch?" asks Mr. Castleman. "I've got lentils with fresh tomatoes and basil."

"Nobody likes lentils, Dad," says Mel with a grimace, reaching for some corn chips.

"Well, your mom is the expert on diet, so I eat them."

"Don't just eat chips, Melvin. Choose something nutritious to go with them, like hummus or fresh salsa. Check the fridge," says Mrs. Castleman.

"See what I have to put up with?" says Mel, rolling his eyes. "I can't just eat chips. I have to eat chips with something healthful."

As we stand at the kitchen island eating, the Mendota *Times* rests on a nearby counter. An article about the cemetery vandalism appears on the front page of the local section. "Here it is," I say, pushing the paper under Mel's nose.

He reads the headline out loud. "Vandalism at Local Cemetery." He stares at me as I skim the article.

"I saw that in the newspaper this morning," says Mr. Castleman. "Looks like it was random destruction in a small area."

"That's weird," I say. "Who would damage gravestones?"

"Not me," says Mel.

"Well, of course not, dear," says Mrs. Castleman.

"Probably kids, though," says Mr. Castleman. "Most likely a prank or a dare. It fits the profile of bored, aimless youth."

"Thanks, Professor Castleman," says Mel.

"It's just a guess based on my years in the field. But psychology is complicated."

Psychology. That's related to psychiatry. Would Mr. Castleman know something about Dr. Oliver?

"The article says somebody may have dug up a grave," I say, still staring at the paper. "Someone named Gwendolyn Oliver, who died in 1999. Have you ever heard of her?"

I look up and Mel frowns at me, shaking his head. He slides his index finger across his throat, but I ignore him.

"Why yes, I recognize that name," says Mr. Castleman. "I must have missed that part of the article. She was the wife of Doctor James Oliver, a professor and researcher at the university."

"How would you know that, dear?" asks Mrs. Castleman. "That was a long time ago."

"Yes, but some things just stick with you. I was an undergrad majoring in psychology. I recall several grad students helped in Doctor Oliver's lab. He was working on a treatment that also involved the psychopharmacology department."

"Did you work with him?" I ask.

"No," says Mr. Castleman, shaking his head. "I was interested in Ed Psych, educational psychology."

"That's too bad," I say.

"Well, not for me. Considering the problems that arose later for Doctor Oliver, him being fired, and later committed to a psychiatric hospital. I'd say I'm happy not to have worked with him."

"A regular shit-show, huh, Dad?" asks Mel.

"You know I don't like it when you use that foul language, Melvin," says Mrs. Castleman.

"Do you know why he was in the hospital?" I ask. "Was he insane?"

Mr. Castleman looks at me and sighs. "Insanity is more of a legal term. I think what you want to know is whether he was mentally ill."

"Okay, sure," I say, my cheeks burning with embarrassment.

"And I don't know the answer to that. I understand he might have been unstable after they shut down his research lab, but I only heard the gossip. His students and colleagues had to scramble to avoid the fallout."

The gears turn in my head. "Do you remember any of the gossip?"

"Well, I don't like to spread rumors, but since it happened so long ago, I suppose it can't hurt. Several colleagues suspected he was having an affair with someone on his staff. Someone involved with his research."

"Wow," I say. "Would that make him crazy enough to dig up his wife's grave?"

Everyone's eyes turn to me, and the flames return to my cheeks. "I mean, do you think it's possible?"

"I don't know," says Mr. Castleman, scratching his head. "It seems far-fetched, but I remember hearing someone in the department mention his release from the hospital."

"Was that recently?" I ask.

"No. At least a year ago, maybe two," he says.

"Do you know if he still lives in Mendota?"

"I think so. I recall a different colleague telling me Doctor Oliver moved to Oak Bluff Nursing Home."

"Sounds like he's too old or sick to vandalize a cemetery," I say.

"Yeah, crazy idea," says Mel, spinning his finger in circles near the side of his head.

I shrug my shoulders and shift my focus back to the newspaper. Everyone else returns to their business, and the only sound is the crunch of Mel eating corn chips.

When I get back to my house, Tara is in her front yard, supervising her brothers. She lounges on a lawn chair, a large floppy hat covering her eyes. I join her on the grass, unable to contain my excitement about all the info I've uncovered.

"Hey, Tara, you've got to hear this," I say, sitting down next to her.

She doesn't flinch. She has earbuds in, and her eyes are closed.

I tap her on the shoulder.

She lifts her head and reduces the volume on her phone. "Hey there," she says. "This better be good since you're interrupting my zone-out time."

"It's important," I say. "I just came from Mel's house."

"How important?"

"Super important. I have news."

"Good news?"

"Yes."

"Tell me you have a six-pack of cold beer."

I shake my head.

"You found a winning lottery ticket?"

"No! It's about Doctor Oliver, the cemetery, and the vial," I say.

"Oh, yeah, our secret mission."

"There's a newspaper article about it, and Mr. Castleman told me some things about Doctor Oliver."

She scoots down and rests her head back against the chair. "Can you tell me later? I've got cramps and my head hurts. I just want to veg out right now."

"You're in a foul mood."

"My life sucks. I'm always working or looking after kids or cleaning the house. Shit, you'd think I was thirty-six, not sixteen."

I stand up. "I'll leave you alone."

"Yeah, leave the bitch alone."

"I didn't say that, Tara."

"I know, but you were thinking it."

"So, now you can read my thoughts?"

"Only the bad ones," she says.

I want to tell her to go screw herself, but keep my mouth shut and stomp back to my house. Some friend. She never listens when I need to talk.

When I reach my driveway, Tara texts. *Talk later*

I debate whether to reply, but do. *Are you joining us for movie night?* I text.

Not tonight

Tomorrow?

Probably not

That settles it. She doesn't want to hang out with me. Well, two can play that game. I don't want to hang out with her either.

Chapter
5

The roar of the neighbor's lawn mower awakens me on Monday morning. My phone says 8:22. I roll onto my side and hug the pillow. The final golf tryout is tomorrow. Do I even care? So far, my scores have been pathetic. I'm almost glad my dad hasn't been around to see my collapse. Last year, at least I broke 100. Lynda shot a 74 on Friday, and three other girls were under 80. I won't make the team.

In the kitchen, I grab a granola bar and some orange juice. "Morning," I say, keeping my back to my mom.

Her computer screen holds her focus, and she doesn't look up. "Morning," she says.

"Busy day?" I ask.

"Yeah. You?"

"Yep."

"Do you need a ride to the golf course?" she asks, taking a sip of her coffee. "I have time this morning."

"No. I'm going to hang out with Mel. He can take me."

"Okay."

I text Mel. *Can u pick me up?*

When?

Now?

Where r we going?

I hesitate before replying. *Not sure*

??

Vet clinic or golf course

C u in 15, he texts.

I'm already in the garage when the car's brakes announce Mel's arrival. I stick my head into the house and yell to my mom. "Bye!" I don't wait for her reply and carry my golf bag to the car.

"Looks like we're going to the golf course," he says.

"No. We're going to the animal clinic."

"Why bring your clubs, then?"

"I want my mom to think I'm at the golf course."

He raises his eyebrows. "Sneaking around again, are we?"

I get into the passenger seat of the Volvo. "In broad daylight."

"You're such a bad girl. I love that about you."

"Speaking of bad girls, did you talk to Tara last night?"

"Nope. Why?"

I turn to face Mel. "She pissed me off yesterday. She's so selfish and stuck in her head."

"What happened?"

"She didn't want to hear about Doctor Oliver or the cemetery or the newspaper article. Can you believe that witch? After all the work I did."

"Somebody's claws are out today."

"She makes me so mad. Clearly, she doesn't care. Maybe we should count her out."

Mel shakes his head. "No way. She was there with us. She stays in."

"But she's not helping."

"Call her today or text her. Or I will. We're in this together."

I press my fingertips to my temples. "Whatever. Right now, I need to focus on meeting Sasha."

"You should probably call her Doctor Hughes," says Mel. "They're doctors, too."

"Good point. And, can you drive me to Oak Bluff Nursing Home this afternoon? I want to meet the other Doctor Oliver."

"Whoa. Don't you think you're moving a little fast? Let's meet one doctor at a time."

I cross my arms over my chest. "Okay, fine, but I'm going to meet him."

"I'm sure you will, but let's take baby steps."

"I'm not a baby."

"I didn't say you were. It's just an expression. You're *so* moody today."

I lean my head back against the seat and sigh. "I can't help it."

"Are you nervous?"

"A little. I might have pit stains." I lift my arm for Mel and he shakes his head. I bend forward and sniff. At least I put on deodorant this morning. My heart is thumping. Am I nervous about talking to Dr. Hughes? Am I upset about missing my last chance to practice golf? Am I angry with Tara? I stare out the window and wish the universe would give me a sign.

"We're here," says Mel, pulling into the parking lot and choosing a spot in the shade away from the door. "Take a few deep breaths, bring your resume, and be polite."

"Thanks, Mom."

"Doctor Hughes could have a lot of information, but you're going to have to be nice to get it."

"I *am* nice."

"Usually," says Mel.

I frown at him. "You'll wait here for me?"

"Right here."

I walk through the clinic entrance, and a bell jingles. The smell of antiseptic stings my nostrils. I paste a smile on my face and approach the front desk. A calico cat relaxes near the telephone, unconcerned about my arrival. A young woman with a name tag that says CHRISTINA sits behind the desk. She has chestnut hair, golden brown eyes, and a tiny diamond stud on the side of her nose.

"Welcome to Shorewood Animal Clinic," she says. "How can I help you?"

"Hi. My name is Penn. I'm looking for a job or some volunteer hours. I brought my resume." I hand her the paper.

"I didn't know we were looking for help," she says, "but let me ask Doctor Hughes. I'll be right back."

I sit on a bench in the waiting room while Christina disappears down the hall. Posters occupy the walls with information about fleas, heartworms, and pet nutrition. Assorted bags of dog food fill a shelf. A bulletin board contains business cards and animal-related fundraising flyers. A large metal scale stands against the wall. I'm startled by the jingle of the door, and a man walks in with a cocker spaniel on a leash. Although he's wearing a business suit, his hair is shaggy and his sideburns remind me of the dog's ears. The guy heads for the front desk, but the dog wants to greet me. As I lean forward to pet the dog, he yanks the pup back in his direction.

When Christina reappears, she speaks to me first. "If you have a few minutes, Doctor Hughes would like to talk to you."

"Okay, sure. I can wait."

"Great. And hello, Mister Paulson and Echo," says Christina. "How are you today?"

"We're here for his flea treatment," he says.

"I see you on the schedule. Let me take your sweet boy to the back. When can you pick him up?" Christina asks, grasping the leash.

"This afternoon, just call me, and I was hoping to have a word with Doctor Hughes if she's available?"

"Yes, of course. Let me get her."

Dr. Hughes glides around the corner at that moment. "Christina, I need exam room two cleaned right away."

"Should I do that first or take Echo?" she says.

"Clean the exam room first." Dr. Hughes takes Echo's leash, and Christina hurries out of the room.

"Hello, Mr. Paulson," Dr. Hughes says with a faint smile. "Nice to see you again."

She bends down to pat Echo's head. "Hi, Echo. How's my good boy? Denise is going to give you a bath today."

A tall woman with an ebony braid down her back appears from the hall and takes the leash. I guess that's Denise.

"Why is the scope missing from exam room one?" asks Dr. Hughes.

"I don't know," says Denise, "but I'll find it after Echo's bath."

"Find it before the bath."

"Yes, Doctor Hughes," she says, taking Echo around the corner.

Dr. Hughes turns and sees me sitting on the bench. I can't tell whether she recognizes me, so I force a smile and stand to meet her. "Hi, I'm Penn."

"I remember you from the other day," she says.

It's probably my hair. "I brought my resume."

"I can definitely use some extra help. Will you wait a moment while I have a word with Mister Paulson?"

"Sure," I say, sitting down again. I text Mel a thumbs-up and smiley face emojis.

Mr. Paulson and Dr. Hughes vanish around the corner, closing the door behind them. The office is quiet again, and the cat lifts its head as if to ask where everybody went. I can make out a faint mumble of words on the other side of the wall and stand up, moving across the room to listen.

"What happened?" says Dr. Hughes.

"It was an accident," says Paulson.

"A screw-up is more like it."

"You've got one, so what's the big deal?"

"The other is missing, and the police are asking questions."

"Not because of me," says Paulson.

"I can't talk about this now," says Dr. Hughes.

I scoot back to the bench so nobody knows I was listening, and text Mel. *Weird guy inside. Paulson. When he comes out, find his car and get license plate*

What guy? Mel texts.

Sideburns. Coming out now, I reply, hitting SEND just as Paulson strides through the waiting room toward the exit. He doesn't look at me, and Dr. Hughes appears a moment later. Any trace of a smile has vanished, and she smooths the hair away from her face.

"Come on back. I'll show you around," she says.

I stand up and follow her.

"You've met Christina and saw the waiting room. We have three exam rooms, a kennel area, surgical room, office, break room, and storage. Denise, who is here today, and Eric are the vet techs. If you have time, you can start right now."

She's offering me a job. It's a sign from the universe.

"Yeah, sure. Let me text my friend who drove me here."

"You don't have a car?" she says.

"Unfortunately not. My parents are making me wait until I'm eighteen to drive."

"Is that going to be a problem? Getting to work?"

I shake my head. "I can ride my bike. It's not that far."

"I can use help in the mornings, say nine to twelve, Monday through Friday?"

"I can do that, at least until school starts."

"Of course. Then maybe in the afternoons. We'll see how it goes."

"That sounds great," I say.

"I'll pay you twelve dollars an hour."

I smile and shake Dr. Hughes's hand.

"Christina will have the paperwork for you to fill out, then find Denise in the back. You can start with cleaning."

"Okay," I say, but my smile disappears quickly. Cleaning.

Chapter

6

Tuesday morning, I wake up in a panic, sweating and panting. My heart pounds and my night-shirt clings to my skin. I had that stupid dream again. The one where I'm running but not getting anywhere. I think somebody is chasing me, but I don't know who or why. In the pale light of dawn, I glance around my bedroom. The familiar cream-colored walls, ancient oak dresser, and overloaded bookshelf comfort me. As my heart rate slows, I close my eyes and try to sleep. No luck. I'm too anxious about my day.

Before I get out of bed, my phone buzzes with a text from my dad. *Good luck with golf tryouts! Not that you need it.*

Unbelievable. He remembered. His message leaves my stomach in knots. I just got the job at the animal clinic, and I've barely thought about golf. I stare into my closet, stalling for time, pulling out clothes for both. When I join my mom in the kitchen, it's already eight-thirty. If I don't leave soon, I'll be late.

"What are you wearing?" she asks, setting her coffee cup down on the table.

"Clothes," I say, opening the refrigerator.

She turns to face me. "Don't you have golf this morning?"

"I'm not going."

"You have to go. I saw the email from your coach. You can't make the team unless you go."

I swallow some orange juice. "I don't care."

"But you worked so hard this summer. You're going to throw it all away?"

"I wouldn't make the team, anyway."

"How can you know that?"

"I got a job instead." I set my cup in the sink and grab a bagel for the road.

"When did this happen?"

"Yesterday. I got hired at Shorewood Animal Clinic, and I need to be there by nine."

My mom looks at her watch. "Am I driving you?"

I shake my head. "I'm riding my bike. See you later."

I'm out the door before she can ask more questions and delay me any further, but she follows me into the garage.

"What are you going to tell your dad?" she asks, as I ride away.

I don't look back or respond.

The morning is a blur of people, appointments, dogs, cats, and disinfectant. I do whatever Christina, Eric, or Dr. Hughes tell me. I clean the exam rooms between appointments. I clean the kennels. I help Christina clean out the filing area. I'm a cleaning lady. The only time I sit down is when I need to use the toilet. Christina loans me a pair of her scrubs and tells me where to buy some of my own. I like the thought of having a uniform and being part of the team.

After I leave the animal clinic at noon, I stop by Mel's house on my way home. His parents are at work, and he's studying in his bedroom.

"You really need a hobby," I say, plopping down onto his bed.

"I have one," he says. "It's called reading. But what I really need is a volunteer gig or a job like you to beef up my resume."

"Since you're so interested in books, why don't volunteer at the library?"

"I can't believe I didn't think of that. I could help people check out books or find research."

"Sounds perfect."

"Nice scrubs, by the way."

"Thanks," I say with a smile. "They're pretty comfy."

"How was work? Did you get any info from Doctor Hughes?"

I shake my head. "The office was really busy. I didn't spend any time with her."

While I sit on the bed, Bebe stretches her paws up to me. I pat the top of her head.

"Not surprising," he says. "You might have to be patient, get to know her, build up trust."

"I know. It was naïve to think that I'd find out about her family on the first day."

Bebe barks, so Mel picks her up and holds her.

"Remember how long it took to find the lady who lost the pendant?" he says.

"True," I say. "This could take longer."

"This situation *is* a bit more complicated," he says.

I nod. "Did you find out anything about that Paulson guy from the clinic? Something about him bothers me."

"I did, but it wasn't easy, or legal I had to get help."

"What kind of help?"

I shift from one side of the bed to the other, so I'm closer to Mel and Bebe.

"A guy in my virtual computer club told me the DMV database firewall gets refreshed just before midnight every night. With the right software and perfect timing, you can see all the data for about fifty-nine seconds."

"And? You found him?"

"His name is Theodore Paulson."

I frown. "He doesn't look like a Theodore."

"A search of LinkedIn shows he works for a company called Feester Incorporated."

"What the heck is that?"

"It's an interesting coincidence. Feester is a pharmaceutical company. They make prescription drugs."

"I know what pharmaceuticals are."

"Just making sure. You had a blank look on your face."

"I was thinking. Do they make TR-97?"

Mel sits down at his desk and types something on the computer keyboard. "I wondered the same thing and looked at their website, but found nothing with a name like that."

"Doesn't surprise me," I say. "You've seen all the ads on TV. Drug companies give their products fancy names. They want it to sound optimistic, not like medicine."

"Even when the list of side effects sounds worse than the actual disease," says Mel with a snicker.

"It's crazy."

"But I also checked out his Facebook page." He points to his computer.

"Paulson's? What's it like?" I glance at Mel's screen.

"He posts a lot of pictures of himself traveling to places like Aspen, Maui, and New York City. He's definitely trying to impress people."

"Scroll down. What about pets? Does he post any of his dog?"

Mel moves the mouse. "I didn't see any dog photos."

"That's odd," I say. "Most people with pets post at least one. Everyone thinks theirs is the cutest."

"Do you want to look?" he asks.

"That's okay. It's probably a dead end." I turn my attention to the dog and sit back down on the bed, scratching her chin. "Speaking of dead ends, how's Tara doing?"

Mel's mouth drops open. "You're asking me?"

"Yeah. How is she?"

"You haven't called her yet? What's wrong with you?"

"I don't know. I wanted her to reach out to me, but I guess I'll call her," I say, grabbing my phone.

"Don't bother calling now. She's working. You know her schedule is Tuesday, Thursday, Saturday."

"I'll catch her at home later."

"Promise?"

"I promise." I draw an X with my index finger across my heart. "You know, someone called the clinic today, and when I answered the phone, the voice sounded familiar."

"They let you answer the phone?"

"Not all the time. Just when Christina is on break. Why are you so shocked?"

"I thought you'd only be doing grunt work."

"Believe me, I do plenty of grunt work and some general office stuff, but the voice on the phone was someone I'd heard before. It gave me a weird feeling in my stomach."

"Who did it sound like?"

Mel sets Bebe on the floor and focuses on me.

"An older woman. She was kind of snooty and impatient, but I couldn't place the voice."

"Was it a teacher?"

"I don't think so."

"Someone famous?"

I shake my head.

"Do you remember the conversation?"

I shift positions on Mel's bed. "She kept asking to speak to Doctor Hughes, and I kept telling her Doctor Hughes was busy. It was like she didn't believe me."

"Did she leave a message?"

"Not like a normal person. She insisted I put her through, but I couldn't. Anyway, during the call, she kept saying 'like I said.'"

"Like I said?" repeats Mel. "Can you imitate her voice?"

I hold my hand up to my ear like I'm talking on the phone. "Like I said, I need to talk to Doctor Hughes right away."

"Oh my god, that sounds like the lady from the cemetery. Remember?"

"Shit! You could be right."

"I'm often right, but I could be wrong in this case. I didn't hear it. It could have been anyone."

"I wouldn't recognize the woman if she was standing in front of me, but her voice was distinctive. I might know it if I heard it again."

"Did she give you her name?" asks Mel. "Like for the message?"

"Helga."

"Yikes! Scary German name."

"She said, 'Tell her Helga called,' and hung up without leaving a number."

———————

Later that night, I stretch out on my bed and call Tara.

"Hey girl, what's up?" I ask.

"Not much. Just hiding out in my room."

"I do that sometimes. Out of sight, out of mind, right?"

"I wish that was actually true."

"Are you feeling better?" I ask.

"Was I feeling bad?" she responds.

"Well, no, but you were in a bad mood the other day."

"I'm always in a shitty mood."

"How was work? Did anyone sneeze on the pizza?"

"No sneezing, coughing, or belching, but there was vomit in the bathroom, and of course, the asshole manager made me clean it up."

"That's so nasty," I say. "What a prick." Animal poop and urine are bad enough, but vomit is the worst.

"Just part of my job description," she says. "Do whatever the prick manager says."

I nod in agreement, even though she can't see me. "Hey, I got a job, too," I say.

"You did? Where?"

"At Shorewood Animal Clinic."

"How many cages did you clean today?" she asks.

"Too many. I can't believe dogs and cats are so messy and smelly. It's kind of disgusting."

"Yeah, little brothers, too. They're so gross."

"At least the animals are cute."

"Do you get a lot of hours?" she asks.

"Fifteen a week. Nine to noon, Monday through Friday."

"How does that work with golf?"

I roll onto my side. "I gave up golf. It's a lame-ass sport."

"I thought you liked it?"

"It was okay, but this is more important." I take my phone off speaker and bring it to my ear. "Sasha Hughes owns the animal clinic. She's a veterinarian."

"Sasha Hughes?"

"You know, Sasha Oliver, daughter of Doctor Oliver?"

"Shit, I didn't know that. Oh my god, I'm so out of the loop. You have to fill me in."

I'm ready to tell her about everything when Tara's dad interrupts.

"Get off the damn phone, Tara! Right now. And get your lazy butt downstairs!"

"Gotta go," she says, and the line goes dead.

Chapter

7

I ride my bicycle to Mel's house again after work on Thursday. I'm eager to meet Dr. Oliver, and today is perfect because Dr. Hughes has appointments scheduled all afternoon. Yesterday, I called Oak Bluff Nursing Home and learned that only relatives or pre-registered guests may visit residents. I could ask Dr. Hughes for permission to visit her dad, but that's just weird. She'd want to know why, and I can't tell her about the vial or what we saw in the cemetery. Then it hits me.

"I'm going to pretend to be the crazy doctor's granddaughter," I say to Mel.

He shakes his head. "I don't think that's a good idea."

"I knew you would say that. That's why I've done my homework on the Olivers, so I can pass as part of the family."

"It's still risky."

"Look, Sasha is an only child, which means I can be her daughter. I'm prepared. Quiz me. Ask me about my 'family,'" I say, making air quotes with my fingers.

"Okay, miss know-it-all. Here's a question for you. When and where was your mother born?"

"Easy. She was born on July twenty-one, nineteen eighty-eight, right here in Mendota."

"You know that makes her a teen mom since you're sixteen."

"It's not that unusual."

Mel frowns.

"What's your grandfather's birthdate?" he asks.

"February one, nineteen fifty-three."

"Who is your 'father'?" he asks, imitating my air quotes.

"Shoot. I didn't think of that, but if she was a teen mom, she probably didn't stay with the guy, anyway."

"How can you say you're prepared?"

"I'm prepared enough. I just want to meet him and talk to him."

"Are you sure? He might be crazy or violent."

"I'll be fine. Besides, he's old. I can run away if I have to."

"It still seems a little cray-cray. Are you going to tell him about the vial?"

I shake my head. "For now, that's our secret."

"Good. But what are you going to talk about?"

"I want him to tell me about TR-97."

"Do you think he'll do that?"

"I have to try."

Mel sighs and glances at his phone.

"Will you at least drive me there?" I ask. "Please?" I bring my hands together in prayer and give him my best puppy dog eyes.

"Okay," he says, "but I'm parking in an out-of-the-way spot where nobody will notice me."

"Deal," I say, and we head to the car.

The lobby and reception area of Oak Bluff Nursing Home remind me of a hotel. Polished marble floors cover the entry, and impressive artwork adorns the walls. I can smell the freesias in the floral arrangement that fills a round table in the center of the room. A desk occupies the far side opposite the entry.

"How can I help you?" asks a young woman behind the desk as I approach.

"Hi. I'm here to visit my grandfather," I say, my mouth suddenly dry.

"How lovely," she says with a smile. "What's your name?"

"Penelope Heavnor, but everyone calls me Penn."

"Welcome Penn. I'm Kathryn. Most people call me Kat."

I smile while she turns her attention to a computer console in front of her.

"Who is your grandfather?" she asks.

"Doctor James Oliver," I say, with a slight quaver.

"Doctor James Oliver," she repeats, looking at me, then typing something on the keyboard. "I'm sorry, but you're not on the family list."

"Really?" I was afraid of this, and I just told her my actual name. "My mom assured me I was on the list. Can you check again, please?"

"Of course. Who is your mother?"

"Doctor Sasha Hughes," I say, looking Kat in the eye.

She studies my face for a moment, then shifts her attention back to the computer screen. I stand still and try not to fidget, my heart hammering inside my chest. I maintain eye contact, but clamp my mouth shut and breathe slowly through my nostrils.

"Let me make a quick call," she says. "Can you wait a minute?"

"Sure," I say as my stomach does a back flip. Oh crap. What's my plan if they call Dr. Hughes? Maybe Mel was right. I'm not prepared for this. I want to bite my fingernail, but clasp my hands behind my back instead, glancing around the lobby. Will the universe act in my favor today? I cross my fingers and listen to Kat speak into the phone.

"I have a guest here to see Doctor Oliver. No, she's not on the list. Penelope Heavnor. She says she's his granddaughter. Not yet. I won't. Okay. Thanks."

I turn to face Kat and she resumes typing on her keyboard.

"Here we go," she says after a few minutes. "There must have been some confusion with the differences in last names. I'll add you to the list. Will you please fill out this form?"

She hands me a notecard that asks for my name, address, and telephone number. "Sign at the bottom," she says. "And I also need to see some identification."

I hand her my old high school ID because it's the only one I have. She scrutinizes the photo where I have brown hair but doesn't question it, placing it face down on the scanner and hitting START. Thankfully, it doesn't have my address on it, because I wrote a fake address and phone number on the form. Not that it matters because they have my name and photo.

"Are you carrying a purse?" she asks.

"No, just my phone," I say, showing it to her.

"That's fine. So you know, by signing the guest card, you agree we can inspect all purses, briefcases, backpacks, and other bags before visiting a resident."

"Why do you do that?"

"To make sure visitors don't bring in dangerous items."

A tall man with dark cropped hair and blue scrubs joins us at the desk. "I'm Jesse," he says.

"I'm Penn."

"Please come with me."

Jesse and I leave the marble floor behind and walk down a long hall, with handrails on both sides. The fluorescent lights hum, and the scuffed linoleum shines in odd places. Pale green walls host black-and-white photos of Mendota, and the room numbers and name plates of the residents. Some of their doors are open, and I can see all the way through to a window. It appears the building is a giant open rectangle with a park-like area in the middle. Residents on the left look outside to the parking lot, while residents on the right have a view of the courtyard.

"So, you're visiting Doctor Oliver today?" Jesse asks.

"Yes," I say.

"He doesn't get many visitors, so this should make his day."

"Oh, good. It's kind of a surprise."

"Have you been here before?"

I shake my head. "This is my first time."

"Well, don't expect too much, okay?"

"Okay," I say. I don't have a clue what he means. I don't know what to expect. I'm pretending to be the granddaughter of a stranger who used to be in a mental hospital.

"He's near the end of the hall on the left in room one-oh-three. You have about forty-five minutes until exercise and dinner."

"Thanks."

I have a ton of questions for Jesse, but my mind goes blank. I focus on walking, breathing, and staying calm, even though my heart wants to pound its way out of my chest.

"Here we are," says Jesse as we approach the room.

The door is ajar, and he knocks before pushing it open.

"Hello, Doctor Oliver, you have a visitor."

No one responds, but Jesse enters anyway. I follow him, wiping my sweaty palms on my shorts.

"This nice young lady is here to see you," says Jesse.

Dr. Oliver sits in a leather recliner by the window. He has gray hair, thick eyeglasses, and wrinkled skin. An open book rests on his lap and he doesn't look up when we enter the tiny room. It contains a twin bed, an empty wooden nightstand, and two chairs. Bare walls painted the same color green as the hallway loom on both sides. A separate door leads to the bathroom. It reminds me of a prison cell, but with a window.

I clear my throat and swallow. "Hi, Doctor Oliver," I say, taking several steps into the room. "It's nice to meet you."

He doesn't reply, and his eyes remain on his book.

"Enjoy your visit," says Jesse as he withdraws from the room, leaving the door open.

"I'd like to talk to you," I say. "Can I sit down?"

"Why do you keep bothering me?" he asks.

I stop moving, startled by his question.

"We've never actually met."

"I know why you're here."

"You do?"

He crosses his arms over his chest. "I refuse to cooperate, so you might as well leave."

"I just want to meet you," I say in my most soothing voice. "It might be my only chance."

Dr. Oliver raises his eyes to look at me. He squints with a furrowed brow, his lips pressed together. I stare back for a moment, then divert my eyes to the floor. When I have the courage to look up again, Dr. Oliver is still staring at me.

"Who are you?" he asks.

"Penn."

"What's your name?"

"Penn."

"What kind of name is that?"

"It's short for Penelope."

He blinks a few times. "Why are you here, Penelope?"

"To talk to you."

"Is your hair purple?"

"Yes."

"Interesting," he says with a cough. "How did you get in to see me?"

"I'm your granddaughter."

"To my knowledge, my only child doesn't have children."

His eyes hold mine, and I look down at his feet.

"I wasn't sure," I say.

"So, back to my question. How did you get in?"

My stomach does a somersault. "I lied and said I'm your granddaughter."

Dr. Oliver's eyebrows rise to the ceiling. "Do you know my daughter?"

"Sort of. Can I sit down?" I ask, pointing to the vacant chair.

"If you like."

"Thanks," I say, lowering myself onto the upright wooden chair. "I work at her veterinary clinic."

"You work there?"

"I just started."

He closes the book on his lap. "And how is that going?"

"Good, I guess."

"Is she a good boss?" he asks.

"So far, yes, but it's hard to tell. Besides my parents and teachers, I've never had a boss."

"Your first job, eh? Everyone starts somewhere."

"I really like animals though," I say.

"Fair enough. So why are you here, Penelope? Is Sasha paying you to visit me?"

"No," I say, shaking my head. "I just wanted to talk."

"Is that another lie?"

He examines my face and I drop my eyes to the floor, but raise them again.

"It's the truth," I say. "Nobody's paying me."

"Okay, Penelope. Since my daughter doesn't allow many visitors, this is a treat for me. What would you like to talk about?"

When he poses the question, my mind races like a hamster on a wheel. Should I ask about his time at Wisconsin State? His research? Should I mention his wife? Is it better to talk about Sasha? Every topic seems too fake and contrived.

"Cat got your tongue?" he asks.

"What is TR-97?"

"How do you know about that?" he asks, sitting up a little straighter.

"I read about it."

"Really? How old are you?"

"Sixteen."

"Why would a sixteen-year-old read about TR-97?" he asks.

"I was curious."

"And what made you curious?"

Crap. I wanted to be the one asking the questions, but Dr. Oliver has taken control. I can tell he was a professor, but maybe he should've been a lawyer.

"I'm waiting," he says, folding his hands over the book in his lap.

I can't tell him about the vial, and it seems wrong to mention that someone dug up his wife's grave.

"I read a newspaper article about vandalism at Westmoreland Cemetery."

"And how does that relate to TR-97?"

"I'm not sure, but the gravestone of your wife Gwendolyn Oliver was damaged. I looked her up on the web, and your name popped up, too, and your research."

"My wife's headstone?"

"I think it was cracked." I take a deep breath. Double crap. I don't think it was damaged. How am I going to keep these lies straight?

"When was this?" he asks.

"I read it in the Sunday paper."

"So, the vandalism happened over the weekend?"

I nod. "Friday night, I think."

"And the newspaper revealed the names on the damaged headstones?"

"I'm not sure about that."

"Then how do you know it was her marker?"

I clasp my hands together in my lap. "I play golf at Glen View, and this past weekend, I hit my tee shot on thirteen into the cemetery. It landed in the area near the vandalism."

"And you want me to believe you took the time during a round of golf to look at the names on the headstones?"

I nod.

"And what were some other names you saw?"

Triple crap. Why did I say that? I'm so stupid. I don't know any of the other names. But would Dr. Oliver? He's been in a mental hospital or living here for the last few years.

"I remember Charles Albert Taylor," I say, making up a fictitious name.

He stares at me, and I hold his gaze.

"So you read some things on the internet about TR-97."

"I'd like to know more about it. You developed the drug to treat veterans with PTSD."

"Aren't you a little young to be interested in a topic like that?"

"I'm not sure age matters. I'm a high school junior. Plenty of kids have PTSD after experiencing school shootings."

"Very well, Penelope, I'll indulge you. TR-97 was a drug I developed and used to treat patients, mostly veterans, with severe post-traumatic stress disorder. It was a multi-prong approach to treatment that involved therapy and medication. I was on the cusp of obtaining approval for the drug from the FDA when I encountered problems."

"So, what happened? You didn't get approval?"

Dr. Oliver studies me again.

"No. TR-97 should have been my greatest triumph as a doctor, but it turned out to be my biggest failure."

"But you had some success. I read about it. You cured people."

"Some patients got better, but not all of them. There were complications and missteps and lawsuits. They never formally approved the drug."

"And you got fired."

"Yes," says Dr. Oliver with a frown. "They let me go, revoked my license, and forced me to destroy the rest of the drug."

"Who did? Wisconsin State?"

"They claimed the drug belonged to them since I worked for the university. It was in my contract. They didn't want to be associated with it and made sure I got rid of it. Of course, the drug company that paid for most of the developmental costs didn't see it that way."

"Is that the lawsuit part?"

He glances out the window, then back at me. "Yes, and no. There were several lawsuits, both civil and criminal. If you're interested, I'm sure you can read more about that on your own. I don't want to get into it."

"But why would the university want to destroy a drug if it was successful?" I ask. "You'd think they'd want to keep it."

"You would think, especially because this drug was different. A genuine breakthrough in treatment."

"How do you mean?"

"Can you keep a secret?" he asks.

I nod, leaning in closer.

Dr. Oliver lowers his voice to a whisper. "I didn't want to develop a drug that only treated the symptoms of post-traumatic stress. We already had drugs for that. I wanted to find a cure, so I created a therapy that reprograms part of the brain, the amygdala. It changes the memory of a terrible event into a positive one, eliminating traumatic events from the mind."

Chapter
8

On Friday morning, I arrive at work early and find the door to the clinic locked. I plop down on the curb and check my phone, waiting for Christina. She arrives a little after nine.

"I can't believe the office is locked," I say to her. "Doctor Hughes is always early."

"She volunteers at the local animal shelter on Friday mornings."

"I didn't know that."

"I'm usually a little late. Denise too."

Christina unlocks the door and disarms the alarm.

"But Doctor Hughes still wants us here working, even if she's gone?" I ask.

"We get to deep clean and organize. Let me check the schedule. There might be a few grooming appointments too."

The computer whirs to life and Christina stares at the screen. The cat jumps up on the desk next to her.

"Nope. No appointments this morning."

I nod and head to the back to clean the kennels.

Later that morning, I'm at the reception desk when Mr. Paulson saunters in with Echo.

"I think my dog has a stomach condition," he says. "He needs a different type of food."

"I can get someone to help you with that," I say, reaching for the phone.

"He also has a bald spot on his hind leg. It might be an allergy or skin condition. I'd like Sasha, I mean Doctor Hughes, to look at it."

Paulson points to the place on Echo. From my angle, it looks like someone used an electric shaver on the dog, but I don't say that.

"Doctor Hughes isn't here right now, but Denise, the vet tech, is. She can look at Echo."

"Why isn't Doctor Hughes here during regular hours?"

"She's working elsewhere this morning. Let me get Denise." I press the intercom button.

Paulson looms over the desk. "I need to see the doctor. Will she be in tomorrow?"

I put the phone down and glance at the calendar. "Yes, Doctor Hughes will be here. Would you like to make an appointment?"

"Late afternoon," he says.

I study the schedule again. "Does two-thirty work? The clinic closes early on Saturdays."

"Fine."

Before I can ask if he'd like a reminder card or text, he disappears out the door, pulling the dog behind him. Christina returns to the reception desk as the jingle of the door ceases.

"Who was that?" she asks.

"Mr. Paulson," I say.

"Again? What did he want?"

"To see Doctor Hughes. I made an appointment for him tomorrow." I point to the computer screen. "Did I enter that right?"

"That's good." She pets the cat who has jumped back up on the desk. "I love your hair, by the way."

"Thanks."

"I've thought about doing that with mine, maybe fuchsia, but I'm too scared."

"It's pretty easy, and the color will eventually wash out."

"Maybe I'll try it. Have you met Opal?"

"Not really." I give the cat a pat on the head. "Does she live here?"

Christina nods. "She's queen of the office."

I watch as Opal rubs her face against the computer monitor and Christina strokes her back.

"She doesn't mind dogs?" I ask.

"Nope. She knows she's the boss."

When I'm ready to leave the clinic at noon, Dr. Hughes arrives, and rather than saying goodbye, she asks me to help her.

"Can you stay longer today? I get so behind with everything that comes in the mail. I can't stand it when it piles up."

"Sure," I say. "What can I do?"

"Come with me to my office," she says.

When we get there, she points to stacks of magazines on the floor. "Start on those journals."

"What should I do with them?" I ask.

"Throw out anything that's more than a year old. Use the recycling dumpster out back."

I sit on the floor and get started while she sorts through the notes on her chair. It's quiet except for the rustle of papers. I want to ask Dr. Hughes about her dad, but Dr. Oliver warned me not to mention my visit. I agreed to keep it a secret, but I want to find out more about their family.

"Did you grow up here?" I ask, interrupting the silence.

She nods. "I went to Central High School."

"That's cool. Do your parents still live here, then?"

"Unfortunately not."

I raise my eyebrows but try not to sound shocked. "Oh, that's too bad. Do you get to see them very often?" I ask.

"I'd rather not talk about it," she says.

"Sorry."

Dr. Hughes sits down in the chair behind her desk. "Some things are best kept private."

This is going to be tougher than I thought. Sasha doesn't want me to know about her dad, and he doesn't want me to mention anything to her. Are they embarrassed because he was in a mental hospital?

"Did you always want to be a veterinarian?" I ask.

"I wasn't sure what I wanted to do when I was your age," she says.

"I don't know what I want to do, either."

"That's normal for high school students. You need time to learn and explore."

"I know I don't want to do what my parents do," I say.

"Knowing what doesn't interest you is helpful, too, but I have to admit I'm curious. What do your parents do?"

I stop sorting the journals. "My mom sells real estate. She works all the time, showing houses, preparing contracts, only to have deals fall through at the last minute and make no money."

"That sounds hectic. And your father?"

"He's a firefighter. Crazy hours, stressful days, sleepless nights. But you get a lot of days off."

"I'm sure that's a tough job, physically and mentally."

I continue grouping the old magazines. The throwaway pile towers next to me. "He's not around much anymore. I wish I had a brother or sister to hang out with sometimes, but no luck."

"You're an only child?" she asks.

I nod. "My dad used to say, 'Why have more when you get it right the first time?'"

"That's a cute saying. I'm an only child as well."

"I didn't know that," I say, feigning surprise. "Did you go to college at Wisconsin State?"

She shakes her head. "The University of California. San Diego as an undergrad, and Davis for vet school."

I close my eyes for a moment and visualize sunshine and beaches and palm trees. "California sounds so awesome. If I ever went there, I'd never leave."

"I thought that way for a while, too. But sometimes it's important to come home."

Dr. Hughes returns her focus to the desk, and I make three trips to the dumpster with the old journals. I want to ask her if she came home because her dad was mentally ill, but she doesn't want to talk about her parents. I'll have to think of something else.

"What's next?" I ask, looking around the office.

She points to the corner. "How about those boxes? I think they're samples or brochures. I need to figure out what to do with them."

I open the first box and find it filled with pamphlets about common problems and infections in animals. I sit on the floor and organize them into groups. As I work, the clinic phone rings. Christina puts the call through to Dr. Hughes in her office. She answers, but it's not a typical veterinary call because she doesn't talk about treatments, lab results, or follow-up care. I slow my sorting so I can listen.

"I've got it under control. He's a dunce. We'll move forward with one. I'm keeping it here. I'll look for that next. I don't need your help, Helga."

Helga? The woman who called before with the distinctive voice? I hold my breath and continue listening, but I feel like an intruder. Before I can give her some privacy, she hangs up the phone.

"Do you want me to leave?" I ask.

"No, it's fine. She's an old family friend who refuses to take 'no' for an answer."

"Is she in real estate?"

Dr. Hughes smirks. "No, but she could be. She could sell ice to Eskimos."

"That's funny," I say.

"If only she had a sense of humor."

I don't know how to respond to that, so I point to the pamphlets. "I've got all these sorted by animal and health issue. Do you want me to put some in the waiting room and each exam room?"

"That would be great, thank you."

As I grab my first stack and turn to leave the room, I bump into the corner of the desk and an assortment of papers falls to the floor.

"Sorry," I say, setting the pamphlets aside and bending down to pick up the papers.

"It's okay," says Dr. Hughes. "I haven't reviewed that pile yet."

As I gather the sheets from the floor, one is the newspaper article about the cemetery vandalism. I stare at it for a moment, knowing Dr. Hughes is watching me.

"Isn't that weird?" I point to the story. "Who would do that?"

"I don't know, but people do strange things sometimes."

She buries the article under the other papers like she's hiding it. It has something to do with her mom. I'm sure the police contacted her about the incident. If I dare, this is my chance to dig a little deeper.

"I heard a rumor that someone dug up a grave," I say.

The corners of Dr. Hughes's mouth droop, and the blood drains from her face. "Who told you that?"

"Friends on the golf team, but they probably made it up."

"What if I told you it was true?"

My eyes spring open. "Why would someone dig up a grave?"

"To find something buried long ago," she says.

"Like the pharaohs in Egypt?"

"Something like that. Would you believe it?"

"Yeah. I would believe it," I say, my heart pounding in my chest. I saw it with my own eyes. Is she going to reveal something about her mom or the grave?

Dr. Hughes scoffs. "Don't believe everything you hear."

I nod my head and my shoulders slump. Darn. I was so close to getting some info about the cemetery. It's going to be a lot tougher than I thought.

I circulate the pamphlets and say goodbye to Christina. I'm still wondering about the article and Dr. Hughes's comment when I reach the parking lot and unlock my bike. A silver sports car draws my attention. All week someone has parked it in the same spot near the birch trees. I don't see it when I arrive in the morning, but it's there when I leave in the afternoon. I'm not that into cars, but this one stands out because it looks exotic. I take a photo and send it to Tara.

Datsun 280zx, she replies. *Vintage*

I text a thumbs-up emoji. Whoever owns it must live or work nearby.

Pretty cool, Tara replies. *Bet it's fun 2 drive!*

I'm still thinking about the car when I notice a note taped to the handlebars of my bicycle. I open it up and read.

MIND YOUR OWN BUSINESS

I glance around the parking lot, but nobody is around. Only empty cars.

Chapter
9

Mel takes the SAT on Saturday morning, and we agree that after the exam, he'll drive me back to see Dr. Oliver. I spend the morning reading about TR-97 and post-traumatic stress disorder. When Mel picks me up, I show him the note from the day before.

"Someone taped it to your bike?" he asks.

"On the handlebars, so I wouldn't miss it."

Mel drives through the neighborhood toward University Avenue. "Do you think it was that Paulson guy?"

"I don't know. That's my first guess because he knows I work there, but I can't connect him to anything else."

"Except he works for Feester."

"But Feester didn't make TR-97," I say. "And Feester didn't fund Doctor Oliver's drug research."

"Wisconsin State funded that, right?" asks Mel.

I lower my window and rest my right elbow on the door frame. "And another company called Treon Laboratories. They funded it along with the university."

"Who else would write the note?"

"Remember, I told you about that car in the parking lot?"

"Yeah."

"It could be whoever drives that car," I say, adjusting my seat belt because it's cutting into my shoulder.

"That's a long shot."

"I know, but who else?"

"What about Doctor Hughes?" he asks.

"I don't think so." I close my eyes and massage my temples with my fingertips. It can't be Sasha. She did come in after me, but wanted me to stay and help her. She would've sent me home right away if she wanted me to mind my own business. What does that even mean?

"You never know," says Mel. "Did you get the license plate of that car?"

I shake my head. "Just a photo. Tara said it's a Datsun *280zx* from the early eighties."

"A what?" he asks.

"Datsun. The company is now Nissan."

"Then it's old. I bet there aren't many on the road anymore."

"Will you look into it?" I ask. "Please."

Mel glances at me. "Send me the photo."

We're quiet for a few minutes, and I stare out the window, feeling the breeze in my face, lost in my thoughts.

"Aren't you going to ask me about the test?" he asks.

"Shit! Sorry, Mel. Did you ace it?"

"Like you care," he says with a grin.

"I do. But I already know you did great."

"At least it's over. I'll find out in six weeks if I need to take it again."

"That's a long time to wait."

"It'll be nice to think about something else for a while," he says as we stop at a red light.

"I *never* want to think about it," I say.

"But, you need to."

I frown.

"Take it in the spring," he says. "I'll give you my study materials."

"Can I borrow your brain, too?"

"You're plenty smart. You just need to prepare."

"Thanks, Mom," I say, rolling my eyes. "I look forward to that."

"What are you going to talk about with the crazy doctor?"

"I'm going to start with family stuff, Sasha, maybe his wife, then ease back into the cemetery vandalism."

"Sounds good, I guess. Are you going to mention the note?"

"Not until I know what it means or who it's from."

"Okay," says Mel as he steers the Volvo all the way through the parking lot to the far side. "I'll wait here for you."

As I enter the nursing home, a blast of cold from the air conditioning hits my face. I shiver, then walk toward the desk, recognizing Kat, the woman from the other day. It's a relief to see a familiar face.

"Hi," I say, showing her my ID. "I'm back to see Doctor Oliver."

She smiles and glances at my photo, then hands me a badge.

"Welcome back," she says and calls an attendant.

I see Jesse down the hall and wave to him.

"You're back for another visit," he says with a smile.

"Yes," I say. "How are you?"

"Good, thank you."

"How's Doctor Oliver?"

"He seemed alert this morning, like he was expecting a visitor, but after lunch he insisted on napping."

"I wanted to visit this morning," I say, "but I didn't have a ride."

"That sounds like me. I take the bus because my wife needs the car for the kids."

"How many kids do you have?"

"Three," he says. "Two girls, ages six and four, and a baby boy."

"That's a big family," I say as we pass a woman walking with a cane.

"Beautiful day," she says to no one in particular. "Such a lovely day."

"Who's that?" I ask.

"That's Dorothy. She enjoys walking," he says.

I look back over my shoulder at her. "She seems happy."

"She thinks life is grand."

"Doctor Oliver is kind of the opposite."

"Not necessarily," says Jesse.

"What if he's still sleeping?" I ask when we're outside room 103.

"Don't worry. He needs to get up, anyway. And I'm sure he'll be happy to get out of bed for a visitor."

Jesse knocks on the door and pushes it open. I follow him inside. Dr. Oliver is lying on the bed in his clothes and shoes. He looks peaceful resting on his side facing us. His eyes are closed, but his breathing sounds a bit like Darth Vader.

"Time to wake up, Doctor Oliver," says Jesse. "You have a guest."

Dr. Oliver remains motionless, like a corpse.

"He doesn't have his hearing aids in," says Jesse, pointing to the nightstand. "He can't hear us without them."

I hope he's right. Jesse nudges Dr. Oliver's shoulder, jostling him a little. Dr. Oliver flinches and opens his eyes.

"Who's there?" asks Dr. Oliver.

"It's Jesse," he says, resting his hand on the doctor's shoulder.

"What do you want?"

"You have a visitor," says Jesse.

"Let me sleep."

"It's time to get up."

"Who sent you?"

"It's okay, Doctor Oliver. Let me help you."

"Stay away from me!" says Dr. Oliver.

The volume of his voice and the fury behind the words slap me in the face. My throat constricts, and I step behind Jesse. The phrase "don't wake the sleeping bear" comes to mind.

"Here are your eyeglasses, Doctor Oliver," says Jesse, moving them toward the doctor's face.

"Don't touch me!" says Dr. Oliver, waving his hands in front of him. Jesse grasps Dr. Oliver's wrist and places the glasses in his palm.

"Let me help you with your hearing aids."

How can Jesse stay so calm? I want to flee from the room, but an invisible force holds me in place.

With his eyeglasses on and hearing aids in, Dr. Oliver looks at me, blinking several times.

"Hi, Doctor Oliver," I say, clasping my hands in front of me and slouching a bit. "It's Penelope."

He stares at me and my eyes shift from his face to the wall behind him.

"Come on, Doctor," says Jesse. "Let's get you up. Do you want to use the toilet first?"

Dr. Oliver coughs and nods his head. He doesn't say a word, but allows Jesse to help him. I wait while they disappear into the bathroom, then study the room. Not one photo or picture hangs on the drab walls. Nothing personal rests on the nightstand or window sill. After the toilet flushes, Jesse offers gentle reminders about hand washing, then guides Dr. Oliver toward the recliner. Once he's settled in by the window, I sit in the chair opposite him.

"There you go, Doctor Oliver," says Jesse. "Enjoy your visit."

I watch Jesse leave, then turn my focus back to Dr. Oliver.

"Sorry to wake you," I say.

"I guess I forgot where I was," he says.

"Did you have a nightmare?"

"I don't remember." He touches his hearing aids and adjusts his glasses. "I'm lost without all this stuff."

"You're okay now?" I ask.

"I wondered if you would visit again."

"I had to wait until afternoon for a ride."

Dr. Oliver stares at me, swaying slightly in his seat. I stare back, gathering the courage to speak.

"I've been working in Sasha's office," I say. "It's been really busy, but she's so good with the animals. Have you ever been to her clinic?"

I wait for a response, but he studies me in silence.

"I can't believe she got to go to school in California. That's so amazing. Just seeing the ocean and palm trees sounds like heaven. Have you ever been to California?"

I'm droning on about nonsense, and even though I've asked a few questions, Dr. Oliver doesn't reply. His face remains blank, his eyes fixed on my face. Is he in a trance? Somehow, I need to get him talking. I don't remember the class, probably English, but one of my teachers told us to avoid yes or no questions because they don't stimulate conversations.

"So, what do you do all day?" I ask.

"I sleep, eat, and use the toilet," he says. "A useless existence."

"What about activities? Do they have those here?"

Before she got sick, my grandma lived at a place where they had exercise, art, music, and games. She was always busy.

"No."

"Why not?"

He shrugs. "They keep us isolated so we don't cause trouble."

"Would you like to do something?" I ask.

"Like what?"

"Play cards?"

"No," he says.

"Listen to music?"

He shakes his head.

I glance around the room. "What about books? You had one the other day."

"Someone occasionally brings me something to read, but then it disappears."

"I can bring you another book. Would you like that?"

"Large print is best."

I nod. "How about a jigsaw puzzle? We have tons of them at home."

His eyes scan the room. "I don't have a place to work on those, and the pieces are too darn small."

Poor Dr. Oliver. He has nothing to do all day. He must be lonely.

"I'd rather solve the puzzle of the mind," he says, tapping the side of his head with his index finger.

"What kind of puzzle is that?" I ask.

"It's the ultimate puzzle that determines who we are, what we think, and how we behave."

"That's what you used to do, right? Psychiatry."

"I miss it, the people, the challenges, and the mysteries." Dr. Oliver sighs.

"I bet it was hard to give up."

"We were so close to getting approval. This close." He holds his thumb and index finger an inch apart. "I wasn't ready to give up, but they forced me."

"Right, sorry. It sounds so unfair."

"My life's work, gone. Just like that." Dr. Oliver's shoulders droop. We're quiet as I listen to the rumble in his chest when he breathes.

"You don't have a television," I say, "but do you read the newspaper?"

"Not anymore. She won't allow it."

"Who won't?"

"My daughter."

"Oh." My heart sinks. He's so isolated.

"So you don't follow the local news?" I ask.

He shakes his head.

"Remember last week I told you about the article in the Mendota *Times*?"

"About the vandalism at Westmoreland Cemetery?"

I nod. "It's turned out to be a genuine mystery."

"How so?" he asks.

"Friends on the golf team told me someone dug up a grave."

Dr. Oliver scoffs. "That sounds like hyperbole."

"The newspaper also reported evidence of grave robbers."

"That can't be right."

"Someone dug up a grave," I say. "Right here in Mendota."

"And the mystery?" he asks.

"Who dug up the grave? And what were they looking for?"

He scratches his head. "I'm sure the police have got it handled. It hardly sounds mysterious."

I don't think he knows about Gwendolyn's grave. Should I tell him? "It might if you knew whose grave it was."

Dr. Oliver studies me for a moment and sighs. "All right, Penelope. I'll indulge you and play along. It was probably somebody famous."

"Not necessarily, but possibly well known."

"Someone in sports?"

I shake my head. "Nope, but it was a woman."

"Someone in politics, then?"

"No, but she died twenty-five years ago."

"That doesn't help," he says, shifting his gaze out the window.

"You knew her," I say, dangling the last clue in front of him. I hold my breath and lean back in my chair. He could explode like when Jesse woke him up.

Dr. Oliver turns his head to look at me. His eyes penetrate my skull and his mouth opens in an expression of surprise, but he doesn't speak. He clenches his fists in his lap, then grasps the arms of the recliner. I imagine the gears turning in his brain. He knows which grave I'm talking about, otherwise he would have asked, "How did I know her?"

"It can't be," he says.

"Yes, it can," I say, feeling drops of perspiration on my forehead.

"Who are we talking about?" he asks.

I struggle to keep my voice steady, knowing I can't give him the answer. I ignore the noise of my heartbeat pounding in my ears. "I think you know."

"Tell me it's not Gwendolyn."

I nod slightly. "It was Gwendolyn Oliver's grave." I grip my chair and wait for the explosion, but it doesn't come.

"Jesus, Mary, and Joseph," says Dr. Oliver. He drops his head into his hands, looking at his lap, then suddenly pivots toward the window. "What time is it?" he asks.

I glance at my phone. "Two fifty-seven," I say.

"You have to leave," he says.

"What? Why?"

"Leave now!"

"I'm sorry I upset you, Doctor Oliver."

Fury fuels his voice. "Right now!"

"But why?" I ask, searching his eyes for an answer.

His face is red and contorted. When I stand, my legs shake. I glance at the door, certain they heard him shouting. They'll send someone to throw me out.

"Get out of here! Before it's too late!"

I shuffle toward the door. The lump in my throat feels like a brick. "Sorry," I say, glancing at Dr. Oliver one last time.

He doesn't look at me. His arms are crossed over his chest, his brow furrowed, his eyes staring out the window at the world beyond.

Chapter
10

I rush out of the nursing home, scurrying across the parking lot to Mel's car. He backed into the space and watches me approach. Shit! I pushed too hard. Why did I go with the cemetery story? I should've asked more about Sasha or his research. Now he doesn't want to see me anymore.

I fling open the passenger door and flop onto the seat.

"Are you okay?" Mel asks. "Your face is all splotchy."

"He threw me out," I say, swallowing my tears.

"What happened?"

"I told him about his wife's grave."

"Oh, shit. Obviously, it struck a chord."

"A bad one." I wipe my nose with a napkin I find on the floor of Mel's car.

"He blew up? Did you get it on camera?"

I frown at Mel and shake my head. "He yelled at me and told me to get out."

"That sucks."

I tip my head back against the seat and stare at the roof. "I blew it."

"Did he want to know how you knew about the grave?" asks Mel.

"I told him it was in the newspaper."

"But they didn't print it in the paper."

"He doesn't read the paper," I say.

"Okay, but he questioned it?"

I turn my face toward Mel. "I also told him friends on the golf team saw it."

"And he believed you?"

"I wasn't going to tell him *we* saw the hole."

"So was he angry that someone dug up his wife's grave, or that someone found something he buried?"

I clench my teeth. "How should I know? We didn't get into the details."

"It makes a difference, though. Did you mention the vial?"

I shake my head. "We didn't talk about TR-97 today."

"But you asked him about it last time?"

"Yeah," I say with a sigh. "Do you have another napkin?"

Mel hands me one and I blow my nose. There must be a connection between the vial and the grave. It can't be a coincidence. But the only logical link is that someone buried the vial with Gwendolyn Oliver's ashes, and that's just weird.

Mel starts the car, and I gaze out the window, trying to clear my mind. Dr. Oliver was definitely upset, but his immediate reaction wasn't anger. He seemed stunned.

"Do you want to get a slice of pizza?" asks Mel.

"Sure," I say. "Cheese fixes everything."

"I think Tara should hear about this."

"Oh Shit! Get down," I say, sliding lower on the seat.

Mel tries to hunch down, but the steering wheel blocks his path.

"What is it?" he asks.

"Sasha just pulled into the parking lot."

"Where?"

"Over to the right. The white BMW."

Mel raises his head and peeks over the dashboard. "I don't see it."

I lift my head high enough to get a view out the window. From across the lot, Sasha gets out of her four-door wagon.

"Thank god she parked over there," I say.

Mel and I hold our breath and watch her walk to the entrance of the nursing home.

"She's going to visit her dad."

"Let's get out of here," says Mel, putting the car into drive.

When we walk into Rocky's, Tara stands behind the counter at the cash register.

"What can I get for you nerds?" she asks with a smile.

"A slice of pepperoni," I say.

"The Motherlode for me," says Mel.

"Anything to drink? It's on the house," she says with a wink.

"Sure," Mel and I say together.

"Can you sit with us for a few minutes? We just came from a visit with the crazy doctor."

Tara looks around. "I can take a quick break," she says. "Grab a booth in the back, and I'll bring you your slices."

We fill our cups with root beer, then slide into the vacant space in the corner. Mel and I sit across from each other, checking our phones while we wait. A few minutes later, Tara glides into the seat next to me.

"So you went for another visit? Both of you?" she asks.

"Just me," I say. "Mel stayed in the car."

"So what happened?"

"I told him someone dug up his wife's grave, and he got angry."

"No shit, Sherlock. Of course he was mad," says Tara. "Who wouldn't be?"

"I don't know what I was thinking," I say, dropping my head into my hands.

"The only person who wouldn't be angry hearing that news is the person who actually dug up the grave," says Mel. "They would have a different reaction."

"What should I do?" I ask.

"What did you think he'd say when you told him?" asks Tara.

"I don't know. I messed up, okay? And now it's over. He doesn't want to see me anymore."

"He said that?" asks Tara.

"He told me to leave."

"So what? It's not like he said get the hell out."

"That's true," says Mel.

"Leave is different from get the hell out," says Tara.

I look at her and scowl. "He said get out of here."

"Okay, that's worse than leave."

"Tell us exactly what happened," says Mel.

When I finish my story, they stare at me in silence, processing the information. My pizza is getting cold, so I take a huge bite.

Tara shakes her head. "I can't believe he guessed his wife."

"You know what this means," says Mel.

"What?" I ask.

"That Doctor Oliver buried the vial."

"You think so?" asks Tara.

"Who else would even consider doing that?"

I rest my elbows on the table. "He admitted TR-97 was his life's work. He also would've had access to his wife's ashes."

"Exactly," says Mel, wiping his hands on a paper napkin.

"But now I can't visit him anymore," I say.

"Are you sure?" asks Tara.

"He yelled at me and told me to leave."

"My sister used to say that all the time," says Mel, taking a bite of pizza, "but eventually she'd let me back into her room."

"This is different," I say.

"Did he say anything else?" asks Tara.

I hesitate and take a deep breath. "Get out of here before it's too late."

"What?" says Mel.

"That's a warning," says Tara, taking a sip of my soda. "Maybe he was trying to help you, not get rid of you."

"I don't know. He was pretty upset."

A Rocky's employee with a mustache and several pimples on his forehead looms over our table, glaring at Tara.

"Robertson, your break is over. Get back to work."

"Gotta go," she says, standing up. "Don't want to get fired from my shitty job."

"We'll talk later," I say to Tara. "I'm getting more root beer. You want some, Mel?"

"How can I resist the lure of sweet sarsaparilla?" he says.

"Is that another SAT word?" I ask, getting up from the booth.

"Spelling bee. I dare you to try it."

"No way." I shake my head and walk to the soda fountain.

While I'm waiting to fill our cups, Mr. Paulson enters the restaurant. I recognize him from his shaggy hair and sideburns. Unless you're Elvis or Wolverine, you shouldn't wear sideburns like that. I ignore him and get more ice, refilling the cups. As I turn to head back to Mel in the booth, Paulson appears next to me.

"Do I know you?" he asks.

"Sort of," I say. "I work at Shorewood Animal Clinic."

"That's where I've seen you."

It's probably the hair. Was my mom right about getting attention?

"What's your name?" he asks.

"Penn."

"You work in the mornings, right?"

"Yeah." I look around him toward the back of the restaurant.

"And ride a bike?"

"Yep," I say, trying to inch away from him. How would he know that?

"I'll see you next week," he says.

"Okay." I hurry to the safety of Mel and the booth.

He grabs his cup. "What took you so long?"

"OMG. The creep is here," I say.

"Where?" Mel leans out of the booth to have a look.

"Don't look now!"

"Too late," says Mel. "He's looking this way."

Chapter
11

I wake up to rain on Monday morning. The drops hit my bedroom window like soft drumbeats, lulling me back to sleep. I drift in and out of consciousness for a while, then force myself to get up.

"Can you drive me to work?" I ask, stepping into the kitchen. "I don't want to ride my bike in the rain."

My mom sits at the table, typing furiously on her laptop. She's still in her pajamas, a good sign that she doesn't have anywhere else to be.

"Mom? Did you hear me?"

"Sure, honey," she says, still focused on her screen. "When?"

"About fifteen minutes."

"Yeah. I should finish this by then."

"I don't want to be late," I say, taking a bite of peanut butter toast. "If you'd rather have me call Tara or Mel, tell me now."

"No, I'll do it."

"You know this wouldn't be a problem if you'd just let me get my license."

My mom stops typing and glares at me. "We've been over this, Penn. Your dad doesn't think it's a good idea, and I understand his concerns."

"But you could let me drive. He wouldn't even know."

She shakes her head. "We'll talk about it later."

"Later means never," I say with a frown.

"Later means later," she says, focusing on her laptop.

"You know everyone else drives. Even stupid people drive. I'm a responsible person with a job. I should be driving."

"I can't talk about it right now. If you want a ride to work, stop interrupting me so I can finish this email."

"Whatever," I say, crossing my arms over my chest. It's pointless. She's not listening. "It's not like Dad would even know if I'm driving. I never see him anyway."

"That's enough, Penn."

"I'll be in the car," I say, grabbing my jacket from the closet and letting the door to the garage close with a bang behind me.

We drive in silence while I stare out the window. Why are my parents so lame? They don't understand anything. When I'm eighteen, I'm going to get my license and leave this place.

When we pull into the parking lot, Sasha stands near her car with a large black umbrella. She has several boxes stacked next to her and is talking to a petite blonde woman in high heels. My mom stops the car near the clinic entrance, and I get out.

"Don't I get a 'thank you' or a 'goodbye'?" she asks.

"Bye," I say, slamming the door and walking away.

Instead of entering the building, I pull the hood up on my raincoat and approach Sasha and the other woman. "Do you need any help?" I ask.

"Yes, Penn. Thank you," says Sasha. "I need to get these boxes into my office."

"More brochures?" I ask, picking one up.

"No, they're books, and they're heavy. So take one at a time."

I carry one to Sasha's office and set it on the floor, then go back outside for another. Sasha and the woman remain under the umbrella.

"Do a book signing," says the blonde woman. She speaks with authority and a hint of arrogance. As she talks, it's impossible not to recognize that voice. It's Helga. She's about my height, but the wrinkles around her mouth and eyes make her look older than Sasha. Her bright red lipstick and thick black eyeliner can't hide her age. I linger nearby and listen.

"I'll sign copies in the office," says Sasha.

"But that's not the same. You need the press and some fanfare. I'll put you in touch with my agent."

"That's not necessary."

"Of course it is. My agent is a genius. She can get you on the news doing a demonstration or something, and if the book becomes a best seller, maybe even *Good Morning America*."

"I don't think I could handle all that."

Overhearing this, I say, "Did you write a book?"

"Yes," both women reply, and I give them a puzzled look.

"My book was just published," says Sasha.

"That's great," I say, grabbing another box. "What's it called?"

"*Training Your Furry Friends*."

"But she needs to get the word out. Nobody knows about it yet," says the other lady.

"You can put a link on the clinic website and sell copies from there," I say.

"How do I do that?" Sasha asks, looking from me to the blonde woman.

"My friend Mel can probably do it. He's great with computers and tech stuff."

Sasha nods. "I'll consider that."

"Like I said, tell your web designer to add something right away. And don't forget to announce it on social media."

It's definitely Helga, the family friend Sasha mentioned last week. The woman from the cemetery. I take another box inside and return for the third. The rain has stopped and they're still talking, but not about the book. I bend down to tie my shoes, hoping they won't notice me.

"I'm going to see James," says Helga with a wry smile.

"He'll be delighted to see you," says Sasha with a smirk.

"Should I relay a message?" asks Helga.

"Tell him someone unearthed new information about his research," says Sasha. "He'll like that."

They both cackle and I cringe.

Unearthed new information? My stomach quivers. Does that mean dig up? I can't stand around any longer without eavesdropping, so I grab the last box and bring it to Sasha's office. Is it a crazy coincidence, or were they talking about the grave and the vial? I'm pondering their conversation when Denise startles me.

"There you are," she says.

"Hi," I say. "Do you need something?"

"We've got a busy day. The sooner you start, the better."

That's a nice way of saying "get to work," so I hustle to the kennel area and start cleaning the cages. It's the worst part of my job because the noxious fumes from the disinfectant make my eyes sting and my throat burn. If I didn't wear gloves, the solution would probably melt the flesh from my fingers.

"Thanks for bringing in the boxes," says Sasha when she sees me.

"No problem," I say. "It's cool that you wrote a book."

"It was a lot of work, but I hope people find it helpful."

I nod and point toward the boxes. "Do you want to put some copies in the reception area?"

"Leave a display copy with Christina. The rest can stay in my office."

"And let me know if you want to talk to my friend about updating your website."

"Okay," she says, turning away from me.

"Was that Helga you were talking to?" I ask.

Sasha pivots to look at me. "How did you know?"

"I recognize her voice. She's called the office before."

"She's definitely more of an expert on books. She's written several, and knows how to sell them."

"What kind of books does she write?"

"Lots of self-help in psychology, meditation, and hypnotism."

I shrug. "I haven't read any of those."

"Probably not, but she gives talks and leads seminars all over the country."

"She's famous?"

"You could say that. When she releases a new book, her publisher makes sure she does a nationwide book tour."

"Wow," I say with a nod. Psychology. I definitely need to Google Helga when I get home. "What's her last name?" I ask. "In case I want to find one of her books."

"Thorstad," says Sasha.

Later that afternoon, I return to the clinic to pick up my paycheck. It wasn't ready in the morning, and I'm excited to have money. It's kind of old-fashioned to get a paper check, but I didn't know my bank account information when I filled out the paperwork. When I pull open the door with a jingle, I find the reception and waiting room areas empty.

"Hello?" I say. Where's Christina? Did she leave already? She knew I was coming back for my check.

Opal is asleep on a pile of file folders on the counter. Like most cats I've met, she ignores my existence. I don't see my check on the desk, so I wander down the hall to Dr. Hughes's office. The door is closed, but I hear her voice. She must be on the phone. No, wait. I hear another voice. A guy. Somebody else is in there with her. I pause for a moment to listen.

"Will you at least look for the files?" the man says.

"Why should I do that?" asks Sasha.

"Because they're valuable, and we agreed to share." It's Paulson.

"But you messed up."

"You're still stuck on that? The good stuff is in the files."

"The university destroyed the good stuff," says Sasha.

"How do you know unless you look?" he says.

I tip-toe back to the reception desk. Valuable files? Is this related to TR-97? I debate leaving and getting the check tomorrow, but I want the money today. I grab my phone and call the clinic. Maybe Sasha will answer, and I can tell her I'm here.

Even though I'm expecting it, I jump when the phone at the reception desk chimes. It rings five times, then rolls to voicemail. I end the call and take one last look around the desk, stroking Opal from head to tail. She gives me a little purr and rolls onto her side. I'm about to leave when the door to Dr. Hughes's office opens, and voices fill the hall. I instinctively hit the top number on "RECENTS" on my cell, then pick up the office phone on the first ring.

"Shorewood Animal Clinic, may I help you?" I say.

"I didn't know you were here?" says Sasha, rounding the corner toward the desk.

"That's okay. Bye," I say into the phone, replacing the handset onto the base.

"Who was that?" she asks.

I shrug. "Wrong number."

Paulson stands behind Sasha with his arms crossed over his chest.

"What are you doing here?" Sasha asks.

"I came back for my paycheck. I guess Christina left early."

"She had an appointment. Let me get it." Sasha turns and heads back down the hall.

"Thanks," I say. While I wait, Paulson studies me with a frown. His stare makes my stomach churn.

"Is Echo with you?" I ask, trying to keep my voice steady.

"Not today," he says.

"He's feeling better?"

"How long have you been here?"

I glance at my phone. "A couple minutes."

"Were you listening to our conversation?"

"No," I say, shaking my head and looking down at the desk. My hands are trembling, so I pretend to tidy the area by the phone.

"You weren't snooping around?"

My throat tightens. "I just walked in and the phone was ringing."

"I swear I saw a shadow under the door."

"I'm just here for my check."

"And here it is," says Sasha, returning to the reception area.

"Thanks," I say, taking the envelope and moving around them toward the door. "See you tomorrow."

Chapter

12

On Wednesday morning before work, I text Mel. *I need 2 go back 2 c Dr. O*

When? he replies.

Today

Afternoon?

Yes. Sasha is busy all day

U sure u want 2 go back?

I have 2 find out if he's still mad

K. Pick u up at work?

Yes. Noon

C u then

At noon, Mel waits for me in the parking lot. I look for the *280zx* in the corner near the trees, but it's not there. I hoist my bike into the back of the car and shut the hatch.

"How was work, honey?" he says with a grin as I get into the passenger seat.

"Kind of a drag," I say. "I'm a glorified cleaning lady."

"That's what happens when you're at the bottom of the totem pole."

I grimace. "Great."

"I'm sure it will get better," he says. "At least you're making money."

I fasten my seatbelt. "One dollar every five minutes."

"You'll be rich in no time."

"Yeah, right."

Mel steers the Volvo out of the parking lot. "Are you nervous?" he asks.

"A little," I say with a nod. "Today could blow up in my face."

"My pits are sweaty, and I'm not even going inside."

"I'm going to bring him this book and pretend like nothing happened, like we never had the conversation about the cemetery and his wife's grave. If he's crazy, maybe he won't remember it, either."

I sink into the seat. But what if he remembers and yells at me to get out? Would I beg to stay and tell him about the vial? I'm glad I didn't eat lunch yet. I'm not sure I could keep it down.

"That's a good strategy," says Mel. "Distract him. But, what are you going to talk about, the weather?"

I fake laugh. "Your name should be Funnyman, not Castleman."

"Seriously, you can't talk about movies or music or sports."

"I want to know more about Helga."

"The woman in the cemetery?"

I nod. "I'm ninety-nine percent certain it was her. With everything I've read about her online, she could have a connection to TR-97."

"Be careful, though," says Mel. "No bold accusations or revelations."

I grip the book in my lap. "I know. I was way too aggressive last time."

"If you want him to talk, you need to move a little slower."

"Good plan."

"Speaking of plans," says Mel, "I have some."

"You do?"

"I'm going to Florida with my family for two weeks."

"Two weeks?"

"Yep."

"When?"

"Saturday."

I turn away from Mel and frown. My shoulders droop. I don't want to make him feel guilty. It's not his fault his parents plan cool trips, and I never get to go anywhere.

"I wish I could be here to keep up with this stuff," he says, "but I have to go."

"I wouldn't expect you to stay home. But we'll miss you."

"I'll miss you, too."

I stare out the window and sigh. "Do you need someone to look after Bebe?"

He shakes his head. "She's going to stay with my aunt."

"Go have fun. Don't worry about me. I'll rope Tara in to help."

"Keep me in the loop, though."

I nod. "You know we will."

We arrive at the nursing home and Mel takes his usual parking spot, backing into the space so he can watch the door. A different receptionist occupies the desk today. She checks my ID and hands me a badge with my name on it. That's a good sign. Dr. Oliver didn't take me off the visitation list. An attendant named Fergus walks with me to Dr. Oliver's room.

"I expected to see Jesse," I say.

"He doesn't work today," says Fergus.

As we walk down the hall, I recognize Dorothy moving toward us with her cane. When we pass each other I smile, and she offers her greeting of "Lovely day, just beautiful."

"Hello, Mrs. Colleran," says Fergus, nodding his head. "Nice to see you."

When we arrive at room 103, the door stands open, and Dr. Oliver sits in his recliner, staring out the window.

"You have a visitor, Doctor Oliver," says Fergus, after knocking.

Dr. Oliver turns toward the door, his face expressionless as we linger near the entry. He blinks several times but doesn't move or speak. At least he's not shouting at me to go away. I step into the room, approaching the empty chair with caution.

"Hi, Doctor Oliver," I whisper, sitting down.

"It's your granddaughter," says Fergus, following me into the room. "Why don't you visit with her for a while?"

When Fergus leaves, I try again. "It's Penelope. I brought you a book."

He stares at me and blinks again. Are his hearing aids in? They must be if he heard us at the door. I place the book on his lap and sit across from him in the upright chair. Dr. Oliver dips his eyes to peek at the title, then turns it over to look at the back.

"I hope you like *The Hobbit*," I say. "It's one of my favorites."

"I read it years ago," he says.

"I hope you'll enjoy it again."

Dr. Oliver nods at me. "Is your name in it?" he asks.

"My name?"

"Inside the cover or in the back?"

"I don't think so. Is that a problem?"

"Please look. You can't leave it here if your name is inside."

I pick up the book and flip through the first few pages. "It's inside the front cover." I show him the book.

"Then don't leave it here."

I frown. "Can I just cross it out?"

"That's not a good idea."

"Okay," I say with a sigh. "Sorry. I'll bring you something else. Maybe a classic like *The Adventures of Huckleberry Finn* or *To Kill a Mockingbird.*"

"I would like that."

We stare at each other and I squirm in my chair. He's waiting for me to say something.

"I just came from work at your daughter's clinic. She's really busy today."

"She likes to be busy," he says.

"She has lots of pets to take care of."

"She always liked animals."

"I do too," I say.

"Do you have a pet?" he asks.

I shake my head. "I want a dog, but my parents won't let me get one. Maybe someday when I'm older."

Dr. Oliver folds his hands in his lap. "I never let Sasha have a pet, either. She really wanted one, but I didn't have time for that."

"They're a lot of work, but they can be great companions."

"Do you think so?"

I pause before replying. "Aren't pets supposed to be good for mental health?" Shouldn't he know that?

He contemplates my statement, nodding his head slightly and sighing. "Sasha brought a kitten home once. A stray she found in the neighborhood. She begged me to let her keep it, promising she'd take care of it. But I ignored her pleas and forced her to bring it to the shelter. She cried for days."

He purses his lips and rubs his forehead. "I didn't even consider that the critter might have brought her a bit of comfort or companionship."

I'm caught off-guard by Dr. Oliver's revelation, and a lump forms in my throat. Should I agree or disagree? "You did what you thought was right," I say. "Kind of like my parents."

"I wonder if things would've turned out differently if I'd let her keep that kitten."

"I guess you'll never know."

Dr. Oliver bows his head. "Losing your mother leaves a hole. A chasm that is infinitely deep and dark. I suppose a pet may have helped."

"She seems fine now, but I guess she was pretty young when that happened."

"Ten years old."

My chest tightens. Ten is too young to lose your mother.

"She understood her mother's illness, the cancer, but not the dying." A tear slides down Dr. Oliver's face, and he doesn't wipe it away. I watch as it drops onto his shirt, disappearing into the landscape of blue cotton fibers. The room is so quiet I can hear the wheezing in his chest as he breathes.

When I speak, my voice is a whisper. "That must have been hard for you, too."

"Gwendolyn was the love of my life. I thought we would grow old together. The only way I could cope with her death was to immerse myself in my work."

"The TR-97 research?"

He nods. "We had just completed the early trials, and it showed so much promise. It was a genuine breakthrough, and I was certain I could eliminate the suffering of so many people."

"I read about the veterans whose lives you changed."

"But I lost sight of what was truly important."

"What was that?" I ask, shifting my position in the chair.

"My daughter. I lost Sasha when the treatment became a success. I handed her off to others, like a stray kitten."

My heart sinks and the pressure of tears builds in my eyes. Poor Sasha. She lost everything.

"But Sasha is here now," I say, trying to sound upbeat. "She went away to college, but she's back in Mendota."

"She came back physically, but not emotionally."

"That's really tough."

"Because of my actions, we're strangers." Dr. Oliver squeezes his hands together in his lap and turns his head toward the window.

"I'm sorry," I say. "Is there any hope?"

He shakes his head. "When she was young and impressionable, I was too busy with meetings and conferences."

"You could apologize."

"It's too late for that."

"It reminds me a teeny bit of my parents. My mom's still around, but she's always working. My dad moved out, and doesn't have time for me anymore."

"I'm sorry to hear that," says Dr. Oliver, another tear skimming his cheek.

"At least Sasha comes to visit you," I say.

Dr. Oliver doesn't respond right away. He continues staring out the window like he's waiting for someone. It could be Sasha or Gwendolyn or a miracle. From my perspective, the view is dismal. A sliver of parking lot, a cluster of dandelions in the grass, and a few spindly birch trees.

"She stops by," he says, "but not because she wants to."

"You mean Sasha?"

"She visits because she feels guilty. I can see it in her face."

Suddenly, the room feels hot and stuffy, the air thick with despair. Sasha must still be angry with her father. I'm angry with mine, but I still want to see him. I need to say something to lighten the mood.

"Did you know Sasha wrote a book?" I ask.

"She did?" he says.

I nod. "It's called *Training Your Furry Friends*."

"Good for her."

"Maybe she'll tell you about it on her next visit. Or bring you a copy."

Dr. Oliver's head sways back and forth a bit. I can't tell if it's an agreement or a dissent.

"I also met someone at the clinic the other day," I say. "Someone you might know."

Dr. Oliver remains mute, lost in his thoughts, gazing out the window.

"I met Helga Thorstad." My voice rises a bit when I speak her name.

"Helga?" he says, turning his face toward me. "I can't believe she's back in town."

"She was helping Sasha with her book."

Dr. Oliver's face reddens, and a vertical crease forms between his eyebrows. "Stay away from Helga," he says.

"Stay away? Why?"

"She's trouble with a capital T."

Before I can ask another question, we're interrupted by a knock on the door. A young health care aide named Bethany enters the room. "It's time for your bath, Doctor Oliver."

"I don't need a bath," he says.

"But we have to keep you clean," she says genially.

"That's nonsense. I am clean."

"Let's not argue today, Doctor Oliver. Your guest can come back another time."

I stand and look at Dr. Oliver. He nods, but I'm confused. Sasha and Helga are friends. Why does Dr. Oliver want me to stay away from Helga?

"Come back soon," says Dr. Oliver.

"See you Saturday morning," I say.

Chapter

13

That night, it takes hours to fall asleep. My mind won't let go of the conversation with Dr. Oliver. He seemed so sad and remorseful. I had never thought about it before, but what if my mom died? Who would take care of me? My dad? Not likely. I'd probably have to live with Grandma and Grandpa up north. That would suck. I'd have no friends, and no mom.

Eventually, I drift off to sleep, but wake up screaming several hours later. My mom races into my room.

"Are you all right?" she asks in a panic, turning on the light. "What happened?"

I shield my eyes from the brightness, then place my hand over my heart. It's pounding like I've been running. "Just a bad dream," I say. I can't tell her about it right now. It makes no sense.

"Sounds more like a nightmare. Do you have a fever?" She places her palm on my forehead.

I shake my head, then wipe the perspiration from the back of my neck.

"You're all clammy," she says.

"I'm fine."

"Are you sure?"

I nod. "I was being chased in my dream." I close my eyes for a moment and try to remember. It was dark outside, and I was running down the street. My legs felt like they were filled with cement. I struggled and fought for each step, but knew I was doomed.

"You screamed," she says. "I didn't know what was going on."

"Nothing," I say. "It's all in my head."

"All right. It's three in the morning. Will you be able to go back to sleep?"

"Probably. I just need to relax for a few minutes."

"Do you want me to sit with you?" she asks.

I gaze at my mom. She has bags under her eyes and a worried look on her face. "I'm okay."

She kisses the top of my head. "All right, honey. I'm going back to bed."

In the darkness, I flip my pillow over, resting my head on the cool dry side. I force myself to think about something happy or serene, like a litter of puppies or gentle waves lapping on the lakeshore. My brain refuses to cooperate, though. I fixate on my dream, even though the longer I'm awake, the faster the images disappear. Who or what am I running away from?

The dream makes me think of my dad. I know he's struggling, and the more I read about post-traumatic stress, the more convinced I am that he has it. His absence, his mood swings, his lack of motivation, all add up. I flip my pillow over again and pull the covers up to my neck.

What's more disturbing is an argument I remember overhearing between my parents the night before my dad moved out. They were in the bedroom and must have thought I was asleep. They rarely argued in front of me, and never like that, but I could hear everything.

My mom sounded hysterical. "What's wrong with you, Jason?"

"Nothing," he said.

"You mope around the house all day."

"I'm fine."

"You don't seem fine."

My dad's voice boomed through the thin walls. "I get things done around here."

"You barely do anything," said my mom. "It's like you're not even here."

"Is that what you want?"

"Of course not." Her voice didn't sound sincere. She wanted him gone.

"Maybe it would be better if I disappeared," he said.

"Don't be a drama king. Just go back to work."

Looking back, my world was crumbling like a dry scone, falling to the floor in pieces before you can even take a bite. I remember grabbing my earbuds and stuffing them into my ears. I found Billie Eilish on my phone and cranked up the volume. She understands anger, loneliness, and helplessness.

Somehow I fall asleep, and in the morning, my mom doesn't mention my nightmare. I'm glad. How would I explain it when I don't understand it.

I stay busy at work, and at eleven-thirty, Dr. Hughes finds me in the break room. "Can you work all day today? Christina needs to leave at noon for an appointment."

"Sure, but I didn't bring lunch. Can I run next door to get a sandwich?"

"Of course. Why don't you do that right now?"

I nod. "Do you want something while I'm there?"

"What's the special on Thursdays?" she asks.

I pull my phone from my pocket. "I don't know, but I can find the menu online."

"Never mind. Just order me a small pastrami on rye with mustard, lettuce and tomato." She hands me a ten-dollar bill.

I take the money and leave the building, striding down the sidewalk to Sandwich Buddies. The air is thick with humidity and feels like a blanket. I'm thinking about turkey and cheddar on sourdough when the 280zx pulls into the parking lot. A man with brown hair and a mustache occupies the driver's seat. What is it with men and mustaches? They're so gross. Thank god my dad doesn't have one. Aviator sunglasses shade the man's eyes, and he drives directly to his spot near the trees. I pause for a moment to see if he'll get out of the car, but he doesn't, so I keep walking. Dr. Hughes expects me back soon.

When I return to the clinic with the sandwiches, the car is empty. I got a decent look at the guy, but he's gone. I bring Dr. Hughes her sandwich, hoping she'll eat with me, but she takes her food to her office and closes the door. I sit alone at the bistro table in the break room, hunched over my phone. It would be easy to spend thirty minutes scrolling through Instagram and Snapchat, but I have several unread texts.

One is from Mel: *Send photo of license plate*

Darn it. I could go back out to the parking lot right now, but I just sat down. I'll get the photo after work.

Another text is from my dad. *Let's play golf tomorrow morning.*

I haven't heard from him in over a week. Not since he showed up at the house to pick up his stuff. He doesn't know I blew off high school tryouts. I doubt Mom told him. It's not the type of news you want to share. I have to reply, but not right now.

The last message is from a private number. Probably a spammer. How do these people get my number? I look at it anyway.

Do I need to repeat myself? MIND YOUR OWN BUSINESS.

I look over my shoulder, even though I'm alone in the room. Somebody knows my cell phone number. Is it the same person who left the note? Suddenly, I'm not hungry. I don't dare reply, but I can't delete it, either. I have to share it with Tara and Mel.

Near the end of the day, I'm alone in the reception area, eager for six o'clock to arrive. The phone has been quiet, Eric is gone, and the appointment schedule is empty. I tidy the desk and play with Opal, tossing her some toys and pulling a feather around on a string. She ignores my invitation to play. I'm about to ask Dr. Hughes if I can leave early, when the door jingles and Helga strides in.

"Well, look who's here," she says with a sneer.

"Welcome to Shorewood Animal Clinic," I say.

"I see Sasha has trained her latest Step and Fetch It."

What did she just call me?

"Can I help you?" I ask, adding my blend of sarcasm.

"Nice try. I'm here to see Sasha."

"I'll let her know you're here." I purse my lips and reach for the phone.

"Don't bother." She waves her arm and struts past me. "I know the way to her office."

What a total bitch. How can Sasha be friends with that woman? No wonder Dr. Oliver told me to stay away from her. I look at the clock again. Only fifteen minutes until closing, so I might as well stay. It's another three dollars for my paycheck.

I pull out my phone and see a text from my mom. *Late meeting tonight. Eat leftover lasagna in the fridge.*

Kk, I reply, then look at the earlier texts from Mel, my dad, and the unknown number. I reach out to Mel first.

Worked all day. I'll call 2night

He replies with a thumbs-up emoji.

Then I text my dad. *I'm busy in the morning. How about afternoon?*

I don't expect a speedy reply. He's not chained to his phone like most people. Instead, I watch the clock as it approaches six. At one minute before, I pick up the telephone intercom.

"Doctor Hughes? I'm leaving."

She doesn't respond. She must be checking on the dogs that need to spend the night. I turn out the lights in the waiting room and proceed to the back.

"Doctor Hughes?" I whisper, pushing the door to the kennel area open a crack. "Are you in here?"

A dog whimpers, so I close the door and walk toward her office. She must be in there with Helga. I can hear the low mumble of their voices and pause outside the door, straining to follow their discussion.

"Just one box?" says Helga.

"That's it," says Sasha.

"I don't believe you," says Helga.

"It's true," says Sasha.

"But there have to be more files." I envision the scowl on Helga's face when she speaks.

"Well, there aren't."

Good for Sasha. She's holding her ground.

"I should come over and look for myself," says Helga.

"That's not necessary."

"You're hiding something. I know it."

"You're one to talk," says Sasha.

"What does that mean?"

"You know what I mean." Sasha's tone is bitter.

"Try me," says Helga.

"The fiasco with my mother's grave."

"What about it?"

"It's in the newspaper," says Sasha. "The police are investigating. What the hell were you thinking?"

During a long pause, I hold my breath. Sasha knows Helga dug up the grave! No wonder Sasha is furious. I should leave, but I'm captivated by the drama. If they suddenly open the door, though, I'm toast.

"Don't worry," Helga hisses. "It will blow over."

"I'm keeping the vial," says Sasha.

"That's not fair. I should keep it."

I lean closer to the door, hoping to hear more, but the conversation stops. I imagine them staring at each other in a stand-off.

I've heard enough, and knock softly on the door, but don't open it.

"Bye, Doctor Hughes," I say. "You can lock the front door after me."

I pause for a moment and Helga says, "She's still here?"

I don't wait for a goodbye, and hurry out of the clinic with a jingle, relieved to be away from them. What kind of person would dig up a grave? That's just wrong.

Muggy stagnant air greets me in the parking lot, like a Saint Bernard breathing in my face. I mount my bicycle and begin the ride home. Beads of sweat form on my back. My shirt clings to my torso. The smell of asphalt and exhaust makes me dizzy. I'm contemplating Sasha and Helga's exchange when a silver sports car turns in front of me, cutting me off. I brake hard and steer out of the way. Asshole! I flip them off and resume riding. What a freaking jerk. And my dad thinks driving a car is dangerous.

As I press the pedals and grip the handlebars, I wonder if that was the *280zx*. I look over my shoulder but don't see the car. It was probably just someone in a hurry or on their phone. But what if it wasn't? As I cycle home, up the long grade of South Hill Drive, I wonder if it was the guy from the parking lot. I push my legs harder, straining and panting up the hill. I can't escape the thought that someone is following me.

Chapter
14

When I get home, I rush to my room and dive onto the bed. I grab my phone and call Mel.

"Hey, Penn," he says, answering right away.

"Oh, my god! I'm freaking out," I say.

"What's wrong?"

"I almost got hit by a car on my bike."

"Are you okay? Did they stop?" asks Mel.

"I'm fine," I say, stretching out on my back. "The idiot just drove away."

"That sucks."

"And I got another message, a text this time, telling me to mind my own business."

"From who?" he asks.

"I don't know," I say. "The number was blocked."

"Oh, shit."

"And you're not going to believe this, but Helga came by the clinic. I overheard them talking."

"Helga and Doctor Hughes?"

I roll onto my side. "Yeah. Sasha suspects Helga dug up her mother's grave."

"She said that?"

"She practically accused Helga, and Helga didn't deny it."

"Whoa."

"Sasha even mentioned the vial."

"How does she know about that?"

"There must have been two," I say.

"Why would they want the TR-97?"

"I don't know, but it must be valuable if you'd dig up a grave to get it."

"The whole thing sounds cuckoo."

"I know," I say, with a yawn. "I'm exhausted."

"Did you get the photo?"

"What photo?" I ask.

"Of the license plate."

"Oh, crap. I totally forgot. Can I get it tomorrow?"

"Sure, but it's my last day at home."

"But you can look it up from Florida, right?"

I hear Bebe barking in the background.

"I suppose, but I'll only have my laptop, and the internet probably sucks."

"I promise, I'll get it tomorrow."

"Are you gonna call Tara tonight and fill her in?"

"She's working late, so probably not. I'll catch her tomorrow."

"Don't forget," says Mel.

"I won't. Bye."

After we hang up, my dad responds to my text. *Afternoon then?*

He means for golf. *Sure*, I text, hoping the tee times are all booked.

After a few minutes, my dad replies. *1:00 tee time. Pick you up at 12:30.*

I can't say no, even though I haven't played in two weeks.

K, I reply.

I'll be horrible, but that's the least of my problems. How I play doesn't matter. I'm going to have to drop the bomb and tell him I'm not on the team.

On Friday morning, while Dr. Hughes is away from the clinic, Christina and I organize the files in the reception area. "What do you think of that Paulson guy?" I ask.

"He seems nice, but he could smile more," says Christina.

I nod. "He sure spends a lot of money on his dog."

"A thousand dollars last month."

I hand her a stack of files. "That's obscene. And Echo's not even sick."

"I know. Can you believe it? I think he has a crush on Doctor Hughes."

"No way. She would *not* date someone with those sideburns."

"Overlook the sideburns," she says. "You can shave those off. I hear he makes bank at some big company. Have you noticed his designer suits and wingtips?"

"Wingtips?" I ask.

"Expensive leather shoes."

I shrug. "I hadn't noticed."

"Check 'em out next time."

"I will."

"While I'm doing this," Christina says, sorting a bunch of papers, "can you bring me all the stray files from Doctor Hughes's office?"

"Of course." I head down the hall and the door is closed. I knock out of habit before opening it and turning on the light. Christina is right. Manila files rest on her desk, the chair, and even on the floor. I start with the desk and chair, looking at the tabs for client last names. When I spent time in her office before, I hadn't noticed the diplomas on the wall and photos on her desk. I study them now, picking up each one. None of them look like Dr. Oliver, but this one looks like it could be Sasha's mother, Gwendolyn.

A loud voice down the hall disrupts my thoughts. Is that Christina? I shift my focus to the files on the floor. As I bend down to pick up NEUMAN, I see a larger one beneath it labeled TR-97. Why is that here? I reach for the file and open it. A stack of type-written papers stares back at me. I'm still holding the folder when Helga barges into the room.

"What are you doing?" she snaps.

"Nothing," I say, dropping the file onto the desk. "Just gathering client files for Christina."

"That doesn't sound like nothing," she says with a frown.

I glance at the TR-97 file and debate whether to pick it up again.

Helga beats me to it, snatching it from the desk. "That's mine. What else have you got in your grubby little hands?"

"Patient files," I say, fanning them out in front of her. When I move to leave the room, she steps to the side, putting her body between me and the door.

"I'm not sure I trust you." She looks me up and down. "You pretend to be innocent, but you have shifty eyes and a dull aura."

Her stare forces me to look down at the carpet. On the floor, under the desk, is a box labeled TR-97 RESEARCH, and another client file hides nearby.

"Excuse me," I say, bending over and grabbing the final folder. "I have to get back to work." I push past Helga and hurry to the reception area. "Here you go." I give my stack of files to Christina. "Sorry that took so long."

"That's okay. I've been chatting with Opal." The cat stretches out in the middle of the floor. Christina brushes her fur, and she rolls from one side to the other. "I suppose you bumped into the Wicked Witch of the West," Christina says, rolling her eyes. "She blew in here on her broomstick like she owns the place."

"She scared the crap out of me."

"Sorry. The phone rang. I didn't have time to warn you."

"Does she do that a lot?"

"Not a lot." says Christina. "But I need to ask Doctor Hughes if it's okay for her to be here."

I frown. "It's not like she even has a pet."

"No, but from what I hear, they've been friends forever."

"Really? The way she acts? I didn't think Helga had any friends."

Christina laughs. "I mean, they go *way* back, like when Doctor Hughes was a little girl."

"Oh." I guess Helga was around when Sasha's mom died.

"I get the impression that Helga was like a mother to Sasha."

I scrunch up my face like I've just smelled dog poop. "That's an awful thought."

Christina shrugs.

"I'm leaving." Helga startles us with her sudden appearance at the reception desk, the TR-97 file tucked under her arm. "And I'm going to suggest to Sasha that she lock her office when she's out. I'm not sure she can trust her staff." Helga glares at me, then exits without another word.

When she's gone, I release the air from my lungs and relax my shoulders.

"What was that about?" asks Christina.

"She's such a bitch. She caught me touching a file that wasn't a patient file. I picked it up, thinking it was, but it didn't have the right label."

Christina rests her hands on her hips. "That doesn't sound so bad."

"Except Helga claimed it was *her* file and took it from me. I know she's going to say something to Doctor Hughes."

"You should wait for Doctor Hughes to come back today. Just tell her what happened, so your story is out there first."

I nod. "Good idea. It was an honest mistake, but I have to leave at twelve."

"I'm sure it's no big deal. You can tell her on Monday. But listen to this. Guess who called when you were back there in the office?"

"Who?"

"Paulson."

"No way."

"Yep. He scheduled another appointment for the end of the day today."

"What's wrong with Echo now?"

"He needs his nails clipped," she says, and we both laugh.

Chapter
15

My dad picks me up promptly at 12:30 P.M. and loads my clubs into the back of his truck.

"How's it going?" he asks.

"Good," I say, opening the passenger door. "How are you?"

"Good. How's your golf game?"

I clench my jaw. "It could be better."

"It can always be better," he says.

We close our doors, fasten our seatbelts, and drive toward Glen View, my stomach in knots. He's going to ask about the team and I don't know what I'm going to say.

"What have you been up to?" I ask.

"Not much," he says.

We haven't talked or texted in almost two weeks, and that's his answer? I know I was angry with him, and maybe I should have reached out, but it's a two-way street. He could have called. He can't be that busy. I stare straight ahead at the road and quietly fume.

"Have you been playing a lot of golf?" he asks.

"Not really," I say.

"Why not?"

I cross my arms over my chest. "I just haven't."

His hands guide the steering wheel, but he swivels his head to study me. "That's all right. Me, either."

"So, what have you been doing?" I ask.

We hit a pothole with a thud, and the truck rattles. "Traveling a little. I went up to a friend's cabin near Spooner Lake. Other than that, I've been running and lifting."

"Are you going back to work?"

He waits an eternity to answer my question. "I haven't decided."

The conversation ends when we pull into the golf course parking lot. As we roll past the rows of cars, a white sedan lurches backwards, nearly crashing into the front of our truck. My dad slams on the brakes and leans on the horn. I brace myself with a hand on the dashboard as he shouts.

"Look where you're going, asshole! You could've killed us!" His knuckles are white on the steering wheel. Flames might erupt from his eyes and ears.

"It's okay, dad."

"That guy was oblivious. He didn't even see us."

I look out the window at the other parked cars and nod. Backing up seems hard, but I wouldn't know.

"He could have hurt us."

I nod my head as he eases into a parking spot. "But we're fine."

After grabbing our clubs and walking to the clubhouse, we check in with the starter in the pro shop.

"How many balls did you bring?" asks my dad.

"Three," I say.

"I'm going to buy another sleeve, just in case."

While he's doing that, I gaze at the racks of ladies' golf skirts, tops, and matching visors. They're all so beautiful and perfect. I touch one with a tropical leaf-pattern on the collar and hem of the skirt. I could be Lynda or Anna in an outfit like this. I'd look like a real golfer instead of a wannabe.

"You don't need that stuff to play well," says my dad, hovering over my shoulder. "It's just for show."

"I know." I turn away from the clothes and glance at my phone. We have fifteen minutes until our tee time. "Range or putting green?"

"Range," he says. "We've got time to share a small bucket."

I stretch a little, then choose my favorite club, the five iron, to warm up. My swing feels awkward, but I try to relax and focus on my wrists and my head, letting everything else flow. My dad fusses with his bag and clubs and doesn't watch me. I grab the driver next and try to follow the same method, but the ball sails off the tip of my club.

My dad turns toward me and frowns. "You better not do that on the first tee."

When it's a few minutes before one, we walk to the first hole. They paired us with a gray-haired man and his young grandson. The boy will probably hit from the women's tees, so it looks like a good fit.

"Be ready for a slow round," says my dad.

"It'll be fine," I say. "They have a cart."

My dad and I walk the course. It's cheaper, and if you play competitively, you walk, so I'm used to it. As we start the round, I make par on the first hole. My dad bogeys. After five holes, I'm only three strokes behind him.

"You're playing well," he says, patting me on the back.

"Thanks."

"When did you play last?"

"About two weeks ago," I say.

"Your coach is letting you have that much time off?"

I hesitate. "Not really. I took the time off."

"Is that a good idea? This game is about repetition. You need to play more often."

"Sure."

"When does the season start?" he asks.

"Next week, I think." I walk a little faster, opening a gap between my dad and me.

He hurries to catch up. "Will you get to play that swanky Maple Hills course?"

"I don't know."

"I would love to play that course. I hear the greens are immaculate."

I deflect my dad's comments and focus on my swing, but I bristle every time he asks a question. I'm going to have to tell him, but how? On the eighth tee, I hit my first shot short, and my ball disappears into the water hazard.

I pound my club into the turf. "Shit."

"Go down one club," says my dad.

I turn to face him. "But I like the five."

"You can't hit the five far enough. Use the four."

"If I hit it right, the five is perfect."

"But you're not hitting it perfect."

I press my lips together and feel my face flaring. "But I always use the five for this yardage."

"Suit yourself," he says, then taps his index finger on his watch.

"Fine." I grab the four iron. When I squeeze the grip and swing, I hit the ball too hard, and it flies over the green into the bunker. "Fuck," I mumble under my breath.

I have to take a seven on a par three. By the time we get to the thirteenth tee, our card shows I'm twelve strokes behind my dad.

"If you hadn't made those mistakes on eight, nine, and ten, you could be on track for an eighty-five," he says.

I shake my head. "I won't shoot in the eighties."

"What was your best score during tryouts?"

"I might have had a ninety," I say, knowing that's not true.

"That's solid. Who's captain this year? Lynda Sinestra?"

"Yeah," I say, even though I do not know.

"She's a senior, right?"

"Yep."

"If I remember it right, you were the number six golfer last season. How's that shaping up? Any new meat nipping at your heels?"

"I wasn't number six, Dad. I was on JV. Everyone on varsity was ahead of me."

My dad hits his tee shot straight down the fairway and it rolls forever. I wish I could do that. I set my ball on the tee and try to clear my mind. Don't hit it into the cemetery. Keep it straight. Loosen your grip. I hit a decent shot near the side of the fairway, but it bounces into the right rough.

"You're not getting any power," he says.

"I'm trying," I say.

"You have to use your core and shift your weight. Accelerate through the ball."

"I know."

"You won't be a top golfer hitting drives like that."

I shove my club into my bag and groan. "Maybe I don't want to be a top golfer."

"Of course you do," he says.

We hoist our bags and walk down the slope toward our balls.

"No, I don't."

"Yes, you do."

"You're wrong," I say, with more volume and intensity than I planned.

"Don't get angry. I'm trying to help you."

"Maybe I don't want your help!" The heat rises in my chest, making my face broil.

"What's that supposed to mean?"

"It means I didn't make the golf team."

My dad stops dead in his tracks and stares at me. "What? You didn't make the team?"

I shake my head.

"How badly did you play?"

"Does it even matter?"

"Yes, it matters. What happened?"

I ball my hands into fists and frown. "I'll tell you what happened. I quit. I didn't finish the tryouts."

"You're not a quitter."

"Maybe I am. Just like you."

He shakes his head. "That's not fair."

"Oh, really?" I ask.

"I'm just taking a leave of absence from the department. I'll be back working in another month."

"Geez, Dad. You don't have a clue. I don't give a crap what you do with your job. I'm talking about us. You quit our family."

My dad shakes his head again. "I didn't quit."

"What would you call it then? A leave of absence?"

"I did not quit!"

"Yes, you did." I burst into tears in the middle of the thirteenth fairway. "You gave up and walked away. That's quitting to me!"

My dad stands limp, arms at his sides, a helpless look on his face. We're holding up the group behind us, but I don't care.

"I'm sorry, Penn. I didn't know it affected you so much."

"How could you not know?"

"I just didn't."

We stare at each other for a moment, and I wipe my eyes with my towel. He gives me a half-hug, and we continue the round in silence. I play better than expected, considering the circumstances. When we get back to the truck, the silence is gnawing a hole in my gut.

"Since I don't play much golf, don't you want to know what I've been doing?"

"Sure, honey."

"I got a job," I say, and tell my dad about working at the animal clinic.

"That's great, I guess."

A hint of smile stretches across my face. "Now I have money for movies and clothes and golf balls."

"If that's what you want."

"And, if I continue working during the school year, I can start saving for college, or a car."

He scowls when I say this, pinching his face into a knot. "How many times do I have to tell you about the car? You're not ready to drive."

I roll my eyes and shake my head. "I don't mean now. I only make twelve dollars an hour."

The rest of our drive is quiet, like somebody hit the mute button on a remote. He's so touchy. Just mentioning the word "car" launches him into another universe. He can't even talk about it. Well, if he won't tell me, then it's time to do some digging of my own. There were dozens of newspaper articles after the accident. I didn't bother reading them, but if I can find information about TR-97, I can uncover the details about that night.

"Are we going to play again?" I ask as we pull up in front of the house.

"How about next week?"

"Okay."

"I'll text you," he says.

I hoist my clubs out of the truck wondering if he'll give me a hug or say 'I love you.'

"Bye, Dad."

"Bye," he says, driving away without a smile or a wave.

———————

Later that evening, when I'm in my room watching Netflix, I text Mel.

I'm an idiot. U leave tomorrow. I didn't c the car in the parking lot today

That's ok

I'll send a photo next week

I know u will

I pause the movie for a moment and text again. *Do u leave early?*

At 6

Way 2 early

I'll sleep on the plane

Have fun. We'll try 2 survive without u

I smile when Mel signs off with a string of smiley faces and beach-related emojis. I wish I could spend two weeks in Florida, but I doubt that will ever happen.

When I climb into bed later, my phone chimes with another text. It's probably Tara or Mel, or maybe even my dad. I check my phone, but the message is from another unknown number.

BAD THINGS happen when you meddle in someone else's business.

Shit. That's got to be from Helga. After the confrontation at the clinic, she's trying to intimidate me. I take a deep breath and read the text again. My hands shake as I switch my phone to silent. I crawl under the covers and pull the sheet up over my head.

Chapter
16

Saturday morning arrives with singing birds and warm rays of sunshine. I read the anonymous text again, and my stomach churns. Helga. She doesn't want me in Sasha's office. I'll figure out a way to deal with that. At least it's better than what I originally thought. I was worried someone didn't want me talking to Dr. Oliver. But since no one knows I visit him, I'm good.

I glance at the Nelson Mandela photo on my phone. I took it last year during a field trip. "The brave man is not he who does not feel afraid, but he who conquers that fear." Reading it gives me confidence, and I push the menacing texts to the back of my brain. I told Dr. Oliver I would return today, so I call Tara, hoping she can give me a ride.

She picks up immediately. "Hey there."

"What's up?" I ask.

"Nothing," she says with a yawn.

"I need to visit the crazy doctor this morning. Can you give me a ride?"

"If you go early. I have to be at work by ten."

"Damn. That's right. I could go early, but then I won't have a ride home."

Tara yawns again. "I would take you, but picking you up is out of the question. I don't get that long of a break."

"It sucks that my parents won't let me drive. And they won't even let me use Uber or Lyft."

"You could take the bus."

I thump my pillow with my fist. "I hate the bus. I want to drive."

"I know."

"Is there a chance I can borrow your car?" I ask.

"But I need my car to get to work," she says.

I glance at the time. "I can drop you off at work and pick you up later."

"Do you even know how to drive?"

"I've been watching you and Mel for months."

Tara sighs. "But driving is different from watching. Trust me, you need to practice first."

"I'll bring you a six-pack of beer if you teach me to drive."

"When?"

"Right now," I say.

"I thought you were still in bed."

"I am, but I'll be dressed in five minutes."

"See you in five," she says.

I smile and look up at the ceiling. A positive force in the universe is shining on me today.

Tara drives me to Westmoreland Cemetery in her Ford *Fusion*, and I practice speeding up, braking, and steering. Tara quizzes me about stop signs, traffic lights, and turn signals. I keep my sweaty palms on the steering wheel and concentrate on the road. We avoid the area near the vandalism.

"Be sure to wear your seat belt," she says.

"Don't worry, I will," I say.

"And forget about music or your phone."

"No music or phone, I promise."

Tara points to the cemetery exit. "You're ready. I need to get to work."

I inhale deeply and guide the car out onto the street. Someone honks and zooms around me, but I focus on staying in my lane. I grip the steering wheel and my arms ache. In less than ten minutes, I turn into the lot near Rocky's and almost make it between the parking lines.

"Not bad," says Tara. "But try to park far away from other cars."

"No problem," I say.

"And don't park on our street. My parents will know something is up."

"I'll park around the corner on Shawno."

Tara grabs her purse and looks at me from the passenger seat. "You know, if something happens to this car, my dad will kill me."

"We'll be even because my dad will kill me if he finds out I'm driving."

We hug and Tara gets out of the car.

"Thanks a million," I say. "I owe you big time."

She winks at me. "You owe me a six-pack."

I give her a thumbs-up. "What time are you off?"

"Four-thirty." She walks away, giving me a half-wave.

After she leaves, the silence in the car is deafening. I sit for a minute and inhale slowly through my nose. I focus on the hum of the engine and the beating of my heart. I can do this. I know I can. I ease my way out of the parking lot onto the street, and it hits me. I'm driving! My face erupts in a huge smile, and I pump my fist.

When I get to the nursing home, I park far away from the door near Mel's spot. I don't back in though, and I wonder for a moment what it's going to be like to put the car in reverse. Tara and I didn't go over that.

I check in at the desk, stick my name tag on my shirt, and wait for an escort. Jesse sees me and waves.

"How are you today?" he asks as we walk toward Dr. Oliver's room.

"Great," I say. "How are you and your kids?"

"Doing well. Enjoying the summer. Do you want to see their picture?"

"Sure."

He shows me a photo on his phone. The two little girls sit on the floor holding their baby brother. They have matching dresses, wide smiles, and doe eyes. One gazes at the baby, and the other stares into the camera.

"They're adorable," I say. "What are their names?"

"Sophia is on the left. She is the oldest. Emelia is on the right, and that's Hector."

"They're beautiful."

Jesse smiles and nods.

When we get to room 103, we find the door open and Dr. Oliver siting in his recliner by the window. Jesse waves me in and leaves us alone.

"Hi, Doctor Oliver," I say, knocking and entering the room.

"Hello, Penelope."

I sit in my usual chair across from him and smile. "It's good to see you," I say.

"It's good to be seen."

"I meant to bring you another book, but I couldn't find either of the ones we talked about."

"That's okay. I'll take anything with larger type."

I cross my legs at the ankle and nod. "What do you want to talk about?"

"I thought you'd be the one asking the questions," he says.

I take a deep, calming breath. "Last Saturday afternoon, when I was here, why did you want me to leave?"

"Last Saturday?" Dr. Oliver scratches the side of his head.

I'm not sure he remembers when he got so upset. I was going to ignore it and pretend it didn't happen, but I can't let it go. I have to know why he told me to leave.

"Yeah, last Saturday afternoon," I say.

"You told me about Gwendolyn's grave."

I shift positions in my chair. "You remember."

"Yes."

"I know it upset you, and I'm sorry. It was wrong to tell you."

"No, it wasn't wrong. A surprise maybe, but not wrong."

"But I *am* sorry, and you let me come back."

"Don't kill the messenger."

"Don't kill anyone, might be a better motto," I say with a nervous laugh.

"That's a good one, too."

My cheeks burn. "Oh, geez. Sorry. I didn't mean you personally."

"It's okay," he says with a slow nod. "You delivered some important information, and I'm grateful."

"Maybe it would have been better if you didn't know."

"No, no. Information is power." He glances around the stark room. "And in here, I can't get any information."

"But Sasha should have been the one to tell you."

He clears his throat. "She visits on Saturday afternoons, but not every week. I didn't want her to find you here. She doesn't think I should have visitors."

"Why not?" That just seems wrong.

"It's a long story."

"I'd like to hear it."

"Maybe some other time."

I lean forward toward Dr. Oliver. "You must be lonely."

"A little, but don't feel bad for me. Few people want to talk to a senile old man."

"But you seem totally normal."

"Thank you for that diagnosis, Doctor Penelope," he says with a grin. "I appreciate it."

"I mean, if you're fine, why were you in a mental hospital?"

Dr. Oliver diverts his eyes, gazing out the window for a moment, absorbed in his thoughts before turning his attention back to me. "The last time you were here, you mentioned Helga Thorstad. Stay away from her."

The thought of Helga's ugly sneer and snide comments makes my stomach twist. I should've called Dr. Hughes right away and told her Helga was snooping around and grabbed that file. Or I should've stood up to Helga at the clinic and told her only staff are allowed in Sasha's office. If it happens again, I'll be ready. I'm not a pushover.

"I'll try," I say. "I don't want to be around her. She's a total bitch, pardon my language."

Dr. Oliver laughs.

"I mean it. What did I ever do to her?"

"I'm sure nothing," he says. "It's just her way."

"She comes by the clinic. I don't think she even has any pets."

"She doesn't, and she never will. She doesn't care about anyone but herself."

"But it seems like she's helping Doctor Hughes, I mean Sasha."

Dr. Oliver's voice is stern. "Helga has ulterior motives. She helps no one but herself."

"You're sure?"

"A leopard never changes its spots."

"A what?"

"You've never heard the phrase? It means it's impossible, for some anyway, to change their character."

We're quiet for a few moments, and I clasp my hands together in my lap. Helga is a bully. She won't change. She behaves that way with Sasha, too. When I heard them talking, at least Sasha had a backbone. I need to grow one too.

"The other day," I say, "I overhead them talking about the cemetery."

"What did they say?"

"Sasha accused Helga of digging up Gwendolyn's grave."

"Interesting." Dr. Oliver pauses for a moment, rubbing his chin. "Many years ago, Helga begged to be involved in the TR-97 research. I hesitated to include her because she wasn't a clinical specialist. She had a psychology degree, but she also had the reputation of making therapy all about herself instead of about the patient. But since she had been so helpful with Sasha after Gwendolyn passed, I gave Helga a chance. I went against my better judgment and allowed her to take part. That was a mistake. A big mistake."

"How so?" I ask.

"How much do you know about the lawsuits against me, and my dismissal from the university?"

"Not much. I know about the patient who died. His family sued you."

"Anything else?"

"Not yet."

"You haven't read about Francine Baker?"

Dr. Oliver's eyes focus on mine, and I shake my head. He pauses, blinks several times, and looks at his lap.

"She was another psychologist, the main treatment specialist for many of the veterans. She and I were friends and colleagues. I should have stuck with her instead of opening the door to Helga."

Dr. Oliver begins to cough. His body shakes and he bends forward in the recliner, gripping the arms of the chair, gasping for breath.

I spring to my feet. "Do you need some water?"

He nods.

I rush to the bathroom and find a small paper cup.

His hand trembles as I give him the water. After a few sips, he thanks me and continues. "Without Francine's help, I'm not sure I would have made it through after Gwendolyn's death."

"I haven't read about her."

"Maybe it's for the best. Her career was ruined, too. She lost her license, and they sent her to prison."

Francine Baker. I need to remember that name and do a Google search. Would she be working with Helga? Would she want the TR-97?

"Do you know if she's still in prison?" I ask.

He shakes his head.

I nod and look outside at the sunshine. I wish I could open the window and let in some fresh air. We have a few casement windows like this one at home, with a crank handle to swing open like a door. Dr. Oliver's window doesn't have a handle, so it's permanently shut. Are they worried a resident might escape?

"I'll try to read more about Francine Baker," I say.

"If you like," he says.

A heavy blanket of silence wraps around us. I want to keep him talking, but need to find a new topic.

"Do you have any brothers or sisters?" I ask.

"I had a brother," he says.

"Were you close?"

"He lived in Montana."

"That's far away."

Dr. Oliver's voice drops to a whisper. "He's gone now."

"Gone?" I ask.

"He's deceased."

I hang my head and look at the floor. "I'm sorry."

"It was a long time ago."

"When you were young?"

Dr. Oliver's eyes drop to his lap and I hear the wheeze in his chest. "I was still in medical school when he took his life."

My lower lip quivers. "That's terrible."

"Our government sent him to Vietnam, and he was never the same after he returned."

"Is that why you worked with veterans?"

Dr. Oliver sits taller in his chair. "Yes, to honor Paul and all the other vets. They need more help than most of us realize."

"Are you a veteran, too?"

He shakes his head. "Just my brother."

"I don't know much about the Vietnam War," I say. "We never get to it in history class."

"Most people can't even pick out the country on a map."

I envision the colorful picture taped to the wall in history class. "I'm probably one of them."

"You should read about it on your own. Our government sent over half a million troops."

"Wow."

"And the average age was nineteen."

I interlace my fingers in my lap. "Not much older than me."

"They were just kids, and many of them came back with some serious scars."

"From gunshot wounds and bombs?" I ask.

"I meant mental scars from their traumatic experiences."

"Is that what happened to your brother?"

Dr. Oliver nods. "When he returned, the big brother I knew was no longer confident or carefree. He withdrew into a world of ghosts, jumping when the door slammed, and fearing the respite of sleep."

"PTSD," I say. Kind of like my dad.

"Paul was a classic case."

"And you wanted to help him."

"Him and all the other soldiers with similar troubles."

"And you did."

"Not nearly enough of them."

Outside the window, a blue minivan pulls into a nearby parking space. A man and two young children hop out. They're talking and laughing. I bet they're going to visit their grandma or grandpa.

"It must have been devastating to have a patient die after treatment," I say, knowing I'm encroaching on dangerous territory. "But you can't expect to save them all."

A cloud of sadness drifts across Dr. Oliver's face. It's an enormous risk bringing it up, but I skimmed some articles about Harold Foster. After his death, his family sued Dr. Oliver, the university, and the drug company.

"You're talking about Harold Foster."

I nod.

"I thought I had healed from my brother's death and moved on, so to speak, but Harold's suicide brought it all back in an instant. I understand now that I may never heal."

"Does all of this have something to do with Helga?" I ask.

"She's part of the mess."

"The lawsuits and getting fired?"

"And she got away, scot free," he says.

"How did she do that?"

A knock sounds on the door, and Jesse enters. "It's time for your medication and a little exercise, Doctor Oliver. We need to boost your activity before lunch."

I look at Dr. Oliver, but he has turned away to stare out the window again. I reluctantly stand to leave.

"When should I visit again?" I ask.

"How about Monday morning," says Dr. Oliver.

"Monday?"

"Is that a problem?"

I hesitate. "I'm supposed to be at work."

"Maybe you should stick to work, then."

My mind races. I need the money, but I want information. Dr. Oliver may be a gold mine.

"I'll see you Monday morning," I say. Work can wait.

Chapter
17

I maneuver Tara's car out of the parking lot, and drive home. When I park on the street, the wheels scrape the curb. Damn. I'll have to tell her, but at least I'm around the corner from our houses. I spend the rest of the morning in my room on the computer, searching for more information about Helga Thorstad and Francine Baker.

Helga's name pops up all over the web with her website, books, and seminars. But I can't find much on Francine Baker. The newspaper reported that both Dr. Oliver and Francine were charged with manslaughter in the death of Harold Foster. Dr. Oliver pled guilty to the lesser crime of criminal negligence, and they revoked his medical license. Francine Baker pled not guilty, and her case went to trial. A jury found her guilty. After that, the trail runs cold. Did people lose interest? Did she die? Dr. Oliver said she went to prison, but I can't find anything to confirm that.

Around two o'clock, I need a break from the screen and ride my bike to Sasha's house. If she's home, I want to explain about the file incident on Friday and tell her I won't be at work on Monday. As I leave the garage, enormous clouds, like mountains of whipped cream, loom in the west. But the sun shines overhead and a light breeze rustles the treetops. I pedal through the neighborhood, passing the swimming pool and elementary school. I traverse the wide streets, coasting under a broad canopy of maple trees. An older man mows his lawn, and the cut grass teases my nostrils. Kids chase a soccer ball in the park. As I enjoy my leisurely pace, the clouds envelop the sun, and a distant rumble of thunder prods me along.

When I reach Dr. Hughes's house, a shiny black Mercedes occupies the driveway. The license plate says "RX GUY." Did she buy a new car? It looks expensive, and I wheel my bicycle around the side of the house and lean it against the garage. As I approach her front door, a gust of wind tousles the tree branches. The ominous growl of thunder creeps closer. I ring the bell and have déjà vu about the last time I stood here, waiting for her to answer. A few moments later, Sasha responds. "Hi, Penn."

I lean toward the doorbell. "Hi, Doctor Hughes. Do you have a minute to talk?"

"Um, sure. Just a minute," she says.

While I wait, the sky darkens, and the rumble grows louder. Lightning flashes over the treetops, and I count the time before another crack of thunder reaches my ears. Six seconds. As the clouds advance, large drops of rain smack the pavement. Crap. Should I go home? I left a bunch of windows open. A bolt of lightning cuts the sky, followed immediately by a thunderous boom. Less than one second. At that moment, the front door flies open.

"Come in!" says Sasha. "You can't be out there in the storm."

"Thanks," I say, leaping into the entry as the clouds unleash a torrent.

"Let me get you a towel."

I stand in the entry, watching the wind whip through the trees, battering the house with rain. Her living room is immaculate, with leather chairs and an angular glass coffee table. The stone fireplace sits bare without a single log.

Dr. Hughes returns with a yellow cotton hand towel, and I blot my face and neck.

"Sorry to bother you," I say, wiping my hands and arms.

"That's okay. Come on into the kitchen."

I follow her down a short hall toward the back of the house. The storm escalates outside as lightning and thunder crash simultaneously. I catch my breath, and the lights flicker.

"I didn't know it was supposed to storm," I say.

"There was a thunderstorm watch earlier, but I turned off the TV," she says. "Maybe I should turn it back on."

Sasha's kitchen looks like a photograph in Architectural Digest with pale wood cabinets and a massive stainless-steel refrigerator. The counters and backsplash gleam. Festive glass lights hang from the ceiling over the island. I'm surprised to see Paulson sitting at the table in the breakfast nook. When his eyes meet mine, Mother Nature unleashes another blast, shaking the house. I squeeze my eyes shut for an extended blink and open them to find the lights out. The gentle hum of the refrigerator stops.

"Oh, shit," says Sasha.

Paulson springs to his feet. "Where do you keep a flashlight?"

"Here in the utility drawer." She pulls open a drawer near the kitchen entry.

It's eerily quiet for a moment, like the rain and wind have hit pause, then the tornado warning shrieks.

I jump and turn toward Sasha.

"Quick, downstairs!" she says, grabbing a flashlight.

I follow her into the hallway, while Paulson takes the other light, and we hurry down the steep steps into the basement. Underground, the concrete floors make the air damp and musty. The space is quiet like a tomb, the faint call of the weather siren barely audible. As Sasha turns to the right, Paulson pauses and shines his light to the left, illuminating stacks of cardboard boxes. With their white labels and neatly fitted lids, they form a wall at least six feet high.

"Over here," says Sasha. "There are beanbags and a few blankets."

While my eyes adjust to the darkness, I move toward the corner and a blue area rug. I plop down on the smallest cushion, leaving the larger ones for Sasha and Paulson. I cross my arms over my chest in a hug, and Sasha hands me a blanket. Although it's scratchy and smells like an old dog, I wrap it around myself.

"Thanks," I say.

"Do you have a transistor radio?" Paulson asks.

Sasha shakes her head. "I keep meaning to buy one."

Paulson continues standing. "That's okay. For now, I still get a cell signal."

I look at my phone. No signal. "How long do we have to stay down here?" I ask.

Paulson responds. "We don't know. That's why having a radio is important."

"Sorry," says Sasha. "Hopefully your phone will give you updates."

"It should, but let's turn on one of the light switches."

Sasha flips the nearest switch. "But the lights aren't working."

Paulson sits down on a beanbag. "If they restore power, the light will come back on."

"Good thinking," she says.

We sit for a few minutes without talking. My ears strain to pick up sounds from outside. I rest my head in my hands and wish I was with my mom or at home in my basement.

Paulson turns his face and body away from me and speaks to Sasha in a low voice. I watch them out of the corner of my eye.

"So what information hides in those boxes?" he asks.

"Nothing important," she replies.

"You looked?"

"It's all junk."

Paulson leans toward Sasha. "There has to be something," he says.

The boxes look similar to the one I saw in Sasha's office. Is Paulson interested in the TR-97 research also?

"It's a dead end," says Sasha.

"I could look."

"Not now," she says, shaking her head and cutting him off. Sasha glances at me. "Let's focus on getting through the storm. Check your phone again."

While they huddle together and stare at Paulson's phone, I study the basement from my beanbag. The space is a lot like mine, partially finished with wood paneling in some areas, but piled with boxes and clutter at the other end. I think of my mom.

Is she home or showing a house? I wish I could text her. And what about my dad? And poor Tara. She's still at work. I'm supposed to pick her up later.

"Penn? Are you okay?" asks Sasha.

I clear my throat. "I'm fine."

"Are you scared?"

I shake my head. "I was just wondering about my mom and a friend who's at work."

"I'm sure they're both safe."

I pull my blanket tighter. "I hope so."

"So, why did you stop by today? You wanted to talk to me?"

"I wanted to tell you two things. First, I wasn't looking through your personal stuff in the office yesterday, in case Helga says something to you. Christina asked me to retrieve the patient files from your office. Some of them were on the floor, and I had to look at them to make sure I got the right ones."

"That's fine. Helga didn't mention it. Was she at the clinic yesterday?"

I nod. "She walked into your office when I was getting the files, and she said one of them was hers."

"A file?"

"It wasn't a patient file. It was bigger and had a different label."

Sasha frowns. "Did she take it?"

"She took it and walked out."

Paulson narrows his eyes and scowls. "She did what?"

"This doesn't concern you," says Sasha, firing an angry look at Paulson.

"I think it does," he says.

Sasha frowns and shakes her head.

Paulson glances at his phone again. "The local weather service just reported a tornado touchdown on the south side of town," he says. "Trees and power lines are down in the area. We're being warned to stay sheltered for a little longer."

"Oh, crud," says Sasha, rubbing her forehead. "I hope the clinic is okay."

"I'm sure it is," he says. "The west side of town is safe so far."

"But it's just my luck. I signed a five-year lease last month. And the gardener planted new flowers in the backyard here last week. I bet they're ruined."

Paulson grunts. "You can easily replace flowers. I'm more concerned about my new car in your driveway."

I remain silent, lost in my thoughts. If my mom is home, she'll go to the basement. She's careful that way. But what do Tara and the other employees at Rocky's do? Hide in the kitchen where there are no windows? And Tara's car? I hope a tree doesn't fall on it.

"Well, that's fine, Penn," says Sasha, turning her attention back to me. "I'll talk to Helga about it. I keep my office unlocked so you and Christina can find what you need, but she shouldn't be there when I'm not."

I nod, but bite my lip and squirm in my seat. Oh, crap. Helga will be furious with me. I just told the teacher about the class bully. "I wanted you to know because Helga was pretty upset with me."

"I'm glad you told me," says Sasha.

"I also wanted to tell you I have an appointment Monday morning, so I won't be at work."

"That's not a problem. We'll see you on Tuesday."

"Okay."

For a few moments, we listen to the wind howl while we wait for a signal that it's safe to go upstairs. What do they do at the nursing home during a tornado? Take the residents into the hall like we do at school?

"I hate to ask this," I say, "but do you have a bathroom down here?"

"Yes," Sasha says, handing me her flashlight. "It's nothing fancy, but go straight back the way we came. It's on the left after you pass the stairs."

I shine the beam in front of me and then onto the floor, following her instructions. I'm intrigued by the boxes, but ignore them. When I pass the stairs, which go up to the left, I turn and see a door. I aim my light in that direction and find a bathroom tucked under the stairs. The room is tiny, with only a sink and toilet. I close the door and rest the flashlight on the floor so the glow rises from the corner. When I return to our sitting area, Sasha and Paulson are standing, hunched over his phone.

"It looks like the storm has passed," she says.

"I think we're clear to go upstairs," he says.

"Great," I say, turning around with the flashlight. "But we don't have power yet."

"It's out in several neighborhoods, including this one," says Sasha.

Paulson steps around me, bumping my shoulder. "I'll go up first."

I let him go ahead, and we climb the stairs. When he opens the door at the top, the house is quiet. "All clear," he says.

From the hallway, nothing looks broken or out of place. Sasha exhales a sigh of relief. In the kitchen, I peek out the window into her backyard. Several large tree branches are strewn about, and a neighbor's umbrella and patio table rest against her lilac bushes. Sasha hurries to the back door to survey the yard. I notice another video doorbell in back.

Sasha slips on some clogs. When she ventures outside to assess the damage, Paulson grabs my arm and pulls me toward him.

"What file was Helga after?" he asks. "Do you know?"

"Ow," I say, as he grips my arm. "That hurts."

He squeezes my arm tighter. "What file did she have?"

"I'm not sure."

"Don't lie to me. I know you saw it."

I shake my head. "It didn't make sense."

"What did it say?"

I try to twist away from him, but his grip is powerful. Should I tell him? Does he know what it means? He asked Sasha about the boxes in the basement. Is there more information there? "TR-97," I say.

"That's it? Just the file?" He's crushing my arm.

"There was a box, too, like the ones downstairs."

He releases my arm and moves toward the back door. I rub my bicep and wince as Paulson opens the door to let Sasha inside.

"Not too much damage back there," she says.

"I better see if my bike is all right," I say, my voice cracking.

Sasha studies my face. "Are you okay?"

I glance at Paulson. He's shaking his head with a furrowed brow, his index finger pressed to his lips.

"I just want to go home."

"Of course. Where is your bike?" asks Sasha.

"Against the side of the garage."

"Let's go out this way, then."

Using a door across from the basement, we descend two steps into the garage. Paulson follows us. Sasha parked her car on the left, near two trash cans. The other side is open except for a snow shovel, some gardening tools, and an empty dog crate. We exit another door to the outside of the house. My bike rests on its side in the grass. I pick it up and spin each wheel, then check the brakes.

"I'll give you a lift home," says Paulson.

"No," I blurt out.

Sasha and Paulson stare at me.

"I mean, it's fine. I can ride."

"It's no trouble," he says.

I shake my head. "I'm good."

"Are you sure?" Sasha asks.

"Yep," I say.

"Be careful," she says.

Paulson takes out his car key. "I should go with her to make sure she gets home safely."

"That's okay, bye," I say, mounting the wet seat and pedaling up the street. My whole body is shaking and I want to vomit. When I glance over my shoulder, I see the black sedan backing out of Sasha's driveway. Shit. He's going to follow me.

My legs are numb, but I keep pumping them up and down. Tears stream down my face. I purposely turn the wrong direction down another street. I refuse to lead him to my house. I grip the handlebars and climb a small hill. In half a block, I glide onto the sidewalk, then disappear between two houses. The walkway will take me to the back of the elementary school. I can go around the building and get out of sight, then take a different route home.

Chapter
18

On Sunday, after Tara and her family return from church, she and I hang out in her backyard. Her brothers play at a friend's house while her mom runs errands. Her dad is out of town. We lounge in our bathing suits on plastic lawn chairs, music playing on a small, wireless speaker. Each of us has a beer tucked in a foam koozy, and we pass a cigarette back and forth.

"Where did you get this?" I ask, inhaling and coughing.

"A guy at work," she says. "I think he wants to ask me out."

"Is he cute?"

"Yeah, but he's twenty. My dad would kill him."

We grab our phones when Mel sends a selfie from the balcony of his family's condo in Fort Myers.

"He's going to get so sunburned," Tara says.

"He better stay under an umbrella." I take a selfie with Tara and send it to Mel.

Cute! he replies.

Maybe you'll meet someone cute on the beach, I text.

Hope so!

"So, how was your visit with Doctor Oliver yesterday?" Tara asks.

"He gave me another idea about who might want the TR-97."

"Who?"

"A woman named Francine Baker. I spent most of last night trying to find information about her."

"And?"

I tell her everything I know.

"She went to prison?" says Tara, pulling her hair back into a ponytail.

I nod. "Doctor O doesn't know what happened to her."

"Why would she want to dig up the serum?" Tara asks.

I lean my head back against the chair and gaze at the clear blue sky. "I don't know."

"What about that creep, Paulson? After what you told me yesterday, my money is on him."

I shiver when she mentions his name and glance at the bruise on my arm. I slipped away from him on my bike, but as soon as I got home, I closed all the windows, locked the doors, and took a scalding shower to remove his prints from my skin.

"He's definitely a suspect," I say. "He's worried about Helga."

"She sounds guilty, too."

"She's so rude." I curl my fingers into fists and imagine myself punching her in the face. "Doctor O told me to stay away from her."

"Did he say why?"

"Just that she's bad news and was involved with the TR-97 research."

Tara swats at a bee buzzing around her beer. "She sounds like a total bitch."

"I'm going to ask him more about Helga tomorrow."

"You're going for another visit?"

I grab the sunblock and rub some on my arms. "In the morning. Can you drive me?"

She nods. "You're skipping work?"

"I already told Doctor Hughes I wouldn't be there."

"Speaking of Doctor Hughes, what about her?" asks Tara.

"What about her?" I ask.

"She could have dug up the grave."

"No way. She accused Helga."

Tara shrugs.

"She wouldn't dig up her own mom's ashes." I cringe at the thought. I can't imagine digging up anyone's ashes, but definitely not my mom's or dad's.

"You never know," says Tara, taking a sip of beer.

"I seriously doubt it," I say.

We're quiet for a few moments, our eyes closed and faces angled toward the sun.

"But so far, nobody knows you have the vial, right?" asks Tara.

"Just you, me, and Mel."

"You haven't told Doctor Oliver?'

"Nope. He thinks I read about it on the internet."

"Okay, good. Can I have the sunblock?"

I hand the bottle to Tara.

"I might have to tell him some time, though," I say. "But not yet."

"Keep it to yourself as long as you can. He *was* in the loony bin."

"But he seems so normal."

Tara turns to face me. "You don't think he's crazy?"

"He seems totally fine, but speaking of crazy, did I show you the text messages I've gotten?"

"What texts?"

I hand her my phone.

Tara reads the messages and frowns. "What are you going to do?"

"Ignore them."

"You could be in danger."

"You think?"

Tara raises her eyebrows and hands me my phone. "There are crazy people out there, like Paulson."

"Okay, but the texts are pretty vague."

"They don't worry you?"

"Not too much," I say.

Tara sighs. "Save them on your phone, just in case."

"In case of what?"

"I don't know, crazy shit. And promise me, if you get one that's a full-on threat, you'll tell someone."

"Like who?"

"Anybody! Your mom, Doctor Hughes, the police."

"Okay, you're right. If it gets more serious."

"Promise?" she asks.

"I promise," I say.

We're quiet for a while, listening to Twenty One Pilots, Billie Eilish, and Halsey's "Without Me." I close my eyes. Who would send me the texts? Paulson? Helga? Thinking about it makes my heart race. I can feel the pounding in my chest. How did they get my number? Dr. Hughes has it in my employment file. My stomach twists and I take a deep breath. One of them is trying to scare me, but why? Do they know I have the vial? That seems impossible. Besides, they're both interested in some kind of file.

"I have some bad news," Tara says when the song ends.

"What?" I ask.

"I'm moving back to Georgia."

"No way! You can't do that." I turn on my side to face her.

She's biting her lip, and the corners of her mouth curve downward.

"NO!" I pound my fist into the grass. "No! No! No!"

"It totally sucks," she says.

"Your whole family?" I don't know why I ask that. Of course it's all of them.

"Yeah."

"Maybe you can stay and live with my mom and me?"

"I wish." She looks at the lawn and plucks a blade of grass. "If we were seniors, I might beg to stay, but with two more years of high school, I have to go."

"Oh my god, that sucks! Does Mel know?"

"Not yet."

"You better tell him," I say.

"I'll call him tonight."

"When are you going?" The knot in my stomach tightens. I know it's going to be before school starts.

"Next week."

"Shit, that's not fair! It seems like you just got here."

"Can you believe it was two years ago?"

I swallow the lump in my throat. "I remember the day the moving van pulled up."

"You helped me unpack my room."

"Two years," I say, my voice cracking and tears welling up in my eyes. "What am I going to do without you?"

"Drink beer alone, I guess." She drains her can, and this makes me smile, but I struggle to suppress my tears.

"You're a real shit," I say.

"Takes one to know one."

When we stand, she puts her arms around me and we cling to each other like we're the last humans on earth. Even though I fight to keep the tears inside, a few trickle down my cheeks. I want to stop time and stay in this moment forever.

We hear a car pull into her driveway, and her mom's voice. "Tara, I need help with the groceries."

We untangle our arms and stroll around the house to the front yard.

Later that evening, while eating Chinese takeout with my mom, I tell her about Tara.

"Can you believe it? She's leaving. This is the worst day of my life." My elbows rest on the table and I drop my head into my hands. The universe can go suck it. I'm not even hungry for my favorite house special Chow Mein.

"Oh, honey. I know it'll be tough for a while, but you'll move on."

I shake my head. "Easy for you to say."

"Well, I'm just glad she finally told you. I have the listing, and we're putting the sign up tomorrow."

"You knew? For how long?"

"At least a week. I've been waiting for Tara to say something to you."

"Are you both trying to torture me?"

She opens a bottle of red wine and pours herself a glass. "Of course not, but I didn't want to be the one to break the news."

"Unbelievable. You guys both suck."

"Now you see why I didn't want to say anything."

I glare at my mom. "It's just like seventh grade when Allie moved away, only worse."

"It'll take time, but you'll figure it out."

"Everyone leaves me."

She takes a sip of wine. "Don't take it personally, Penn."

"But why can't Tara stay here?"

"Because her dad is taking command of the military base back in Georgia. They have to go."

I gaze at my mom. "She could live with us. It would be great to have a sister."

"Aww, sweetie, that's a nice thought, but she needs to be with her family."

I shake my head. "She's keeping her family together while mine is falling apart."

"I knew you'd be upset. Losing a best friend is never easy."

I raise my arms above my head and shake them at the ceiling. "It's just the worst possible timing. Grandma died. Dad is gone, and now Tara's leaving. Who's next? You? Mel?"

"Nothing I say is going to make you feel better, except your dad isn't gone. He just doesn't live in this house."

"Is there a chance he'll move back in?" I ask.

"I don't think so, honey."

"Why not? Can't we get family counseling or something?"

My mom clears her plate from the table. "If he's truly willing to work on it, then maybe, but I can't deal with his moods swings and volatile rants. We can't even have a civil conversation anymore."

"But we can help him," I say.

"He has to start by helping himself."

"Does he have PTSD?"

"What makes you say that?"

I close the Chow Mein container. "I've been reading about it, and his symptoms match the description."

"Isn't that a war-related problem?"

"It can be, but any traumatic event can trigger it. Students have it after surviving a school shooting."

My mom puts her plate in the dishwasher. "You're thinking about the accident, aren't you?"

"I've read the newspaper articles. It all fits."

"I don't think it's a good idea for you to read about that. The details are pretty gruesome. A lot of young people died. That's why Dad doesn't want you to drive."

I bring my plate to the sink. "I know, and that's why Dad hasn't been working. He needs to deal with his trauma so he can move on."

"Aren't you the little doctor of the family?"

"I'm just saying, there are people in Mendota who can help him."

"He would need to see an actual doctor for that, and you know him. He either doesn't think he needs help, or he thinks he knows more than the doctors."

"It's so frustrating," I say.

Mom opens the refrigerator and I hand her the leftover food containers.

"Speaking of frustrating," she says, "why does my beer keep disappearing?"

"I don't know. I shared one with Tara today."

"You shouldn't be drinking."

I point at the bottle on the table. "Says the person who is always drinking."

"That's different. I'm an adult. You're sixteen."

I grab a paper towel to wipe off the table. "It's not a big deal. It's not like I'm driving anywhere."

"Well, it's a big deal to me, so stop."

"When did you get so uptight?"

"That's enough, Penelope. No more beer."

I roll my eyes and raise my hands to surrender. "Whatever."

"And don't take that sassy tone with me."

"Fine. No more beer."

"That's better, or there'll be hell to pay."

Chapter
19

The next morning, I get dressed in teal green scrubs for work. If my mom is still home, I want her to think I'm going to the clinic. When I get to the kitchen, her coffee mug sits half-empty and cold. I decide not to change clothes.

Tara drives me to the nursing home, and I ask her to take the long way to the east side of town. I want to spend as much time with her as possible.

"I really can't believe you're moving." I say.

"I know," she says with a sigh.

"You've known for a while. How come you didn't tell me?"

She keeps her hands on the steering wheel, but turns her head to look at me. "I was hoping for a miracle. You know. Maybe my dad would change his mind."

I nod. "I get it."

"Sorry."

"It's okay." My favorite song from The Growlers comes on the radio, so I turn up the volume. "What're you going to do while I'm in there?" I ask.

"I don't know. Maybe get a coffee and watch TikToks," she says. "How long are you going to be?"

"Thirty minutes at least. Maybe an hour."

"Just text me. I won't be far."

"Okay. I'll let you know."

I walk inside Oak Bluff and stroll to the reception desk. A gray-haired woman occupies the chair. She narrows her eyes and frowns at me.

"Employees should use the other entrance," she says.

I turn and look behind me, but nobody is there.

"I'm a guest," I say, handing her my ID, "here to see Doctor James Oliver."

She scrutinizes it and types something into the computer. "Sorry," she says. "Your attire threw me off."

"That's okay," I say, glancing down the hall at Jesse. He waves, ambling closer.

"You're dressed like me today," he says with a smile.

I look down at my scrubs and shrug. We walk side-by-side down the hall, our footsteps silent because we're both wearing sneakers.

"You know," I say, "I was cleaning out my closet yesterday and found a bunch of Groovy Girls dolls and clothes. I'm never going to play with them again. Would your girls like them?"

"I'm sure they would love them."

"I'll bring them next time."

We get to room 103, and the door is open.

"Hello, Doctor Oliver," says Jesse. "Your young visitor is here."

I wave at Dr. Oliver, who sits in his recliner, watching the door. "Bye, Jesse," I say, as he continues down the hall.

I'm two steps away from my chair when Dr. Oliver asks me to close the door.

"Close it?" I say.

"Yes, please."

That's weird, but I do as he asks and return to my seat.

"We need some privacy today," he says.

"We do?"

He lowers his voice to a whisper. "The door has eyes, and the walls have ears."

My eyes wander around the dismal room, and I scoot my chair a little closer. "What's going on?" I ask.

"My daughter came by yesterday and shared some news."

I lean forward so I can hear him better.

"There are people interested in buying my research files."

"The TR-97 files?"

He nods. "A pharmaceutical executive wants his company to take another crack at the treatment, using my old research as a starting point."

"That's great," I say without enthusiasm. I bet he's talking about Paulson.

"Sasha is skeptical."

"Are the files in Sasha's basement?"

Dr. Oliver wrinkles his brow and stares at me. "How did you know?"

"I guessed. I was at her house on Saturday during the storm. When the tornado siren went off, we took shelter in the basement."

"And you saw them?"

"I saw a lot of boxes, and Paulson was definitely curious."

Dr. Oliver folds his arms in his lap. "Who is Paulson?"

"He's the guy from the pharmaceutical company. He brings his dog to the clinic all the time, but it's pretty obvious he just wants to talk to Sasha."

"What else do you know about him?"

"He works for Feester."

"Those sons-of-bitches."

I clear my throat. "You've heard of them?"

"They're the ruthless bastards that sued me and the university."

"Wait. That was Feester?"

Dr. Oliver adjusts his eyeglasses. "They acquired Treon Laboratories, which funded my original research, then took over. I'm not sure I want them to have the files."

"Well, they won't get the most important one," I say, remembering the file that Helga snatched from Sasha's desk.

"What do you mean?" asks Dr. Oliver.

"I saw a box labeled RESEARCH and a TR-97 file in Sasha's office at the clinic."

"Why would she bring it there?"

I shrug. "Maybe she was going to show Paulson, but I don't think it's in the office anymore. Helga took it."

"Jesus, Mary, and Joseph, not Helga," says Dr. Oliver, turning toward the window and resting his head in his hands.

"Is that bad?" I ask. He doesn't answer right away, but stares out the window at nothing in particular.

"Helga is worse than Feester. At least Feester will compensate me, continue the research, and use the drug to help others. They will profit, but they'll use it for good. Not Helga. My mind isn't devious enough to figure out why she wants it."

"Maybe she wants to sell it and profit as well."

"She doesn't have the right. It doesn't belong to her."

"Oh."

"I've known her a long time. She has an evil plan, I'm sure of it."

A sparrow lands on the windowsill outside. For a few moments, we watch it hop around, then fly away.

"Then why does Sasha let Helga into her office? I mean, it's weird."

"I guess they've remained close. After Gwendolyn died, Helga took over as a surrogate mother, doing the shopping and cooking."

I frown. Sasha has had to deal with Helga all these years.

Dr. Oliver sighs. "I didn't object to her involvement. At the time, it seemed like a good fit."

I glance outside, wishing the bird would come back. "What are you going to do?"

"I told Sasha to wait for a full written offer before revealing anything, but it sounds like Helga already has her hand in the cookie jar."

Darn it. That bitch has the file. If she brings it back to the office, maybe I can take it from her.

"Except," says Dr. Oliver, bumping the heel of his hand against his forehead, "if I remember correctly, the crucial information is not in the RESEARCH box or that TR-97 file."

"Really?" I say, sitting up straighter. "Where is it?"

"In a different file, in a different box."

"In the basement?"

He nods.

"You're sure?"

"I packed the boxes myself."

My shoulders slump. "But that was a long time ago."

"True, but I've always been a bit paranoid and secretive. When they forced me out, I took my time with those files."

"That's great. Maybe Helga won't get it."

"Eventually, she will," he says with a sigh, looking out the window again. "Sasha will give it to her, unless we get it first."

Butterfly wings flutter in my stomach. We can still defeat Helga. "You could ask Sasha to bring it to you."

"I could, but then she'll know."

I lean forward, my eyes fixed on Dr. Oliver. "She'll know what?"

"That she didn't grab the correct file in the first place."

We're silent again, and Dr. Oliver returns his gaze to the window. My brain whirs to life with ideas about how I can help Dr. Oliver. I need another excuse to go to Sasha's house. Maybe I could bring her stuff she forgot at the clinic, or ask if she'd like my mom to give her an estimate of how much her home is worth. I peek at my phone. It's been twenty minutes. Should I text Tara?

"I'd rather destroy the file than have it fall into the wrong hands," says Dr. Oliver.

"Whose hands are the wrong hands?" I ask.

"Anyone's but mine."

"You don't think Sasha would help? She could sell the information to a different company than Feester."

"She could, but I'm not sure I trust Sasha."

"Why not?"

"Because," he says, then stops and rubs his temples. "She doesn't want to help me."

I'm so confused. I really don't understand their relationship, and for whatever reason, Dr. Oliver doesn't want to tell me. It must be something awful. I cross my legs and wait. We have to convince Sasha to help. She has the boxes and the files. I glance at my phone again. Twenty-five minutes.

Dr. Oliver clears his throat. "Whoever dug up the grave has half of the puzzle. The other half is in the file."

The butterflies multiply in my stomach and feel more like hummingbirds. I visualize the Christmas ornament box in my basement. I have half of the puzzle.

"So, they buried something with your wife?"

"With her ashes."

"What?"

"Two vials of TR-97."

I uncross my legs and plant my feet on the ground. Two vials. "You buried them?"

"When she was sick, Gwendolyn had a premonition. She told me it was a controversial drug, and I should protect it."

Mel was right. I stare at him without speaking. The two vials were buried with his wife's ashes.

Dr. Oliver grasps the lever on the side of his chair and pulls. The footrest swings upward, pushing his feet into an elevated position. "It was an unorthodox choice, I admit, but I couldn't think of a safer place."

"Who else would know that?" I ask.

"I didn't think anyone knew."

"But someone had to know. You don't just dig up a grave at random."

"My best guess is Sasha," he says.

"Not Helga?"

He shakes his head. "The ashes fascinated and horrified Sasha. She couldn't help but look in the urn at her mother's remains. She might have seen me hide the vials."

"Oh." I say, biting my lip.

"I suppose Helga could have found out about it from Sasha."

I sit back in my chair and think for a moment. I'm certain Helga was the woman in the cemetery that night. I heard her voice, and Sasha asked her about it.

"I'm pretty sure Helga has a vial," I say. "She has half of the puzzle."

Dr. Oliver nods. "Then we have to do everything possible to get the other half."

"The file?"

"Yes."

"But how?" I ask.

"I have a plan," he says. "It won't be easy, but it's crucial to stopping Helga."

The flutter in my stomach escalates to the flap of a dozen bat wings. "What is it?"

"Get the file so they can't put the pieces of the puzzle together."

Chapter
20

I walk outside and text Tara. *I'm ready*. My hands tremble as I hit SEND. My head and stomach buzz like a hornet's nest with excitement and trepidation.

B right there, she texts.

I wait, pacing the sidewalk in front of the nursing home. Can I do what Dr. Oliver asked? Is he crazy? Does he know how much trouble I might get in? Tara arrives a moment later, and I plop down in the front seat next to her.

"You're pretty quiet," she says, glancing at me while I gnaw on my thumbnail.

"Dr. Oliver wants me to bring him the file," I say.

"What file?"

"*The* file. The one with the secret info about TR-97."

Tara lowers the volume on the radio. "There's a secret file?"

"I guess."

"Are you going to do it?"

I taste blood in my mouth from the torn skin on my thumb. "I don't know. I have to get it first."

"Where is it?"

"In Sasha's basement."

Tara slams on the brakes. "How does he expect you to get that?"

The car behind us honks.

I clasp my hands in my lap. "He says I should get it while she's at work."

"Holy shit! He wants you to break into her house?"

"Sort of."

She presses the accelerator and we move forward into traffic. "Is he going to give you a key?"

I shake my head. "He told me where she used to hide one."

"That's crazy, Penn. It's illegal."

"Even if I use a key?"

"It's breaking and entering, or trespassing, or something. If you get caught, they'll arrest you."

"What if I don't get caught?"

Tara frowns and grips the steering wheel. "You're seriously thinking about doing it?"

"He needs the file."

"Who cares? You need to avoid a criminal record."

"But, I think I can do it."

Tara glares at me and shakes her head.

"Remember last year in English," I say, "when I stayed after class and snuck your paper into Ms. Angle's desk drawer so it wouldn't be late? If I can do that with her in the room, I bet I can get the file."

"As much as I appreciated your effort, and that fact that I got full credit for my paper, I don't think it's the same thing."

I sigh. Tara's right. This is more dangerous. I want to help Dr. Oliver and defeat Helga, but it's insane. No wonder he was in a mental hospital. "You're right. That would be stupid."

"Damn right," Tara says, pulling up to the curb and parking in front of her house. "There must be another way."

I nod. "Are you working tomorrow?"

"Double shifts Tuesday and Thursday."

We stand on the sidewalk near the car. I watch a maple seed helicopter to the ground. "Then you leave Friday?"

"Early Friday. It's a long-ass drive to Georgia."

"I'm going to miss you."

"Me, too," she says, giving me a quick hug before she walks toward her front door. I wait in the driveway until she waves and disappears into her house.

What am I going to do? Dr. Oliver is certain Helga will get the file unless I get it first. And he doesn't want Sasha to know about it. There has to be a way to do it and not get caught.

I text Mel. *How's Florida?*

Sunny. Hot. I look like a lobster

Send a photo. I'll b the judge

He sends a selfie, and I burst out laughing. His nose and cheeks are apple red. *Lol. Melvin the red-nosed tourist,* I text with red-faced emojis.

Lame attempt at humor

What does the rest of u look like?

2 many shades of red

Bummer

What've u been up 2? he asks.

I sit down on the concrete step n front of my house. *Saw Dr. O today*

Is he still crazy?

Xtreme. He wants me 2 break in2 Sasha's house

WTF?

He needs an important file

Certifiable

A blue jay lands on a tree branch in the yard. It whistles and jeers. Is it a sign from my grandma? I wish I could talk to her.

I know, I reply.

Ur not going 2 do it, right? he asks

No

U sure?

Absolutely not going 2 do it

K, good, he texts.

But

But what?

I bet I could, I text.

Don't b crazy

The scream of a siren startles me and I look up. The Blue Jay flies away and an ambulance races down a nearby street. I return my focus to my phone.

The chem supply closet last yr? The hcl I took 2 keep u from failing the lab?

Yur supposed 2 forget that!!!

Just sayin. I include a flush-faced emoji.

Don't do it
K, btw
What? he texts.
Can u tap a phone?
!?
Need 2 know who Helga talks 2
Over my head
Kk, I text.
Talk later. Got 2 go

After dinner that evening, while my mom scrubs the pots and pans, I load the dishwasher. "What's the deal with all the video doorbells?" I ask. I spent the afternoon researching different types, trying to find Sasha's model, but I need more firsthand information.

"What do you mean?"

"It seems like everyone has one."

She nods. "They're popular."

"Why?"

"Because you can see who is at your door, and you don't even have to be home."

I drop our dirty knives and forks into the utensil basket. "So when someone rings the doorbell, it alerts your phone."

"A camera on the doorbell sends an image and sound to your cell phone or computer. Some have motion sensors that let you know when someone is at your door, even if they don't ring the bell. Others let you see your whole front yard, all the way to the street."

"So you can see who walks by?"

"More importantly, you can see which neighbor lets their dog poop in your yard."

"That's gross."

She grabs a towel and starts drying a pan. "The more expensive models allow you to unlock the door for someone, say a housekeeper or child getting home from school, without giving them a key."

The plates clang against each other as I fit them between the wire racks of the dishwasher. "Do they record inside, too, or just outside?"

"Just outside. You'd need a separate security system for inside."

Sasha's house has two video doorbells. Can she see who passes on the sidewalk? Through the backyard? Are they always recording? I didn't see that type of doorbell on the garage side door, though, so Dr. Oliver was right. That entry point seems promising. But what about a security system inside? I didn't look for that and I forgot to ask him.

"You register for school tomorrow, right?" my mom asks, opening a bottle of white wine.

"In the afternoon," I say with a frown.

"It's hard to believe. Your junior year is already here. Where did the time go?"

I shut the dishwasher and shove my hands into my pockets. "Did you fill out the paperwork?"

"I did it online and ordered you a yearbook."

"Not that I'll be in it."

She pours herself a glass of wine. "Maybe you can write for the school newspaper?"

"It's too late. I had to apply for that last spring."

"Well, how about student government?"

I smirk. "No way." Nobody would vote for me except Mel.

"You need to get involved. Make new friends."

I shake my head and clench my jaw. "Tara hasn't even left and you're telling me to make new friends?"

"It's just a suggestion. Do you miss golf?"

I grab a towel and wipe the table. "Not really."

"At least you'll have some tough classes this year. You'll be busy."

"Three cheers for homework."

She sits down at the table and pulls her laptop close. "You know it's important."

"So I can go to college."

"Exactly. College is the goal."

"I can probably keep working at the animal clinic when school starts."

"Are you considering it?" she asks.

"I don't know," I say, rinsing my hands in the sink. "I like making money, but it sucks doing the grunt work."

"That's why you need a college degree, so you can be the boss."

"I guess so." I dry my hands and return the towel to the hook.

"I'm proud of you for taking the initiative and getting a job. That says a lot about you."

"That I'm poor?"

She shakes her head. "That you're willing to work for what you want and not just expect it to be handed to you. Plus, it looks good on a resume."

"Whatever."

My mom's phone rings, and she looks at the screen. "Sorry, I have to take this." She pours a little more wine, then answers the call, walking out of the room.

I watch her go, then grab a glass from the shelf. I pour myself some wine, too, then retreat to my room. When I get there and flop down onto the bed, my phone pings. It's another text message.

STOP SEEING THE DOCTOR . . . OR ELSE

Chapter
21

I wake up at dawn on Tuesday, fighting to break free from my dream. Why does this keep happening? I roll over in bed, my heart thumping. I can't remember how the dream starts. Where am I? Is it at night? It makes no sense, but it seems so real.

I take a cool shower and put on my light blue scrubs for work. As I slather peanut butter on an English muffin, I tell myself to ignore the most recent text. I won't see Dr. Oliver today anyway. It's just a normal Tuesday.

After locking my bike outside the clinic, I glance around the parking lot. Dr. Hughes parked her car in its usual reserved spot, but no *280zx*. I need to get that license plate for Mel. When I enter the building with a jingle, I find an empty waiting room and Christina behind the reception desk.

"Hey, there," she says.

"Hi," I say. "Where is everybody?"

"There aren't any early appointments today."

"That's kind of nice."

She moves a stack of papers and nods. "We missed you yesterday."

"I bet. Someone else had to do the grunt work."

"Not me, though," she says with a wink.

"Of course not," I say, proceeding to the back to clean the kennels. About thirty minutes later, shouting erupts in the reception area. I drop the disinfectant and dash into the hall. I can't see the waiting room, but I hear a male voice.

"You have to help him!"

"Doctor Hughes!" yells Christina.

"He's hurt badly," says the guy.

Eric rushes past me. "Bring him in here." He motions with his arm toward the surgical room. "Quickly," he says.

I'm blocking the hallway, so I duck back into the kennel area. Someone hurries by and Dr. Hughes follows. I open the door again and lean into the hall. I can hear them talking.

"What happened?" asks Dr. Hughes.

"He just bolted into the street," says the guy. I know that voice and suck in a deep breath.

"Was he struck by a car?" she asks.

"Yes."

"Get him up on the table," says Dr. Hughes.

"It's going to be okay, Echo," says Eric. "We'll take good care of you."

I step into the hall and my heart free falls into my stomach as I watch Dr. Hughes and Eric grab things from the cupboards and drawers. I shuffle closer to the surgical room and peek inside. Echo lies on the table, a bright light shining on him. Drops of blood stain the floor, and when I look around the corner into the room, Paulson meets my gaze. He has blood on his hands and all over his white dress shirt. I swallow hard to keep the food in my stomach.

He walks past me, out of the surgical room and down the hall.

"You can wash your hands in here," says Christina, opening the door and showing him the bathroom.

He looks down at his shirt. "Thanks. I'm a mess."

"What happened?" I ask, hurrying after him.

He turns to face me. "I was walking Echo before work, and he must have seen a squirrel or something. He took off, and the leash came out of my hand. He ran out into the street, just as a car was coming around the corner."

I study Paulson for a moment. Despite the dramatic story, Paulson yawns and looks at his watch. I'd be hysterical if this happened to my dog. I'm on the verge of crying because it's Echo, but he seems detached.

"Doctor Hughes will take care of him," says Christina.

Paulson disappears into the bathroom.

I lean against the wall so I don't faint.

After Paulson washes up, he says he'll be right back. "I have a spare shirt in my car."

I chew on my fingernail and wait with Christina in the reception area.

"This is awful," I say.

"Poor Echo," says Christina.

When Paulson returns with another white shirt, someone else occupies the bathroom. "I'll change in Sasha's, I mean, Doctor Hughes's office," he says, breezing past us down the hall.

Christina and I look at each other with raised eyebrows.

"Is that a good idea?" I ask.

"I don't know. I guess they're friends." She shrugs her shoulders and answers the ringing telephone.

"I'm going to check on him." I bet Paulson is going to snoop around Dr. Hughes's office. He wants that file too. I follow him and find the door closed, so I put my ear close to listen. It's quiet and I consider knocking. As I reach for the handle to see if it's locked, the door flies open.

"I thought someone was out there," he says, narrowing his eyes. "You were spying on me."

"No," I say, shaking my head and moving backward. "Just checking to make sure you're okay."

"I'm fine," he says, smoothing the front of his shirt with his hands. "You should mind your own business."

My mouth hangs open. Is Paulson sending the texts? "I thought you'd be worried about Echo."

"Well, I'm not," he says, stepping closer. "Doctor Hughes can handle it. But I want to know why Helga has the TR-97 file."

"The what?"

"The file you mentioned on Saturday."

I glance down the hallway. "How would I know?"

"You're here a lot. You might know."

I shake my head again.

He leans his face and body closer, and his coffee breath invades my nostrils. "You know something."

"I don't," I stammer, looking at the floor.

"I saw you staring at the boxes in Sasha's basement."

I try to retreat, but my heel bumps into the wall.

Paulson grabs my arm. "Tell me what you know, or you're going to be in big trouble."

"Ouch!"

He grips my arm tighter, and I wince.

"Helga has the research."

"She does?"

I nod, trying to pull away.

He twists my arm. "How do you know that?"

"I saw the box in Doctor Hughes's office," I say. "And overheard them talking. But now it's gone."

"The research is gone?"

I nod again.

"They were talking about TR-97?"

"I think so."

I squirm, but he holds me against the wall. "What day was that?"

"I don't remember."

We hear a noise in the reception area, and he releases my arm. I dash around him and run to the bathroom. I'm going to burst into tears, and I don't want anyone to see. When I emerge a few minutes later, Christina is hovering near the door.

"Are you okay?" she asks, touching my shoulder. I flinch and hug myself tightly.

"I don't know," I say, wiping my eyes with a tissue.

"What happened?"

"Paulson." My voice cracks. "He grabbed me."

"That bastard!" she says, looking down the hall. "What a prick! I'm going to kick him in the nuts."

"No! Don't. Please." I throw my arms around Christina to hold her in place. "It wasn't like that. He just grabbed my arm."

"I don't care what he grabbed. He shouldn't be touching you." Her jaw clenches and she growls.

"I'll be okay. I'm sure it won't happen again."

"It better not," she says, holding my face in her hands, staring into my eyes. "If it does, you need to scream bloody murder, okay?"

I nod.

"You promise?"

"Yes."

"Good girl."

I press my fists into my eyes, then take a deep breath. "How's Echo?"

"I haven't heard."

Dr. Hughes enters the reception area a few minutes later, and I can tell by the look on her face that Echo is gone.

"Where is Mr. Paulson?" she asks.

"He might be in your office," says Christina with a frown.

"Is Echo okay?" I ask.

She shakes her head. "He didn't make it."

Dr. Hughes walks away, and as much as I try to hold them back, the tears cascade down my face like raindrops on a window. Christina wraps her arms around me.

"Poor Echo," I sob.

"He was such a little sweetie," she says.

The rest of the morning, I struggle with work. I can't believe Echo is dead. I don't see Paulson again, which is a relief, and when noon arrives, I can't wait to leave. Cheerful sunshine and a lively breeze welcome me outdoors. I close my eyes for a moment, breathing in the fresh air, then exhaling my sadness and grief. Other than a few flattened squirrels and birds, I've never seen a dead animal. At least Echo looked peaceful. I'm thinking about my grandma, unlocking my bike, when that voice spoils the mood.

"You little snake," she says. I turn and see Helga, hands on her hips, dark sunglasses shielding most of her face.

"Are you talking to me?" I ask.

"Of course I am, you little snitch."

"What's that supposed to mean?" I place my hands on my hips to match Helga's stance.

"Don't be coy with me. You told Sasha I was in her office."

"I thought she should know."

"Well, she doesn't care because I was just retrieving my property."

"Are you sure about that?"

Helga frowns. "You're a nosy one. Always around at the wrong time. She mentioned you were in her basement this weekend."

"We went down there during the storm."

"How convenient you were at her house."

I cross my arms over my chest. "I didn't plan it that way."

"Sure you didn't, and now you're going to tell me you weren't snooping around there, either."

"I wasn't. We just waited for the storm to end."

"Like I believe that."

"It's the truth."

Helga crosses her arms over her chest and taps her foot. "Not likely."

I glare at her but say nothing.

"Just you and Sasha?" she asks. "Like you're best friends."

"It wasn't like that," I say.

"No one else was there?"

"Um." I'm suddenly stuck. Should I tell her about Paulson? Does she already know? Is she testing me? Paulson clearly doesn't like Helga, so maybe the feeling is mutual.

"Listen, you little hussy," she says, pulling a small silver gun from her purse. "Stop lying." It looks like a toy, but something tells me it's real. "Tell me who was there, or I'll make your life miserable."

"Paulson," I say without hesitation. The gun scares the shit out of me, and she seems crazy enough to use it. "He was there, too."

"I thought so. That two-bit scam artist," she says under her breath, tucking the weapon back into her bag. "Just stay out of my way. It's none of your business."

I'm still holding my breath when she turns and moves toward the clinic entrance. When she disappears inside, I expel the air from my lungs and shudder. If my heart was beating any faster, it would explode from my chest. I'm still shaking when I mount my bicycle and race home. That was close. Too close.

Chapter
22

On Wednesday morning during work, I accidentally break the latch on one of the dog cages and drop a bottle of sanitizer all over the floor. I also forget to clean the third exam room.

"Are you okay?" asks Denise. "You seem distracted today."

"I'm okay, just clumsy," I say.

"Slow down or take a break if you need one."

I nod and take several deep breaths. The bat wings flapping inside my stomach make me feel nauseous. I plan to get the file from Sasha's house this afternoon. She scheduled appointments until six o'clock, and I talked Tara into helping me. Thankfully, Helga and Paulson don't show up at the clinic.

When I get home, I change into blue jeans and a plain white T-shirt. I can't eat a single bite of lunch because of the turbulence in my stomach. Around one, Tara comes to my house.

"Are you sure you want to do this?" she asks. "It's pretty insane."

I nod my head. "I'm sure."

"You can change your mind. No shame in backing out."

I think of Dr. Oliver. I can't let him down, and I can't let Helga or Paulson win. "I have to get that file."

"He told you where to find it?"

"He told me which box to look for, and then which file inside the box."

Tara chews on her fingernail. "What happens if you can't find the right box or the file?"

"I don't know. I'll decide what to do if I get to that point."

"So what do I need to do again?" she asks.

I sit down at the kitchen table. "Drive me to the end of the street. I'll walk up to her house from the bottom of the hill. You come right back here and park in your usual spot. Then go to my room and stay there until I get back."

"I'm not picking you up?"

I shake my head. "I'm walking. My alibi is that we're together at my house all afternoon."

"Will you be able to text or call me?"

"No, my phone has to stay here. Post something on Instagram for me. Let's get a photo now." Tara and I press our heads together for a selfie. "Cross-eyed," I say, and take the photo. It looks totally innocent and goofy. It's perfect. "Post that later when you get back here."

"Is your passcode on?"

"Let me disable it. And text Mel from your phone while you're here. Text him from mine, too."

"Got it."

"But don't tell him where I am. He can't know."

Tara nods. "What if someone calls you?"

"Don't answer my phone. Let it go to voicemail."

"What if your mom comes home?"

"If you hear her, lock my bedroom door and put on some music."

Tara folds her arms around herself in a hug. "How long is this going to take?" she asks.

"From the time you drop me off, it should be twenty to thirty minutes max."

"What if you're not back in thirty?"

"Just keep waiting. Don't come looking for me."

"Shit, I'm so nervous. Can I have a beer?"

"My mom left an open bottle of wine in the refrigerator," I say. "You can have it when you get back here."

"Okay," she says. "You ready?"

I nod. "Let's go."

I get out of the car, slipping the backpack over my shoulders, then closing the door. Tara drives off, and I walk up La Crosse Lane. I stick to the sidewalk on Sasha's side, knowing I'll duck behind the hedge at her neighbor's house. My heart pounds like a bass drum inside my chest. The plan is in my head. I keep walking at a steady pace. If I see someone, I just keep going, no stopping. I walk with purpose, but not like I'm in a hurry. Thankfully, I don't see anybody, and not one car passes me in either direction.

When I get to the hedge, I dart to the right, scurrying down the side of the house. Like Dr. Oliver said, the garden gnome waits for me near the door to the garage. As I approach the statue, I lift my eyes, searching for a camera. Nothing but rain gutters and siding. But what if the key isn't there? What do I do then? Look elsewhere? Go home? I remove the thin cotton gloves from my pocket and put them on, then grab the ceramic gnome by the neck and tip it sideways. I exhale and take the key, inserting it into the lock above the doorknob. It slides in and I hold my breath, turning it to the right, releasing the bolt.

Leaving the key in the lock, I turn the knob and push the door open. After stepping into the empty garage, I wait for my eyes to adjust to the darkness, then close the door. When I get to the two steps near the interior door, I remove my shoes. I'm going to wear socks in the house. I inhale a deep breath through my nose to steady my nerves, then reach for the doorknob and twist. It doesn't budge. I need the key for this door, too? I slip my shoes back on and retrieve the key from the outside door. I push it into the lock opening, but it doesn't fit. Shit! He didn't tell me there were two locks! I set the key down on the top step and look around. It's got to be here somewhere. Nobody hides a key outside, but not inside. Scanning the side of the door frame, I spy a small nail and another key up high. I grab it and unlock the door to the house.

After removing my shoes again, I slide a black ski mask over my head and crack open the door, peeking inside. I wait a moment and listen for the beep of an alarm. It's quiet except for the hum of the refrigerator, so I step onto the wood floor in the hallway.

On my left, mounted high in the corner near the front door, is a device with a small red blinking light. A camera. I turn my face away as the garage door closes behind me with a click. And then I hear whimpering. I lean to the left and peer around the corner. A large crate with a dog occupies the middle of the living room. The dog looks at me, pushing its nose against the cage. Please don't bark. That's probably a pet-cam. I've seen ads for them in the magazines at the clinic.

My head tells me to leave, but the thrill of beating Helga and Paulson pushes me forward. I dash across the hall, open the door to the basement, and fly down the stairs. I need to be quick in case Sasha comes home. I flip on the light at the bottom and turn left toward the tower of boxes. Dr. Oliver said to look for the one labeled GENERAL. I scan the stacks from top to bottom, starting on the left. They're in no particular order, but I spot the box in the third column. Four others rest on top of it. I remove them first and set each one aside before opening the target box. It's crammed with loose papers, and I push them out of the way. They slip to the bottom and some spill out onto the floor. Shit. It has to be in here.

I grab more papers, but my gloves create a problem. The cotton makes it difficult to grip the sheets. I take off my right glove and sift through the contents of the box until I find it. A thick file labeled MISCELLANEOUS. The front includes hand-written notes and a circular coffee mug stain. When I stuff it into my backpack, zipping it closed, the barking starts.

My throat constricts. Is someone here? Did Dr. Hughes come home? OMG. Stay calm. I grab the loose papers and shove them back into the box. I press the lid closed and return it to the tower, placing the other boxes on top of it. I slip the backpack over my shoulders, turn off the light, and run up the stairs, pausing at the top to catch my breath. The barking continues. When I reach for the doorknob, my right hand doesn't have a glove. Shit! I left it downstairs, but I can't go back. I need to get out of here. I crack open the door using my left hand and take a step into the hall, keeping my face turned away from the camera. As much as I want to check on the dog, I know that would be foolish.

Once I'm in the empty garage, I breathe a sigh of relief. She's not here. I use my gloved hand to relock the door and return the key to the nail, then sit to put my shoes on. I pick up the key for the outside door and stride across the barren concrete. Once outside, I lock the bolt and stash the key back under the gnome.

I slink behind the neighbor's hedge and remove my ski mask and the other glove, shoving them into my backpack. I head for the sidewalk, moving away from Sasha's house, retracing my footsteps back down the hill. I don't look back, but I want to scream at myself. Where did I leave the glove? I walk faster and round the corner at South Hill Drive, knowing it's probably in the box with all the loose papers. Dammit. I'm such an idiot. That's a huge mistake. At least I didn't leave it on the floor. I'm confident it's out of sight—until someone opens that box.

I cross the street, only a few blocks from home, when a car zips past me. I recognize the vehicle. The silver *280zx*. Was it following me? I race around the corner of Marinette Trail, abandoning the sidewalk and cutting across the grass. As my house comes into view, I see my mom's car parked in the driveway. Now I can't go in through the front door or the garage. I stay on the opposite side of the street, walking past my house, then double back toward it. My bedroom windows face the front and side yards. I approach the side and tap on the glass, knowing it's going to startle Tara.

She whips around and rushes to the window, cranking it open. "Oh my god, you scared the shit out of me!"

"Sorry, but I saw my mom's car. I need to climb in through the window."

Tara opens it as a wide as possible, but a screen separates us.

"Pull the screen inside," I say. "There are little buttons up high and down low. Push those, and it should come loose."

While she's doing that, I try to figure out how to climb up to the base of the window. It's higher than I thought. Once she has the screen off, I remove the backpack and toss it inside.

"I might need help," I say.

"What can I do?" she asks.

"Hand me the desk chair. I can stand on it, then pull it back inside."

The plan works, and I'm safe inside my bedroom, with the chair and screen back in place. "How long was I gone?" I ask.

Tara looks at her phone. "Almost forty minutes."

"Sorry if you were worried."

"I was so nervous, I drank all the wine." She holds up the empty bottle.

I burst out laughing.

"But I posted to your Instagram account and texted with Mel."

I pull off my t-shirt and unzip my jeans. "Good. When did my mom get home?"

"About fifteen minutes ago."

"I'm going to change clothes and get something to drink. Come with me. She'll see us together."

We go to the kitchen, and my mom sits at the table working on her laptop, a glass of red wine within reach. She looks up when we enter.

"Hey, Mom," I say.

"Hi, Mrs. Heavnor," says Tara.

"Hi, girls," she says, returning her eyes to the computer screen.

"Is there any more lemonade?" I ask, searching the refrigerator.

"We drank it yesterday, but you can make more."

"Is it the powder?"

"No, it's frozen. There should be another can."

I open the freezer and spy the lemonade concentrate on the middle shelf. I pop it open and scoop the slush into a plastic pitcher, filling it with cold water.

"We're going to need ice," I tell Tara, and she opens the freezer again.

In the door, she spies a bottle of Absolut and points to it. I look to make sure my mom remains focused on her computer, then nod my head, grabbing three glasses from the cupboard. I hand Tara the small one and make a pouring motion. She knows what to do. The vodka looks like water. I fill the two larger glasses with ice and some lemonade. I also point to a bag of pretzels on the counter, and Tara takes that back to my room. I follow her, closing the door and locking it.

"I can't believe we did that with your mom sitting right there," says Tara, sitting down on the bed.

"She's oblivious when she's working," I say.

"That's so cool."

I shrug.

"Let's pour these drinks," she says. "I can't wait to hear what happened."

"Okay, but first, a toast to secret missions." I raise my glass.

Tara raises hers. "To best friends on secret missions," she says, and we clink our glasses, taking a sip. Tara's grimace mirrors what my face must look like as the alcohol assaults my taste buds, burning my throat.

I eat some pretzels and open my backpack, showing Tara the file, and telling her what happened.

"Was the red light on the camera blinking?" she asks.

I nod.

"Then it might not have been a real camera."

"I hope not."

"When a camera is recording, I'm pretty sure the light is solid red. Or is it the other way around?" She takes another sip of lemonade.

"Let's hope for the best. What about the glove I lost? I'm pretty sure I left it in the box in the basement."

"There isn't anything you can do about it now, but you need to get rid of the other one."

I hold it up for her to see. "What should I do with it?"

"Let me handle it. I'll bring it home, cut it up into tiny pieces, and throw them away at work tomorrow."

"And the mask?" I hold it up, then toss it on the bed.

"I can get rid of that, too. I'll pack it with my moving stuff, then destroy it when I get to Georgia."

"Thanks."

"That's what friends are for." She raises her glass and we take a gulp of the vodka lemonade.

"Here's the file." I pull it out of my backpack. "Should we open it?"

"Duh. You didn't go to all that trouble for us *not* to read it."

I sit down on my bed next to Tara. The folder contains an assortment of handwritten notes on Dr. Oliver's stationery, a bunch of computer printouts with columns of numbers and technical data, plus the names and trauma summaries of several patients. Most of it we don't understand, but we're captivated reading about the veterans. We find their stories sad but hopeful.

"Who wrote all those?" asks Tara.

"Maybe Francine Baker," I say, pointing to the bottom of the page. "See the initials?"

"She was their psychologist?"

"I guess. Doctor Oliver said they worked with the same patients."

At the back of the file, we find a document titled TREATMENT PROTOCOL. It's bound on the left side and sealed with round white stickers on the other three sides. Tara and I stare at it.

"That looks top secret," she says.

"He definitely didn't want anyone to read this," I say, turning it over in my hand.

"Are you going to open it?"

"Not unless I can find more stickers to seal it back up."

"What do you think it says?"

I set the document on the bed between us. "It could be about the patient who committed suicide."

"Or it might contain information that no one has seen before."

"My gut says this is what Paulson wants, and Helga was hoping to find in the TR-97 file."

Tara grasps my hand and squeezes. "Then you better keep it safe."

Chapter
23

The early light of Thursday arrives too soon, piercing the window shade in my bedroom and delivering sharp jabs to my forehead. My mouth feels like I ate sand. I have to go to work, but the thought of riding my bike makes my stomach lurch. I call Tara while I lie in bed.

"Good morning, sunshine," I say.

"Why are you calling so early?" she says. "My head is killing me."

"Vodka will do that. Can I borrow your car today?"

"Why? What's up?"

I stare at the ceiling. "I need to deliver the file to Doctor Oliver."

"I'd let you, but I have to be at work by ten."

"If you give me a ride to work at nine, I'll walk to Rocky's at noon, get your key, and drive from there."

"Okay, but you have to come back and pick me up from work at eight tonight."

"At eight? I was thinking you only worked until five."

"I wish. The prick manager added a few extra hours to my shift."

I massage my temples with my fingertips. "I don't even want to go to work today, but I have to."

"Me either," she says. "But I need the money."

The room spins and I brace my hands on the bed. "Me too."

"If you drive, be careful parking. Not anywhere near our houses while I'm gone."

"Never mind. It's too complicated. My head is throbbing. I'll just ride my stupid bike."

"Sorry."

"It's not your fault. Call me tonight when you're home. I'll bring you a couple of beers."

"I'll need them," she says.

"Talk later," I say.

I'll have to keep the file in my backpack at work. Not my first choice, but it should be fine. Nobody looks through my stuff, anyway. If I leave it at home, I have to come all the way back for it. I find a large envelope from my mom's real estate company and shove the papers inside, sealing the flap. The outside is blank. In case someone opens my backpack, I want it to look like an actual piece of mail. I write my dad's name on the outside and a fictitious address.

Later at the clinic, when I finish my first-of-the-morning chores, Sasha pulls me aside. My stomach somersaults and sweat erupts under my arms. I follow her into her office, my brain buzzing, and grip the doorframe for support. Oh my god, she knows I was in her house. She saw the security video. I'm in so much trouble.

"Yesterday was kind of traumatic," she says. "Losing a patient. Are you alright?"

She's talking about Echo, and I breathe a sigh of relief. "I'm okay, just sad. I can't believe Echo died."

"It's tragic, but he had major head trauma. We couldn't save him."

"That must be hard."

"It's difficult to lose one, but Echo died before he even got here. There wasn't much we could do for him."

I hang my head. "I'm sorry."

"It happens sometimes in this job. But Christina told me you were pretty shaken up."

I look up. Did Christina tell Dr. Hughes about Paulson? I can't deal with that right now.

"I've never seen anything like that before," I say.

"Well, try to put it out of your mind. Echo didn't suffer."

"Okay," I say with a nod, meeting Dr. Hughes's eyes.

"Is there anything else?" she asks.

I want to ask if she knows Helga carries a gun, but I don't want to get into that either. "It was weird that Mr. Paulson didn't seem upset. I was bawling my eyes out and he seemed fine."

"He was still in shock."

I nod again, but don't speak.

"Everyone reacts differently in that situation," she says.

I hear the telephone ringing at the reception desk. Although I'm sad about Echo, I'm thrilled that Paulson has no more reasons to come by the clinic. I hope I never see him again.

"Well, that's it," she says. "If you're doing okay, I've got patients waiting."

"I'll be fine," I say, but my heart is still pounding.

At noon, I say goodbye to Christina and grab my backpack to check the contents. The envelope is still there. I stroll outside to find mostly overcast skies. Is it supposed to rain? I check the weather app on my phone. Forty percent chance this afternoon, increasing to eighty percent tonight. I better get going in case those odds increase.

As I unlock my bike, I notice the 280zx in the parking lot occupying its usual spot. With no one around, I ride over and snap a photo of the license plate, then send it to Mel.

Here it is, I text. Hope u can help

I don't get an immediate reply, so I tuck my phone away and pedal south. On the way, I stop at the university copy center. I want to copy the file, even the Treatment Protocol, before I give it to Dr. Oliver. I found some round white stickers at the clinic. If I carefully peel off the original ones, I can make it look credible. Since those papers are bound on the left side, I copy them one at a time, laying each page on the glass. When I get near the end, I find a small bronze key taped to a blank sheet. It could be for a cabinet or a padlock. If I pull the tape, it will ruin the folder and Dr. Oliver will know, so I photocopy the side with the key, then finish copying the last pages.

After tucking both sets of papers into my backpack, I turn around to leave, and Paulson strides into the copy center. Our eyes meet as he enters, and my stomach does a back flip. Did he follow me here? I look at the ground and try to move by him, clutching the pack close to my chest. He stops just inside the entrance.

"This is a surprise," he says with a smirk.

"Hey," I say with a frown, glancing around. Is there another exit?

"How's it going?"

My eyes scan the area for another door. "Fine."

"Did you just come from the clinic?"

"Yep, but I'm late." Several other people linger nearby making copies, and one uses the fax machine.

"Have you seen any more boxes at the office? Like the ones in the basement?" he asks.

"Nope."

"Can you look for me?"

"I need to go."

"Will you at least look?" he asks, taking a step toward me.

"Get away from me!" I shout.

The woman at the fax machine stares, and the guy at another copier turns to look.

"And stay away!"

I lunge for the door and leave the building, hurrying toward my bike. Thank god I didn't lock it near the entrance. But he might follow, so I'm prepared to run. I avoid looking back until I reach my bike. When I glance over my shoulder, the copy center door is closed, and nobody stands outside. I exhale slowly, letting my heart rate slow. I need to get to Oak Bluff.

When I check in at the nursing home, the gray-haired receptionist asks me to open my backpack. I unzip it for her and show her the contents.

"Let me page an attendant," she says.

"I know where the room is," I say, eager to see Dr. Oliver.

"All visitors must have an escort," she says.

"Okay." I step off to the side and study the floral art in the lobby. I don't want to break the rules or draw attention to myself. A worker named Fernando greets me.

"Hi," I say.

"Who are you visiting today?" he asks.

"Doctor Oliver in one-oh-three."

"Yes, of course. This way."

We walk side by side down the hall. He hums a song I don't know as we pass a room where someone is yelling: "My sister Frankie should be here! Where is she? Frankie? She's late!"

I glance at Fernando, but he keeps walking, ignoring the woman's outburst. I shut my mouth and try to do the same.

"Doctor Oliver is probably finishing his lunch," says Fernando, knocking on the door to announce our arrival. "You have a visitor," he says.

Dr. Oliver sits in his usual place, but a hospital table stands in front of him. He has eaten only a few bites of a roast beef sandwich, pasta salad, steamed broccoli, and apple juice.

"I'm finished," he says, trying to push the table away. Even though it has wheels, it won't budge.

Fernando releases the brake with his foot and rolls the table out of the way.

"Are you sure you're done?" asks Fernando, taking the bib and napkin from Dr. Oliver. "You have food left."

"Yes, I'm finished, and tell the cook the beef was tough, the broccoli undercooked, and the salad bitter. How do you expect me to eat this garbage?"

"I will tell him," says Fernando with a smile.

I take a seat in the upright chair across from Dr. Oliver, setting my backpack on the floor near my feet. I don't speak until Fernando departs with the table. "Do you want me to close the door?"

"Yes," he says with a nod.

When I return to my chair, I ask how he is doing.

"Fine, but I see you have a backpack today."

I nod.

"Does that mean you brought me something?"

I unzip the bag and remove the envelope, leaving the copies. "Here's the file."

His eyes widen as he stares at the package.

"It was mostly like you said. I don't think anybody knows."

"Well done, Penelope. That's fantastic. Let me see it."

I hand him the envelope, and he glances at the name and address, then pulls the flap open, removing the file. He holds it for a moment, feeling its weight, running his hands across the smooth surface. When he parts the heavy paper, I pray the correct information rests inside.

Dr. Oliver reads the top sheet, flipping the pages, nodding his head. The corners of his mouth curl upward as he reviews the contents. He nods again when he reaches the Treatment Protocol document. After a few minutes, he looks up with a smile.

"It's a miracle," he says. "Thank you."

"You're welcome."

"I really thought I lost these notes forever."

I grin. "Not lost, just hidden."

He returns his attention to the first few pages.

"Are you going to keep the file here?" I ask.

He nods. "I have a secret pocket in my chair." He taps the right arm and slides his hand down inside near the cushion, making it disappear. "It should fit just fine."

"I want it to be safe."

"It's safe with me." He taps the arm of the chair again and looks at me over the top of his glasses. "But you're concerned?"

"A little because I've received some strange text messages lately, telling me to mind my own business and stay away from you."

"Oh?"

"Should I be worried?" I glance at the file in his lap and at my backpack.

"Not necessarily, but be careful."

"Careful?"

"About Sasha."

"I thought Helga was the one to look out for?"

"Both of them. Don't let them know about our visits."

"I won't, but Helga seems a lot more dangerous."

"Why do you say that?"

"Because she already has half of the puzzle, and she carries a gun."

Dr. Oliver sits up straight. His fingers grip the file. "What?"

"In her purse. She pointed it at me the other day."

"She showed you the TR-97?"

I shake my head. "She showed me her gun and told me to stay out of her way."

"But you think she has the serum?"

"Yes."

"Why do you think that?"

"We talked about it. It's her or Sasha, but Helga insisted the TR-97 file in Sasha's office was hers. Remember?"

"But the serum wouldn't be in the file, so we still don't know who dug up the grave."

Should I tell him I was in the cemetery that night? That Helga was there too? If I do, that means I haven't been completely honest with Dr. Oliver. He may not trust me anymore. "I also overheard Sasha and Helga talking last week. Sasha thinks Helga had something to do with the cemetery incident."

"I guess that's possible."

I need to convince Dr. Oliver without telling him everything. "I think it was Helga, or she had someone to do it for her. She doesn't seem like the type to dig in dirt."

"Have there been any other newspaper articles about the incident?"

"Not that I've noticed, but I haven't looked recently." Shoot. I need to be more diligent about that. They could have printed something that I missed.

"I don't understand why Helga thinks you're such a threat," he says.

I shrug and shake my head. "Me, either. But she wanted to know about Paulson."

"The pharmaceutical guy?"

"She called him a scam artist."

Dr. Oliver gives a dismissive wave of his hand. "He's the least of my worries."

I pause for a moment. I'm worried about Paulson. How much should I tell Dr. Oliver? "He scares me."

"Then stay away from him," he says.

"I'm going to avoid both of them."

"Good idea."

Dr. Oliver opens the file again, reading the top sheet of paper. I stare at him and bounce my legs. The questions in my head whirl like a fidget spinner. Is it time for me to ask my real question? The one I've wanted to ask since I first learned about Dr. Oliver and TR-97? I guess it's now or never.

"My dad has PTSD," I say, interrupting the silence.

Dr. Oliver lifts his eyes and fixes his gaze on me. "He does? What's his name?"

"Jason."

"Heavnor? Like on the envelope?"

"Yes."

"Is he a veteran?"

I shake my head.

Dr. Oliver rests his hands on his lap on top of the file. "What about him then?"

I tell him all about my dad, the accident that changed him, his mood swings, depression, and my desire to help him. "I know if he gets better, he and my mom won't divorce, and we'll be a family again."

Dr. Oliver remains quiet, absorbing the details. He wrings his hands and swivels his head to look out the window. I lean forward in my chair, clasping my hands in front of me, waiting for his reply.

"Has he been seeing a psychotherapist?" asks Dr. Oliver.

"I think so," I say.

"I know some experienced ones, and can give you their names."

"But what about using your treatment? Can't we use TR-97 and give him a positive memory instead of the traumatic one?"

Dr. Oliver looks at me, opening his mouth to speak, but stops. He closes his eyes and rubs his temples with his fingertips.

"Please, Doctor Oliver," I say. "He really needs help."

A firm knock sounds on the door, and Fernando enters the room. "It's time for your bath," he says.

"Can't you see I'm busy?" says Dr. Oliver.

"Your guest can return another time," he says.

"I don't need a bath. I just had one yesterday."

"Not according to your chart."

"Well, your chart is wrong."

"Say goodbye to your visitor, Doctor Oliver. Tomorrow is another day."

I stand and grab my backpack. "Does it have to be right now?" I ask Fernando, stepping toward him. "Maybe it could wait until later?" I wave my arm behind my back to signal Dr. Oliver. I want him to slip the envelope into the secret pocket of his chair.

As expected, Fernando won't tolerate a delay. "We keep to the schedule. It's bath time."

I turn and say goodbye, then stroll to the door. Dr. Oliver hid the file, and it should be safe, but I still don't know if he can help my dad. I'll have to visit again soon.

When I exit the building and approach my bicycle, I'm shocked to see that both tires are flat. How did that happen? I look around the parking lot filled with empty cars. I don't see Paulson's or Helga's, which is a relief. I spin each wheel and look for glass, a nail, or a slice in the rubber. Nothing. Someone let the air out of my tires. Who would do that?

I look around again. It seems silly to call the police or report it to the receptionist. I would risk drawing attention to myself and my visit. Instinctively, I grab my phone and text my mom.

She replies right away. *Busy now Can help after 4.*

It's only two. I can't wait two more hours. Mel is gone. Tara is at work. Crap. I have to text my dad. *R u around?*

I wait a few minutes, unlocking my bike. I could push it for a while or call him? I decide to call, and my dad actually answers the phone.

"Hi honey," he says.

"Hey, Dad. What are you doing?"

"Nothing much."

"Can you pick me up?" I ask.

"Yeah, sure. Where are you?"

"Oak Bluff Nursing Home."

"What are you doing there?"

I glance around the parking lot again. "I'll explain when you get here. I have bike trouble."

"Okay. I'll be there in twenty minutes."

"Thanks," I say.

"See you soon."

When I end the call, I'm startled by the screech of tires. I whip my head around and see some crazy driver peeling out of the parking lot. It's the *280zx*.

Chapter
24

Sometimes twenty minutes seems like forever. As I wait for my dad, I scan the parking lot and the street, suspicious of every car. Was the guy in the silver sports car following me? Did he let the air out of my tires? Oh my god, what am I going to tell my dad? He'll want to know why I'm here, and what happened to my bike.

Like a mirror of my mood, the sky darkens, and a few drops of rain dampen the pavement. My dad arrives just as the clouds burst. I move my bike to the curb, and he jumps out to lift it into the back of the truck. I scramble into the passenger seat to avoid getting drenched.

"I've got great timing," he says, climbing into the driver's seat and closing the door.

"Thanks," I say.

"Happy to do it. What're you doing way over here, anyway?"

"A favor for my boss."

"Does somebody in the nursing home have a pet?"

I shake my head. "She needed something dropped off with her dad and couldn't get here today."

He flips on the windshield wipers and pulls out of the parking lot. "That was nice of you, but people usually call a courier service for that. Is she paying you?"

"I don't know."

"She should pay you for your time."

"I'll ask tomorrow."

He glances over his shoulder toward the truck bed. "What's wrong with your bike?"

"My tires are flat."

"Both of them?"

"Yeah."

"That's strange."

"Or unlucky."

"Was it glass?" he asks.

I fasten my seatbelt. "I'm not sure."

"You really have to watch where you're going."

"I know," I say with a nod, eager to change the subject. "Have you had lunch? I'm starving."

"We could go to Culver's?"

"That's perfect. I'd kill for a double butter burger with cheese."

"All right," he says. "Let's do it."

We drive in silence for a while, and the rhythm of the windshield wipers keeps pace with the song on the radio. I stare out the side window, watching the water droplets slide down the glass.

"Do you want to get the bike fixed?" he asks.

"It can wait," I say, without thinking. That was stupid. I have a pump at home, but will the tires hold air?

"I know a shop downtown. We go right by it."

"I guess I should. I need it to get to work tomorrow."

"Let's drop it off and then go eat. By the time we're stuffed, the bike will be ready."

The rain slows to a sprinkle as we park, and I wheel my bike into Yellow Jersey Cyclery. My dad follows.

"Can I help you?" asks a young guy with a goatee.

"My tires are flat. I might need new ones," I say, showing him the problem.

"What happened?" he asks.

"I'm not sure, but can you put some air in them?"

"Yeah. The pump is in back." He wheels my bike away and I glance around, looking for my dad. He's near the front of the store looking at a tandem bicycle.

"This looks fun," he says.

"For old people," I say.

"Are you saying I'm old?"

"I'm saying it's not the right bike for you."

"Nice recovery. What did the guy say?"

"He's checking my tires."

"You're in luck," the goatee guy says, walking back into the showroom. "The tires seem good, a little worn in places, but rideable. Of course, I can replace them."

I look at my dad. "Should I replace them?"

"Yes," he says with a nod. "I want you to be safe, and I'll pay for it."

"Okay," says the goatee guy. "Give me about thirty minutes."

"Great," I say.

"Do you want your chain cleaned or brake pads replaced?"

"No, thanks," I say. "Just the tires."

"You got it. Can I get a name and phone number for the work order?"

I give him the information and turn toward my dad.

"Thank you," I say.

He smiles. "No problem. Come on. Let's go get burgers."

While we eat, I fixate on Dr. Oliver's question. Is my dad seeing a psychotherapist? I want to know, but how do you ask a parent that question? How do you ask anyone that question? It's too personal and accusatory. Are you mentally ill? The thought makes my insides quiver like Jell-O. I never see my dad anymore, so how would I know? We barely talk, and when we do, it's not about important stuff. He's like a shadow I glimpse out of the corner of my eye.

"So," I say, "how're you doing?"

"Good," he says, bobbing his head up and down. "I love these burgers, and the onion rings are the best."

"I don't mean with lunch. I mean you. How are *you*?"

He stares at me with a blank expression. "I'm fine."

That's such a bullshit answer. "Yeah? Have you played golf this week?" I ask, trying to shift the conversation away from what's directly in front of us. We played last Friday, but with everything that's been going on, it seems like a lot longer.

"Not since we played."

"I thought we were going to play this week," I say.

He takes a bite of his burger. "Since you're not on the team, I didn't know if you were still interested."

"I still like golf. I just don't want to play competitively."

"But that's the fun of it," he says.

"Not to me. I like the challenge of it and being outside." It's also the only time I get to see you.

"I'll try to get us a tee time this weekend," he says, "or next week for sure, in the afternoon."

"Okay," I say, and we return our focus to the food. What will it take to get him to talk? It's not like I want him to spill his guts, but I want to hear something that's not superficial.

"So, when does school start?" my dad asks, interrupting my thoughts.

"About ten days," I say with a frown.

"You're not looking forward to it?"

"Not really."

"Why not? High school can be the best years of your life."

I shake my head. "God, I hope not."

"I thought high school was fun."

"You would. I've seen your old yearbooks. You were athletic and smart and popular. I'm none of those things."

My dad studies me, and a small crease forms between his eyebrows. His dimples appear as he presses his lips together. I know why my mom fell for him, but he's forty-five now. High school couldn't have been that great.

"You just need to get involved," he says. "Find your crowd. Do your thing."

"Sure," I say.

"Is there something you can look forward to?"

"I don't know. Being done?"

"I meant homecoming or the school play or joining a club?"

I sigh. "Nothing will be fun without Tara. She's moving back to Georgia."

"I didn't know that."

I set down my burger. Suddenly, I'm not hungry anymore. "She leaves tomorrow."

"You probably want to get home then."

"She's at work. I'll see her later tonight."

Another long pause envelops us, and I imagine this happens on a bad first date. We sip our drinks and plunge the last of the French fries into the ketchup. I'm running out of time. I need to say something.

"You should meet Doctor Oliver."

"Who's that?" he asks.

"My boss' dad. He lives at the nursing home."

"You saw him today."

I nod. "He's really smart."

"And you want me to meet him?"

"He was a professor at Wisconsin State."

He stuffs the last onion ring into his mouth. "Okay."

"He's a good person to talk to."

My dad gives me a blank stare.

"He's helped lots of people."

"With what?"

"PTSD," I say, taking a sip of my root beer.

My dad doesn't reply. The corners of his mouth turn down and his dimples disappear. He gazes at me with a furrowed brow, narrowing his eyes like he's having trouble understanding me.

"You know, post-traumatic stress," I say, trying to make it sound totally normal.

My dad stands. "We should go." He takes his tray to the trash bins. "Your bike is probably ready, and you want to get home."

I remain seated, watching my dad retreat from the table. I failed. He's a brick wall. After a moment, I get up and clear my trash, then head for the truck.

We pick up my bike and drive home without speaking. Classic rock music on the radio fills the void. We don't even comment on the sunshine and dry pavement during the ride. I wish I knew what he was thinking. I know it's hard for him to talk to me, but is he talking to someone? He leans in for a hug when we get to the house, and I meet him halfway.

"Thanks for the tires," I say.

"You're welcome, honey."

I want to talk longer, encourage him to meet Dr. Oliver, but I can't take my eyes off the moving van on the street in front of Tara's house. Boxes of all sizes fill the driveway, waiting to be loaded. Three large, sweaty men grunt and point as they carry furniture from the house to the truck.

"See you later," he says, getting back in the driver's seat.

"Later," I say, barely able to breathe as I'm caught in an undertow of sadness.

When I eventually roll my bike into the garage, I get a text. I bet it's from my dad, asking me if I'm okay, or saying we'll talk later. Instead, it's from an unknown number.

YOU'RE DONE WITH THE DOCTOR

I groan and shove the phone back into my pocket. Another message. Someone *is* following me, but at least I delivered the file to Dr. Oliver.

Chapter
25

Just before nine that evening, I sneak a six-pack of beer over to Tara's house. My mom will be angry, but who cares? My best friend leaves tomorrow. As I walk through her house, my footsteps echo in the barren rooms. A few picture hooks cling to the walls, and over-stuffed bags and suitcases lie about. Tara's bedroom is like a cave with an air mattress on the floor, topped with a pillow and blanket. We close the door and pop open two beers, raising them for a toast.

"Here's to you," she says, "for dropping that cigarette and burning a hole in the carpet." We stare at the scar on the floor, and I blush. We each take a swig. I hadn't thought of that night in a long time. We were freshmen. It seems like a lifetime ago.

"And here's to you," I say, raising my can, "for gouging the wall when we rearranged the furniture to cover the hole in the carpet."

Tara laughs, and we take another drink.

"And you should see the stain on the bathroom floor," she says, "from the black nail polish we spilled and couldn't clean up fast enough."

"Oh, that was horrible," I say. "Good thing you had an extra bathmat."

"You never know when an ugly bathmat might save the day." We finish our first beers and open two more.

"How was your last day at Rocky's? Did they throw you a party?"

"More like threw me out. The prick manager was happy to get rid of me."

"But you were so pleasant with the customers," I say with a grin.

"Just doing my job," she says, sticking out her tongue and crossing her eyes.

"I had an interesting day."

"What happened?" I tell Tara about visiting Dr. Oliver, my flat bike tires, and the car that peeled out of the parking lot. I also show her the most recent text message.

"That's creepy. But now that you gave him the file, you don't have to visit him anymore."

I sit down on the floor. "I know, but I still have the vial, and I need to find out if he can help my dad."

"With TR-97?"

I nod. "It's still in my basement."

"And Doctor Oliver doesn't know you have it?"

"Nobody knows except us."

"Well, I won't tell anybody." She tips her can for another gulp of beer.

"I know. Mel won't, either."

Tara finishes her second beer and cracks open another, sitting down next to me. "Speaking of, have you heard from him lately?"

I shake my head. "I sent him the license plate for that car, but nothing so far."

"I hope he hasn't drowned."

"Or been struck by lightning."

"Or eaten by an alligator."

We roll onto the mattress laughing, spilling beer onto the floor.

"Oops," says Tara. "One more donation to the carpet gods."

"School is really going to suck without you," I say.

"Tell me about it. My life is going to suck. New house, new school, new kids, new neighborhood. Yuck, yuck, yuck, yuck."

"I'm sure you'll make friends, but what am I going to do?"

"You have Mel."

I grab her hand and hold it. "True, but you're the best."

"When it gets tough for you, just think of me. I start from ground zero."

"I know. I'm being selfish, but you'll find somebody."

She squeezes my hand. "I suppose."

"My parents told me to join a club," I say, rolling my eyes.

"I'll join the beer pong club, or create one if they don't have one," she says.

"If anyone can do it, you *can*." I raise my beer. "No pun intended."

Tara grins and shakes her head. "You're such a nerd."

"I'm crazy like Doctor Oliver."

"I think we're all crazy."

"Crazy cool," I say.

We both sit up and finish our beers.

"Keep in touch on Instagram, okay?" she says. "And call me sometime."

"I will, and I'll tell Mel goodbye for you."

"Thanks. I miss you already."

We hug and I pinch my eyes shut to hold back the flood. I don't want to let go, but she has to get up early, and her mom wants lights out. When I walk home, I take the empty cans and throw them into our recycling bin. I gaze up at the dark sky and ask the universe if I'll ever see Tara again.

When I step inside, my mom sits at her usual place at the kitchen table, sipping from a cocktail glass. "Where have you been?" she asks.

"Next door. Tara leaves tomorrow."

"Oh, that's right. I'm sure it was hard to say goodbye."

"The hardest," I say, my voice cracking.

"I can make you an ice cream sundae?" she says.

My shoulders droop and my eyes focus on the floor. I'm not six years old. Ice cream can't possibly dull the ache in my heart. "I'm going to my room." In my sanctuary, I close the door and fall onto my bed, letting the tears flow.

The next morning, I wake up in my clothes. I didn't bother with pajamas, my face, or my teeth before bed. It all seemed so pointless. Tara is long gone since it's already after eight. A hot shower clears my head, and I decide to skip work. I leave a message for Christina on the clinic answering machine, telling her I woke up with a sore throat. My mom left a note for me in the kitchen. She's got two open houses today and won't be home until later.

I drop a slice of bread into the toaster and leaf through the newspaper my mom left on the table. Dr. Oliver asked if there were any more articles, so I had better look. On the last page of the local section, I spy a small blurb about the cemetery vandalism. I need to talk to Dr. Oliver again. I throw on some clothes and check the bus schedule. My bike can stay in the garage today.

While I wait in the lobby, Jesse helps a resident at the end of the hall. I wave to him and he walks toward me, saying hello. "Back again, Miss Penelope?"

I nod. "Doctor Oliver seems to like the company."

"Yes, he does."

"And I brought these for your daughters." I hand Jesse a plastic bag with four Groovy Girls dolls, some toy furniture, and lots of clothes.

"Thank you so much. Sophia and Emelia will love them."

"I'm glad they'll have a home."

As we walk down the hallway, we pass a hunched, frail-looking woman using a walker. Fergus strolls beside her with a strap around her waist.

"I'm tired," she says. "I don't want to walk anymore."

"But you need your exercise, Missus Gerhardt," says Fergus. "It's very important."

"That's baloney. I want to lie down."

"This is good for you," says Fergus.

"Where's my room? I want to sleep."

"Just keep walking a little farther."

"You're working me to death."

I look at Jesse, and he smiles, nodding. That must be Agnes Gerhardt. If the names plates are correct, she's in 110. I pass it when I walk from the reception area to Dr. Oliver's room. I've heard her yelling before.

When we reach 103, the door is open, and Dr. Oliver occupies the recliner.

"Hi, Doctor Oliver," I say, entering the room before Jesse can knock or announce we're there.

"Good morning, Penelope," he says.

"Enjoy your visit," says Jesse, continuing down the hall.

"Should I close it?" I ask.

"Yes, please," says Dr. Oliver. With the door shut, the room is so quiet I hear the wheeze in Dr. Oliver's chest when he breathes. "These days, I can't help but wonder who is going to walk through that door." He shakes his head. "Will it be a relative, a friend, or a ghost?"

Is he talking about Gwendolyn? Does Dr. Oliver imagine his wife walking into the room?

"It's a friend," I say.

"No work today?" he asks.

"Not today."

"It's Friday, isn't it?"

I sit down in my chair. "Yes, but I wanted to see you."

"What's on your mind?"

"Did you read the file? Was it the right one?"

He nods. "I read it. What a gift. It brought back so many memories of my work, the triumphs and the failures. I was on the right track, making great strides in medicine."

"That's fantastic," I say, thinking about my dad. This treatment can help him. I know it. If he can change that one traumatic night into something positive, we'll all benefit. "And it's safe from Helga?"

"Much safer here than in Sasha's basement. And if Helga has the serum, as you suspect, it's useless without the information in this file."

"That's a relief."

"What else?" he asks.

"I saw an article in the newspaper this morning about the cemetery vandalism."

"Oh?"

"It said they repaired the headstones and removed the paint. According to the police, they didn't find any fingerprints at the scene, and no witnesses have come forward. Unless new evidence surfaces, they're going to close the case."

Dr. Oliver rests the tips of his fingers on one hand against his fingertips on the other. "Interesting," he says. "The article didn't mention the digging? Just the damaged markers?"

"I noticed that. What do you think it means?"

"They might still be investigating the incident and not want to give anything away to the public."

"How so?"

"It's a psychological ploy. By not mentioning it, it makes a guilty party feel more complacent, like they're off the hook. Then they're more likely to relax and say something incriminating or make a mistake."

I inhale slowly through my nose and stare out the window. Is someone following me because they saw me in the cemetery or connected me with Mel and his car? What if the police are investigating me?

"Are you okay?" asks Dr. Oliver. "You're quieter than usual."

"I was just thinking about the threatening texts I've received."

He nods.

I shift positions in my chair. "I'm a little worried. The most recent one said 'You're done with the doctor.'"

"Who are they from?"

"I don't know. They're sent from different cell numbers."

"So they're from different people?"

"Not necessarily. It could be the same person using a pre-paid phone, so you can't trace the number."

"That sounds ominous."

I gnaw on my thumbnail. "Yeah."

"What are you going to do?"

"I'm not sure. They don't threaten me directly, but I'm worried about you." I study Dr. Oliver's face, his milky blue eyes, bushy gray brows, and wrinkled forehead. "And I think I'm being followed."

"By whom?" he asks.

"I don't know, but this strange car parks near the animal clinic and has passed me a few times in my neighborhood."

"You're sure it's the same vehicle? So many of them look alike."

"I'm sure. It's a unique car."

"Could it be a coincidence?" he asks.

"I suppose. But it's kind of weird, and someone let the air out of my bike tires the last time I was here."

"While you were visiting me?" he asks, gripping the arms of his chair and sitting up straighter.

I nod. "My gut tells me I'm being followed."

"It's important to listen to your gut."

I glance out the window, then back at Dr. Oliver. "My gut also tells me you're not crazy."

"I appreciate that assessment."

"That didn't come out right," I say. "I asked you before, but you didn't answer. Why were you in a mental hospital?"

Dr. Oliver sighs. "That's a long story, and a complicated one, but I'll give you the abridged version." He clears his throat. "After my public disgrace, I had a breakdown. Losing my wife, career, and reputation was more than I could handle. When Sasha moved home, she couldn't tolerate my moods and insisted I get help. I agreed, thinking it would be for a few weeks, maybe a month. But once I was admitted to Monona Hospital, they sedated me. She had me declared incapacitated, and a judge appointed her as my conservator. She kept me in there for two years."

I feel like someone punched me in the stomach. "You couldn't get out?"

"Not until she broke my spirit. Then she forced me to move here."

"That's terrible. You couldn't go home?"

"This became my home, although it's more like a prison with the strict routine and lack of visitors. She won't even allow me to have any books or photos that remind me of my former life."

"None of your wife?"

He shakes his head. "Nothing."

"Oh, my god. That's awful. I'm so sorry."

I want to get up and hug him, but we're interrupted by a loud voice in the hall. Dr. Oliver and I turn our heads toward the door.

"He has a guest," somebody says.

Before Dr. Oliver can reply, the door swings open and Helga barges into the room. Fergus watches from the hall.

"Well, well, well. What have we here?" Helga asks, focusing her gaze on me. "A little party, and you didn't invite me?"

The blood drains from my face and my mouth hangs open. I'm frozen to the chair.

"What are *you* doing here?" asks Dr. Oliver.

"Does it matter? I want to know how that urchin got in here," she says, pointing at me.

"None of your business," says Dr. Oliver.

I clamp my mouth shut and glance at him, but his attention remains on Helga.

"Looks like I've discovered a little secret," she says with a smirk. "It would be a shame if anyone else found out."

"It doesn't concern you," says Dr. Oliver.

"Oh, but it does. Sasha asked me to come by and check on you. It looks like you're still alive."

"Like you care," he says.

"Oh, don't be such a sourpuss. I care a great deal."

My mouth is dry and I feel my chest constrict. I need to get out of there, but is it safe to leave Dr. Oliver alone with her? I stand, searching Dr. Oliver's face, hoping my eyes convey my thoughts. He nods at me, and I mumble goodbye, hurrying out of the room.

"What? No hello or goodbye for me?" says Helga with a scowl. "That trash has no manners."

I rush out the door, past Fergus, and down the hall to the exit. When I get outside, I stop and take a deep breath, resting my hands over my heart. Fergus will look after Dr. Oliver. But why did Helga have to show up? She'll ruin everything.

I hurry to the bus stop and gaze down the street, searching for the Mendota Metro, but there are no buses in sight. I pace back and forth near the bench, then sit down, pulling out my phone to check the bus schedule. My hands are shaking as I search for the right route. When I find it, a black car pulls up alongside the curb. I look up. It's Paulson. My heart jumps and I spring to my feet, scooting around the bench, putting a barrier between me and the car.

"Hey, Penn. I thought that was you. What are you doing on this side of town?" Paulson asks after rolling down the passenger window.

"Just waiting for the bus."

"Can I give you a ride?"

"No, I'm good." I switch my phone to camera mode in case he does something crazy and I need to record it.

"I can take you home."

Hell, no. You couldn't pay me to get in the car with you. "The bus will be here soon," I say.

"I'd like to talk to you about something. We could get a slice of pizza. My treat."

"No, thanks." My armpits dampen and I search the street for the bus.

"It's really important," he says. "I need your help."

"I'm busy," I say, looking over my shoulder toward the parking lot. Should I run back to the nursing home? Should I call my dad? While I consider my options, a bus arrives, honking at Paulson to move his car from the curb. I scurry to the door of the bus and jump inside onto the bottom step, not even looking to see if it's the right route. I collapse onto the seat behind the driver, hoping Paulson doesn't follow.

Chapter
26

Mel calls me that night while I'm watching Netflix on my laptop in my bedroom. "Hey there," I say, answering the call. "How's the sunburn?"

"Better. I've got aloe. How're you?"

"Okay, I guess. It's been a strange week."

"What's going on?"

I pause the show on my laptop and lean back against my pillows. "A bunch of weird stuff. I have dark circles under my eyes."

"I can add one more layer of weirdness."

"If you're moving to Florida, shoot me now."

"It's nothing like that," he says.

"What then?"

"I got the info on the owner of that car."

I sit up straighter in bed. "Who does it belong to?"

"Somebody named Roger Wilcox. He's a private investigator."

"Seriously?"

"Yep. He has his own business."

I close my eyes and hang my head. "Ugh."

"How bad can it be?"

"He's been following me. He knows where I live, that I work at the animal clinic, and that I visit Doctor Oliver at the nursing home."

"He might not know you visit Doctor Oliver. You could visit someone else."

"That doesn't make me feel much better. Besides, if he doesn't know about Doctor Oliver, he will soon. Everybody will. Helga saw me there today."

"What?"

I stretch my legs out on the bed. "She showed up in his room while I was there."

"How did *she* get in?"

"Sasha probably approved her as a guest because she's a family friend."

"Maybe it's not so bad," says Mel. "Visiting Doctor Oliver isn't a crime."

"I know, but when Sasha finds out, she'll want to know how *I* got in. Remember? I told them I'm his granddaughter."

"Maybe she won't find out."

"You know Helga's going to tell her."

"If she does, maybe Sasha won't care."

I shake my head. "One week on vacation and you're mister laid-back?"

"I'm trying to be an optimist," he says.

"I think the sun is getting to you. I need a legitimate reason for my visits with Doctor Oliver. Something innocent, because Doctor Hughes will probably ask me about it on Monday."

"We'll come up with something. Are you sure Wilcox is following you?"

I stand up and look outside my bedroom window, scanning the street. "I've seen him everywhere. He was at the nursing home and the clinic. He nearly hit me when I was riding my bike home, and he once passed me when I was walking near my house."

"Damn. That's too frequent to be a coincidence."

"Do you think he's the one sending me the texts?"

"You've gotten more?"

I glance at my phone. "Two this week."

"And you didn't tell me?"

"I didn't want to worry you. Tara knows."

"I'll try not to be hurt by that. Are they from the same number?"

I pace around my bedroom. "Different numbers."

"It could be him, or whoever he's working for."

"How do we find out who he's working for?"

"Beats me, unless you followed him and he met Helga or Paulson. That's who you're thinking, right?"

I sit back down on my bed. "They're the most likely suspects."

"Let me think about it. Maybe I can call him and try to find out."

"Would you do that?"

"It's worth a try."

"Don't use your phone though," I say. "Buy a prepaid phone so he can't trace it."

"Now you sound like a criminal."

I roll onto my back on the bed. "I'm trying to keep you safe. What if the investigator found me because of your car?"

"Shit. Do you think so?"

"I don't know. The latest newspaper article said the cemetery vandalism case had no witnesses, but Doctor Oliver thought they said that so the guilty party would relax and make a mistake."

"Okay," he says. "I won't use my phone."

"Speaking of phones, I'm going to delete the TR-97 photo from mine," I say, pulling up the photo and clicking on the trash can icon.

"That's a good idea. And delete the browser history on your phone and computer."

"I'll do that now."

"No mistakes," he says.

My phone vibrates, and I look at the caller. "My dad is calling. I should take this."

"Okay. Talk to you soon," Mel says, as I switch calls.

"Hi, Dad."

"Hi, honey. How are you?"

"Good."

"I've got an eleven o'clock tee time tomorrow. Do you want to play?"

"Sure."

"I'll pick you up around ten. That'll give us more time on the range before we start," he says.

"I'll be ready."

I go to bed early that night but can't fall asleep. I'm fixated on Paulson, the private investigator, and seeing Helga at the nursing home. She's going to tell Dr. Hughes, and then what? Will she be angry? Surprised? Ambivalent? Fat chance, but I've got bigger problems. I'm being followed. Should I tell my mom? If I do, I'll have to explain everything, and I don't want to do that just yet. I'm so close to helping my dad. My mom would probably want me to go to the police. If they talk to me, they'll ask all kinds of questions, and I'm not ready to spill my guts.

Around one in the morning, I'm irritated by my tossing and turning. I get out of bed and go downstairs to the basement. I want to make sure the vial of TR-97 is still there. Keeping the lights off, I use my phone to guide me. When I lift the lid on the Christmas ornament box and dig around, the socks aren't here. Oh shit! Did my mom find them? Did someone else take them? Nobody except Mel and Tara knows I have the vial. But if a private investigator ran Mel's license plate and followed him, maybe they connected him to me.

Trying not to panic, I glance to my right and see another box labeled Christmas ornaments. I open it and find my crew socks and the TR-97. I study the bottle for a moment, turning it over in my hand. Should I bring it back upstairs to my room? No, leave it here. It's safer hidden in the basement. I fold it back into the socks and close the lid on the box. It's the one with the green label, not red.

Around dawn, I wake up in a cold sweat, my heart racing. How many times can I suffer through that stupid dream? I doze for another hour, then get out of bed and shower. The house is quiet, and I wander out to the kitchen. My mom left a note telling me she's at an early meeting. I don't know when she'll be home, so I find a pen and write on the bottom of it: "I went golfing with Dad."

When my dad picks me up, I barely recognize him. His face is scruffy, his shorts torn, and his t-shirt shows several stains on the front. He hasn't even combed his hair.

"Rough night?" I ask, getting into the passenger seat of the truck.

"I haven't been sleeping well," he says.

"Are you sure you want to play today? It's going to be crowded."

"I could use the fresh air."

I nod and gaze out the window. The rest of the drive is silent.

When we pull into the parking lot at Glen View, it's packed. As my dad searches for a spot, I spy the black Mercedes with the vanity plate: "RX GUY." That's Paulson's car. What is he doing here? I search the area but don't see him, and cross my fingers that he's already out on the course. Because of the crowd, we have to park way in the back near the dumpsters.

"Here are some tokens," says my dad, putting several coins in my hand. Then he lifts my clubs from the back of the truck. "I'll meet you at the range."

"I could wait for you," I say.

"Go on ahead. I'll be a minute or two behind."

"Okay," I say, hoisting my golf bag onto my right shoulder. As I walk toward the clubhouse, I scan the lot. The sun is so bright I have to squint. I'm craning my neck to my right when Paulson pops out from behind a Sprinter van on the left.

"I didn't know you played golf," he says.

"Are you following me?" I ask, picking up my pace.

"No," says Paulson, falling into step next to me. "This is my first time here. I usually play at Maple Hills, where I'm a member, but a friend wanted to play here this morning."

I don't look at him or respond.

"So, what's been going on at the clinic?" he asks.

"Same old stuff," I say, walking faster.

"Does Helga still come by?"

"Sometimes."

"Have you seen her recently?"

"No."

"Let me give you my number," he says, pushing a business card toward me. "Call or text when she's there. It's really important."

I turn away and shove my free hand into my pocket.

"I'll pay you."

"I don't need your money," I say.

"If you bring me the box with the research files, I'll give you five hundred dollars."

"I don't know what you're talking about."

"Come on, Penn. You told me you saw the box at the clinic. You've got to help me."

"No, I don't." I stop to shift my golf bag from my right shoulder to my left. As I do this, Paulson grabs my bag and pulls it to the ground. "Get away from me!"

"Take my card." He waves it in front of me.

I lean back out of his way and pull my golf bag, but he holds onto the strap so I can't lift it.

"Get the hell away from my daughter!" my dad roars, running up behind me. He looks like a football player about to tackle his opponent. His face is crimson, and his eyes shoot daggers. His hands are balled into fists.

Paulson lets go of my bag and takes a couple of steps backward.

"Is this asshole bothering you?" my dad asks, spit flying from his mouth as he glares at Paulson.

"I'm okay," I say, not wanting to provide any more details. If he knew, my dad might strangle Paulson and wind up in jail.

"Why was he touching your bag?"

"He was giving me a business card," I say.

Dad waves his arm. "Get out of here, pal. She doesn't need your stinking card."

"My mistake," says Paulson, raising his hands to surrender. "I thought she was someone else."

"Does he know you're only sixteen?" My dad is talking to me, but staring at Paulson.

I shrug. "I don't know."

"But, you're okay?"

"Fine," I say, giving Paulson my most evil stare.

He takes the hint and slinks away, disappearing between the parked cars.

I sigh with relief and take a deep breath. "I better get us a spot on the range."

"Do you know that creep?"

"Not really." If you only knew, you would have ripped his head off with your bare hands. "I've seen him at the vet clinic."

"He better stay away from you." My dad's hands remain clenched into fists.

"I'm pretty sure he will," I say with a satisfied smile.

When I find an open slot on the range, I relax my shoulders and stretch a little, remembering all the basics about a good golf swing. I take a few balls out of the bucket and use my wedge to warm up. A teammate from last year is several stalls down. She's focusing on her swing, so I wait to interrupt her. After her next drive, I approach with a wave.

"Hey, Madison. How're you doing?"

"Good, Penn. How're you?"

"All right. I can't believe summer is almost over."

She frowns. "I know. It went so fast."

"Are you warming up or just practicing?" I ask.

"I'm going to play with my dad. We have an eleven o'clock tee time," she says.

I look at my phone for the time. "That's great. So do my dad and I."

"Awesome! I'm so glad I get to play with you. I barely saw you during tryouts."

I nod. "You were better off. I played so horribly."

"Me, too. You know I didn't make the team, either."

"I didn't know that. I'm sorry."

She shrugs. "It's okay. I'm just trying to find the fun in the game again."

"That's a great goal. I want to find the fun again, too."

Despite my lack of sleep and seeing Paulson in the parking lot, I'm only six over par after nine holes.

"You're doing great," says my dad, giving me a fist bump. "Keep it up."

A smile stretches across my face. Despite his disheveled appearance, my dad is upbeat today. I savor the compliment and also the protection he provided in the parking lot. Paulson probably crapped his pants when my dad charged in. "You're playing well, too," I say.

My dad nods and gives me a thumbs up.

Although it's great to spend time with my dad, the best part of the round is hanging out with Madison. We talk about normal stuff like school, clothes, and boys. We laugh and joke and encourage each other.

"You have to come to the party at Hoyt Park tonight," she says, lining up her putt.

"Who's going to be there?" I ask.

"Pretty much everyone. It's a junior class gathering to kick off the school year."

Madison sinks her putt and I place my ball on the green near my marker.

"That sounds fun. What time?" I ask.

"Around nine. One of the hockey players is bringing a keg."

"I'll try to make it, but I don't have a car."

"I'll pick you up," she says.

I tap in my putt and pick up my ball from the cup. "That would be great. At nine?"

"More like eight-thirty. I'll text you."

Until I'm standing on the thirteenth tee, I haven't thought about Dr. Oliver, Helga, or TR-97 while we've been playing. What does the cemetery look like now? Are Gwendolyn's ashes back in the ground? Does someone know we were there that night? I clear those thoughts from my mind while the guys hit first, then Madison and me. Her drive is a beautiful high arc that lands in the center of the fairway.

"Really nice," I say, teeing up my ball. I angle my stance a little to the left. I don't want to hit it to the right near the cemetery. Keep it in the fairway, even if it's short. I swing my driver and the ball soars up and to the left, bouncing once on the fairway, then disappearing into the tall grass near the sand trap.

"Ooh. Tough one," says Madison, "but you've got this."

I'm not unhappy with my shot. It may have ruined a fantastic round, but I avoided the cemetery. That's all I asked for.

When my dad drops me off at home later, I'm excited about the party. Should I wear a miniskirt or a low-cut top? No, jeans and a T-shirt are better. I might wear mascara and eyeshadow though. What if someone brings pot? Will I take a hit? I find my mom parked at the kitchen table when I walk in.

"You took my beer again," she says.

"I went golfing," I say.

"My six-pack of Stella is gone."

"Oh, that. It's been gone since Thursday. I took it over to Tara's. We had a little send-off party. I didn't think you'd mind."

My mom stands. "Well, I *do* mind. I told you before, no more drinking."

I cross my arms over my chest. "But it was Tara's last night."

"How could you? If her parents find out, they could fire me."

"They won't find out. She's already gone."

My mom frowns. "But you deliberately disobeyed me."

"Sorry. It won't happen again."

"You're damn right it won't because you're grounded."

"That's so unfair! I have plans tonight."

"No, you don't. You're staying home."

"But Mom, I finally got invited to a party. This is the first one all summer."

"And you're not going."

I raise my hands in prayer and face my mom. "Please? Just this once? Ground me tomorrow."

"You're grounded today, and that's final."

I clench my jaw and feel my face burning. "That sucks. Everyone is going to be there."

"I don't care."

"When did you become such a bitch?" I ask.

"Go to your room and don't come out until you can show me some respect."

I give her the finger and stomp to my room, slamming the door and locking it. What a royal bitch. She's ruining my life. I punch the pillows on my bed until my arms ache, then change into some old shorts and a T-shirt. I open my laptop with a sigh and flop onto the bed. If I'm stuck here, I might as well watch Netflix.

About two hours later, she knocks on my bedroom door. I don't respond, and she knocks again.

"What?" I ask, still irritated by her ambush.

"I made tacos for dinner," she says.

"I'm not hungry."

"I'll put the leftovers in the fridge if you change your mind."

"Does that mean I can leave my room?"

"Of course. You can use the bathroom and go to the kitchen. You just can't leave the house."

"Got it." I sense she's standing outside the door, waiting to see if I'll open it. I ignore her and resume watching the movie. Thirty minutes later, I get a text from Madison.

Pick u up at 8:20. I want 2 b early

I debate whether to reply "yes." I could sneak out my window, but then I'd have to leave it wide open. I could just walk out and see if my mom stops me.

Instead, I text Madison. *I can't go. I'm grounded*

Bummer, she replies. *What happened?*

Long story

Maybe next weekend

Maybe, I text, knowing I'll probably be stuck at home.

On Sunday morning, I wake up with a headache. It hurts to open my eyes. I never ventured out to the kitchen for food or water, and I'm paying for it now. My mouth is so dry you could strike a match on my tongue. I swipe through the Instagram posts from last night's party. It's a mosaic of red cups, glazed eyes, and goofy smiles. Somebody posted a hockey player shot-gunning a beer. A couple of football players take hits from a bong. They partied for an hour before the cops showed up. That's trouble I don't need, but I missed all the fun.

I wander out to the kitchen. My mom stands at the stove, frying an egg with a strip of bacon. I fill a glass with water and open the fridge, grabbing the plate of soft tacos.

"Do you want an egg?" she asks.

"No, thanks," I say. "I'm eating the tacos."

"For breakfast?"

"Yep." I add more cheese and heat the plate in the microwave. "Can I take the newspaper?"

"Since when do you read the paper?"

"Since today." I grab the *Times* and return to my room, closing the door and locking it. I skim through the paper but find nothing about the cemetery. Since I have all day, I guess it's time to review the Treatment Protocol. The copy is still in my backpack.

On the first few pages, I stumble over the technical jargon. Long phrases confuse me so much I forget how the sentence even starts. I learn that "TR" stands for "trauma remedy," not somebody's initials, as I originally thought. The treatment involves many steps guided by a psychologist and a medical doctor. I cringe seeing the words "intramuscular injection." When I flip through to the later pages, I see a chemical formula for TR-97. Even though I took chemistry last year, I don't know what half of the symbols mean.

Turning a few more pages, I read a case study on a test subject—somebody named Joseph Wagner, age 31, a Gulf War veteran. He lost a leg and sustained burns to forty percent of his body when a roadside bomb exploded during a convoy. Francine P. Baker was his psychologist and worked with him for two years before trying TR-97. I skim the next few sections, which provide details of Wagner's treatment. The objective was to replace the traumatic memory with a more positive outcome, one they had discussed during therapy.

I flip another page and freeze when I see her name. Once the patient was ready, James B. Oliver, M.D., administered a dose of TR-97. The report then describes a therapist hypnotizing the subject, inducing an initial tranquil state, then guiding him to the heightened emotional state of the trauma. Helga Thorstad took part as the hypnotherapist.

Chapter
27

On Monday morning, I'm late for work. I dawdle at home, looking through the newspaper and checking my phone. I change my shoes twice and pump more air into my bicycle tires. I take a longer route, but still end up at the same place. Christina is cheerful, but I have to force my enthusiasm. Opal follows me around the clinic. She never does that. As I spray each kennel with disinfectant and wipe it clean, she sits on the counter watching me. When I enter an empty exam room, she is a furry statue in the doorway.

"What are you looking at?" I ask, turning to face the cat. When I address her, Opal looks away, deciding it's a good time to groom her back. Of course, when I show interest, she ignores me. What is it with cats? They're so frustrating.

I avoid Sasha most of the morning, but at ten minutes before noon, she calls me into her office and closes the door. Oh, shit. Here it comes.

She doesn't waste any time. "I understand you've been visiting my father at the nursing home."

I take a deep breath, and it feels like someone is wringing out a wet rag in my stomach. Of course, Helga would tell her. I haven't done anything super wrong, but if that's true, why do I want to run away?

"Yeah," I say. "I just learned about the connection between you and Doctor Oliver the other day. You have different last names, so I didn't put the two together."

"I changed mine when I turned eighteen," she says. "And it's a good thing. Otherwise I would be another Doctor Oliver."

I nod. "But I thought your parents didn't live around here."

Her stare is frightening. If she was Medusa, I would be stone. "My mother is deceased, and I can't take care of my father."

She turns and walks to her desk, sitting down in the chair before changing the subject.

"So it's just a coincidence that you work here and visit him?"

"Small world." I shrug my shoulders and pretend like it's no big deal.

"Why do you go see him?"

"For volunteer hours."

"It's a school-sanctioned activity?"

"Sort of. I belong to a club. We talk with elderly people and keep them company."

"I've never heard of it."

I shift my weight from one foot to the other. "It's pretty new."

She rests her hands on top of the desk. "So, what do you talk about?"

I keep my eyes on Dr. Hughes. "Anything that comes up. Current events, their life, family, history."

"You talk to my father about his life and history?" she asks.

"If he wants."

"And what does he tell you?"

I clasp my hands together in front of me to keep them from shaking. "That he was a doctor, a psychiatrist who taught at Wisconsin State. That he has a daughter, I guess that's you. His wife died years ago. I think he said he had a brother. Stuff like that."

"Did you know he was in a mental hospital for two years?" she asks.

I shake my head. "He didn't tell me that."

"I wouldn't expect him to."

"Is he okay now?"

"It depends on what you mean by okay," she says. "He's not violent, but he is delusional."

I feel my eyes open wider, like I've heard a scary noise. "He is?"

Dr. Hughes nods. "He has false beliefs and ideas about things, particularly his work as a doctor."

"He doesn't talk much about being a doctor," I say.

She smirks. "I'm surprised. That used to be all he talked about."

"He said he misses the challenge of it and helping people."

A vertical crease appears on her forehead between her eyes. "That doesn't sound like him. He's usually all ego and no compassion. And he makes up stories, exaggerating the truth to inflate his ego."

I keep my gaze on Dr. Hughes and do my best to look innocent.

"Just remember," she says, interlacing her fingers, "if he talks about his ground-breaking research and saving the world, it's mostly lies."

"Okay." I struggle to keep my eyes on Dr. Hughes and focus on the wall behind her.

"He thinks he can play God."

I stay quiet but nod, wondering if Dr. Oliver has been lying to me all this time.

"Have you talked with other Oak Bluff residents?" she asks.

I shake my head. "I was supposed to talk with someone named Agnes Gerhardt, but she didn't want visitors."

Dr. Hughes blinks several times. "Did you know only relatives and approved guests are allowed at Oak Bluff?"

"I thought I was an approved guest."

"Technically, you're not, but I suppose it's okay. It seems harmless."

I remain quiet with my head bowed slightly. Should I mention seeing Helga there? Would Dr. Hughes already know that? I'm sure that's how she found out I was visiting her father.

"If you don't want me to visit him," I say, "just let me know. I can probably talk with someone else. Doctor Oliver has other visitors, like Helga."

Dr. Hughes purses her lips. "Helga is an approved guest."

I nod.

"It's fine," she says. "I just wanted you to know that my father isn't all there upstairs." Dr. Hughes points at her head.

I bite my lip and nod again.

"That's it," she says. "You can go."

I leave her office and walk to the reception area. Holy shit, that was close, but I think she believed me. A wave of relief washes over me, like a defendant who has just heard the jury announce "not guilty." The universe just gave me a hall pass.

I say goodbye to Christina and unlock my bike, looking around for the *280zx*. It's not there. Good. I'm going directly to the nursing home.

As I approach the entrance to Oak Bluff, I prepare myself for the possibility that they'll turn me away. Dr. Hughes said my visits were okay, but Helga is a different story. She'll try to keep me out. I know it. When I walk into the building, a man occupies the chair behind the reception desk.

"Hi," I say, giving him a weak smile.

"Hello," he says. "May I help you?"

"I'm here to visit Doctor Oliver."

He types something into the computer, then studies my face. "I'm sure he'll be happy to see you, Penelope." He hands me a name tag.

"Thanks," I say. I am so lucky Dr. Hughes didn't check with the reception desk for the paperwork about my visits. If she had, she would have caught me in a lie because there isn't a school club.

Fergus appears in the lobby and walks with me down the hall. As we approach Agnes Gerhardt's room, she stands in the doorway yelling.

"Where is she? Frankie! She should be here! Where's Frankie?"

"I'll help you in a minute, Missus Gerhardt," says Fergus.

"Beware," she says, pointing at me. "She's a witch."

"No, no, Missus Gerhardt," says Fergus, shaking his head. "She's a nice young lady. I'll be right back to help you."

I turn to Fergus. "Is she all right?"

"Yes, just high-strung, but she has a good heart."

"She's always yelling and complaining," I say.

"It's nothing to worry about. She means well."

We keep walking, but I can't resist turning my head to see if Agnes is watching me. Our eyes connect, and her stare makes my skin crawl. What's her problem? Is it the purple hair? I shrug it off and focus on my visit.

When we get to the room, Fergus knocks on the open door.

"Hi, Doctor Oliver," I say, strolling into the room.

He occupies his usual place in the recliner with the table in front of him. His feet rest on the floor with low socks and slippers. His ankles are the size of softballs.

"Hello, Penelope," he says.

Most of the food remains on his tray untouched: pasta with marinara sauce, green salad, and cauliflower. Only the bread plate is empty.

"Not hungry today?" asks Fergus.

"I had this yesterday," says Dr. Oliver.

"If you're finished, let's get you to the bathroom so you can visit with your guest."

While Fergus assists Dr. Oliver with standing and shuffling to the bathroom, I stare out the window at a Robin hopping around in the grass. When Dr. Oliver settles himself in the recliner with his feet raised, Fergus leaves us alone.

I can't take my eyes off Dr. Oliver's swollen ankles. "Are you okay?" I ask, staring at his feet.

"Yes," he says without explanation.

"I've never seen ankles that big."

"Well, now you have." He looks me in the eye and I get the hint. Change the subject.

"Doctor Hughes, I mean Sasha, found out I visit you," I say.

"I'm sure Helga told her."

"She, Sasha, was a little bothered by the news."

"She doesn't understand why anyone would want to visit me."

"At least she wasn't too upset."

Dr. Oliver tugs on the sleeve of his sweater. "Now, that's a surprise."

"Because I'm not an approved guest?"

"Because she wants to control everything in my life, including who I talk to."

I cross my legs at the ankle. "If that's the case, why does she let Helga visit you?"

"It's her way of tormenting me."

"Does she think you're still friends?"

He shakes his head. "Given our history, I seriously doubt it. Sasha knows how I feel about Helga."

I shake my head. Sasha knows they're enemies but approves Helga as a guest, anyway? That's twisted. "Have you ever met Agnes Gerhardt?" I ask.

"Who?"

"Your neighbor down the hall in room one-ten."

Dr. Oliver studies me for a moment but remains silent.

"Have you met any of the other residents?" I ask.

"Dorothy," he says.

"The woman who walks?"

"She has dementia, and she often pokes her head into my room thinking it's hers."

I nod. "I've seen her in the hall before."

A heavy silence fills the space between us. He stares at me, but I can't think of anything to say. I know why I came back here today, but I've lost the courage to speak up. I fear the truth. And from the look on his face, maybe Dr. Oliver can sense it.

"Penelope, we can chit chat all day. I've got plenty of time, but I'd rather know the truth. Why are you really here?"

While I contemplate a response, my cell phone buzzes. I ignore the call and focus on Dr. Oliver. It's time to be completely honest. I inhale deeply and swallow the lump in my throat.

"I need to know if you can help my dad. We talked about him before. He has PTSD, and TR-97 can cure him. I'm sure of it."

"So that's it."

"Yes."

He sighs. "Believe me, I would like to help, but there are many hurdles to clear."

"But if you meet him and tell him about the treatment, he might listen to you."

"I wish it was that simple."

"But he really needs help." I uncross my legs and plant them on the floor, leaning forward.

Dr. Oliver blinks several times. "There are plenty of therapists who can start working with him to uncover the trauma. That's imperative."

"But I've read the newspaper articles and know all about the trauma. He responded to a head-on collision on the Beltline. Several cars burst into flames. He witnessed the charred body of a teenage girl and a decapitated boy. Another passenger had a crushed ribcage. He tried to pull them from the wreckage and save them, but he couldn't."

"I agree your father was likely traumatized by an event like that. But the treatment is complicated. He may remember events differently than the newspaper accounts."

"But you can cure him, right? If he doesn't remember the accident, he can go back to work and my parents won't divorce."

Dr. Oliver shakes his head slowly. "I'm afraid it's not that easy. It takes time and a team, and a willing patient. Plus, I would need the TR-97."

"But we can be the team. We can help my dad remember the scene, so he saves them."

"It doesn't sound like he's ready. Your father has to be the leader in the treatment process."

I scoot forward in my chair. "I can get him to participate. I know I can."

"Even if you could, I'm here in this place." Dr. Oliver glances around the room. "They've revoked my medical license, and TR-97 never received federal approval."

"So you can't help my dad?" I hear the strain in my voice and feel the early sting of tears in my eyes.

"I don't think so," he says with a sigh. "Not without a willing patient and the TR-97."

I clasp my hands together in front of me. "What if I told you I can get the TR-97?"

Dr. Oliver narrows his gaze. "From Helga?"

"No." I pause and suck in a deep breath. "I have one vial."

"You have the serum?"

My throat constricts. "One of them."

His face reddens as he grips the arms of the chair and rises a bit from his seat. "Did you dig up my wife's grave?"

"No." I shake my head. "I found it in the cemetery when I was looking for my golf ball."

"Is that the truth?"

"Swear to god," I say, crossing my index finger over my heart.

He leans back in his chair. "So that's why you've been so interested in TR-97. Since the day you walked through that door, I have wondered. I didn't buy the story that you just read about it on the internet, but I couldn't figure out the connection."

I bow my head and look at the floor. "Now you know."

"Well, this changes things. Until you brought me the file, I actually thought you might work for Helga."

I frown and shake my head. "Never."

"And Sasha isn't paying you?"

"Only to work at the clinic."

He nods.

"I'm doing this for my dad. I want my family back."

"Will you bring me the vial?" he asks.

"If you agree to help my dad."

We hold each other's gaze for a moment.

"I can't make any guarantees," he says. "Remember, your father has to help himself first."

I cross my arms over my stomach like a hug. "Then why should I bring it to you?"

"First, because it belongs to me. And second, if I have it, at least your father will have a chance. Without the serum, the likelihood of me helping your father is zero."

I look at Dr. Oliver and my lower lip trembles. "Okay. I'll bring it to you."

"And you'll be safer getting rid of it," he says.

"Why do you say that?"

"Because she's still after the information, and she won't stop looking until she finds it. She's already threatened me, and if she suspects you, it could get ugly. I want you outside the danger zone."

"But what about you?"

Dr. Oliver places his hand over his heart like he's saying The Pledge of Allegiance. "I'll be okay. If you bring me the vial, I can protect you. I have a plan."

"What is it?" I ask.

"Someone here can help us."

"Somebody here?" My brain clicks through the different people I've seen at Oak Bluff, knowing there are many more I haven't met.

Dr. Oliver rests his hand in his lap and nods. "Someone I trust."

"But how can I trust you?" My voice cracks again and I sound like I'm whining.

"If you want to help your father, you're going to have to trust somebody."

I glance out the window, then back at Dr. Oliver. "But if I bring it to you, you'll be in more danger."

His voice remains calm. "Not any more than I am right now."

"And you promise to help me?"

He crosses his heart with his finger. "I promise."

A knock rattles the door, and I freeze. Fergus opens it and walks in with medication for Dr. Oliver. "It's time for your pills and some exercise."

I stand to leave and am again tempted to give Dr. Oliver a hug, but stop short and pat him on the shoulder. "I'll see you soon." I leave the room knowing I spilled my guts. He knows how much this means to me. I really hope he can help.

When I get outside, I check my cell phone and open a text from my dad.

Want to play golf on Thursday?

Yes, I reply. *Afternoon*

My dad texts a thumbs-up.

I also have a voicemail from an unknown number. I click on it and listen. It's a female voice. "That was your last visit with the doctor."

Chapter
28

I race home from the nursing home like a competitor in the Tour de France. When I'm safely inside the garage, I play the message again. Do I recognize the voice? I listen one more time, then grab a soda from the refrigerator and retreat to my bedroom, locking the door. I need to call Mel.

"Hey, Penn. I was gonna call you tonight."

"Can you talk now?" I ask, looking out the window to the front yard.

"Yeah. What's up?"

I sit down on my bed. "I went to see Doctor Oliver again. He wants me to bring him the vial."

"You told him?" I can hear the surprise in his voice.

"I want him to help my dad."

"He said he would do that?"

"Sort of." I bring my thumbnail to my mouth and nibble on the cuticle.

"What did he say?"

"That bringing him the serum was the best chance of helping my dad."

"And you think it's a good idea?" he asks.

"Don't you?"

"I don't know," he says. "The serum is old, and he's old, and maybe crazy. He's not really at the top of his game."

"How would you know? You're on a beach in Florida. You haven't met him or even talked to him."

"Don't be mad. I'm just playing devil's advocate."

I flop onto my back. "But you're gone, and Tara is gone, and I've got no one right now except Doctor O."

"I'm worried about you, Penn. You sound a little desperate."

"I'm fine."

"But this whole thing seems a little out of control."

I sigh. "Doctor O is smart, and he makes sense. If you met him, you'd understand."

"Just be careful. Think it through."

"I will," I say, propping a pillow behind my head.

"When are you bringing it to him?" he asks.

"Tomorrow."

"Is your dad going with you?"

"No."

"Then what's your plan?"

I exhale loudly. "I don't have one yet."

"Maybe you should wait and bring it another time, or not at all."

"But it's the only way to help my dad."

"Are you sure?"

I shake my head. "It's the best chance I've got. I have to take it."

We're silent for a few moments. I won't tell him about the latest voicemail. He'll just get angry and make me promise to avoid Dr. Oliver.

"By the way," Mel says, "I called Roger Wilcox, the private investigator. I used a pre-paid phone and a voice-changer app."

I sit up and my pillow falls to the floor. "How did it go?"

"I pretended I wanted to hire him, asking for information about what he does, how much he charges, and if he'd be willing to provide references."

"Good thought. He might say a name we know."

"That's what I was thinking, but he told me to review the testimonials on his website."

I frown. "Oh. They probably have fake names."

"Most likely."

"Then what?"

"I got frustrated and told him I was your father and demanded to know why he was following you."

I press the phone against my ear. "What did he say?"

"He denied knowing anything about it and hung up."

"Oh well. Thanks for trying."

"Sorry I turned it into a dead end."

I sigh again. "That's okay. It was a long shot, anyway."

"Listen, I need to go, but let's talk again later, okay?"

"Yep. Bye, Mel."

When the call disconnects, I text Tara: *How's it going? I miss u*

She replies right away: *I miss u! I'm in hell. School started. I'll call u 2night*

School started? Crap. We start next week.

———

When I wake up on Tuesday, I glance at the newspaper while waiting for my bagel to pop up from the toaster. Buried on page five of the local section is a blurb about the cemetery: "The Mendota Police Department states that a witness has come forward in the cemetery vandalism case. The witness reported seeing a car parked in the area the night of the destruction."

The hair on my arms stands on end. Someone reported seeing Mel's Volvo. Shit. What am I going to do? Mel is going to freak out. I abandon my bagel on the plate and pace around the kitchen. Don't panic. It might not be that bad. Mel is out of town. They won't question him until he returns from Florida. I glance at my phone. Eight-forty. I can't do anything about it right now. I have to get to work.

When I arrive at the clinic, the waiting room is full. I hurry to the back and start my daily routine. Eric needs help with flea dips for two dogs. Christina asks me to answer the phone while she uses the bathroom and takes a smoke break. I assist Dr. Hughes as she inspects the incision sites and sutures of two kittens spayed yesterday.

"They're so cute," I say.

"So innocent and vulnerable," she says.

"When do they go home?"

"Not until tomorrow. I want to observe them one more day."

I hold one kitten. "They're just tiny balls of fur."

"Will you put some clean newspaper in their cage?"

"Of course."

"And give them fresh water and a little wet food."

"Okay." I place the kitten back inside the cage.

"And when you're done with that, go to the storage room and see if we have any E-collars. Now that the anesthesia has worn off, I don't want them pulling at the sutures."

"What am I looking for?" I ask.

"An E-collar? The cone of shame?"

I nod. "Right."

"I'm not sure we have any small enough, but it's worth looking. Let Christina know if you can't find any. But if you do, Eric can help you put them on the kittens."

Dr. Hughes hurries to her next appointment, and I open the storage room to look for the cones. An overhead light is burned out, so I wait a minute and let my eyes adjust to the gloom. I glance at the shelves loaded with boxes and bins. None of them have labels. I'm too short to see the highest ones, and shift the step stool to the side for a better look. When I move the stool, the TR-97 Research box catches my eye. It's tucked in the corner on the floor.

I glance over my shoulder to make sure no one is around, and lift the lid off the box. It's empty except for a vial of TR-97. I reach to pick it up, but stop myself. Don't be a fool. She'll know it was me.

I close the box lid and step up onto the stool, turning my attention to the top shelf. No E-collars. As I step down and slide the stool to the right, I'm startled by a voice behind me.

"Now you're snooping in the storage area."

I don't need to turn my head to know it's Helga.

"Doctor Hughes asked me to look for E-collars," I say, continuing my search.

"Sure she did. Just like she wanted you to look for files in her office and visit Doctor Oliver."

"It's the truth."

"I doubt it. Sasha is far too trusting with her staff, but I know better. While she's busy working, you're pawing through her personal property."

"I don't think swabs, bandages, masks, and gloves are very personal," I say.

She stands in her high heels, hands on her hips, staring at me with a sinister grin. She doesn't have her purse with her, which is a relief.

In the next bin, I find a bunch of E-collars in several sizes and grab them all.

"Interesting that you mention gloves," Helga says, extending her arm. She's holding a dark piece of cloth between her thumb and index finger. "Do you recognize this?"

"No," I say, looking her in the eye.

"Are you sure?"

"What is it?"

"Oh, come on, you little snake. You know."

"No, I don't." I keep my eyes steady and my voice calm. Is that the glove I left in Sasha's basement?

"You know exactly what this is." She swings it back and forth in the air. "And I'm prepared to go to the police with it."

"You can go anywhere you want with it," I say, in my bitchiest voice, then push past her into the hall to find Eric. I'm in so much trouble.

I avoid Helga and Dr. Hughes the rest of the morning. Just before I leave at noon, Eric asks me to re-fill the hand sanitizer in each exam room. I return to the storage room to find the gel packs. I also look inside the RESEARCH box. The vial is gone. Dammit. Helga must have taken it. I hear her and Dr. Hughes arguing in the office and pause near the door.

"I saw you on the video," says Dr. Hughes.

"What video?" asks Helga.

"From my house."

"That's impossible."

"Don't deny it. It was you with the ski mask and backpack."

"Ridiculous," says Helga.

"You broke into my house."

"I did not."

"I have proof," says Dr. Hughes.

"It wasn't me," says Helga, "but I bet I know who it was."

Oh shit. Sasha has a video security system at her house. I need to get out of here before she questions me. And I need to destroy my old backpack.

Later that day, I ride the bus to Oak Bluff with an original *Nancy Drew* mystery, *The Quest of the Missing Map*. It's one of my favorites and has larger type in hardcover. I think Dr. Oliver will like it. I also have the vial in my pocket. Like Dr. Oliver said, I have to trust someone, so the sooner I get the serum to him, the better.

"Good afternoon," says the gray-haired lady at the reception desk. "May I help you?"

"I'm here to see Doctor Oliver," I say.

"Identification please." I hand her my ID and wait. After a few moments, the words I'm dreading reach my ears. "I'm sorry, but you're not on the visitation list."

"What do you mean? I was just here yesterday."

"You do not have permission to enter."

I look down the hall and see Jesse. He waves and strides toward me.

"But how's that possible?" I ask the woman.

"I don't make the rules," she says. "I just follow them."

Jesse approaches and gives me a hug. "You're back to see Doctor Oliver."

I frown. "Yeah, but I guess I can't. They're denying me access."

"Is this true?" Jesse asks, looking at the receptionist.

"Correct. She has to leave."

"Are you sure it's not a mistake?" he asks. "She is good company for Doctor Oliver."

"It says so right here." She taps her fingernail on the computer screen. "Penelope Heavnor is not allowed inside the building."

"I've never heard of such a thing," Jesse says, shaking his head.

"She must leave now, or I'll call security to escort her out."

"Don't bother with security," I say, holding up my hands. "I'm leaving. Will you walk me out, Jesse?"

"Of course," he says. "I can't believe it."

"It's a mess," I say.

"I'm sorry to see you go, but thank you again for the dolls. My girls love them."

When we get to the door and step outside, I pause for a moment, looking at Jesse. "Do you have a piece of paper and a pen?"

"Yes." He reaches into his pocket and retrieves a notepad and pen.

I scribble a single word on the paper, tear it off, and shove it into my pocket. "Since I can't go inside, will you give Doctor Oliver a message?"

"Of course," he says.

"Give him this book and tell him I came by today, but they turned me away. Then tell him I'll bring him the other half of the puzzle."

"The other half of the puzzle?"

I nod. "Yes."

"Do you want me to give him the note?"

"No." I hand him back the pad and pen. "Just deliver the book and the message about the other half of the puzzle."

"I'll tell him as soon as I can."

Jesse takes the book and gives me another brief hug before saying goodbye. He returns inside, and I stroll toward the bus stop, wondering what to do. When I look down the side of the building, the sidewalk extends all the way to the back, past Dr. Oliver's room. His is the second from the end, and I follow the path, locating his window. Glancing to my left and right to make sure I'm alone, I press my nose against the glass and stare inside. It takes a moment for my eyes to focus, but Dr. Oliver rests in the recliner. He might be sleeping. I tap on the window, and his eyes spring open. I wave at him and smile. After a few seconds, he seems to recognize me, and nods his head as an acknowledgement. I hold up the paper that says "FRIDAY."

I hold it there until I'm sure he's seen it, then pull away from the window when the jangle of laughter hits my ears. Scanning the area, I see no one and realize the voices are coming from the back of the building. I follow the noise and peek around the corner. Fernando and another worker are smoking and talking outside the employee and service entrance.

That night I call Tara. "Do you have a southern accent yet?" I ask.

"You tell me," she says.

"Not yet, but you'll be saying 'y'all' in no time."

"I'll start saying it just to bug you."

I close my bedroom door. "So, how's the new school?"

"Okay. Bigger than Central, and people actually dress up for class."

"They do?"

"The girls wear sundresses with makeup and heels, and the guys wear slacks and button-down shirts."

I glance into my closet, which contains only one dress and no heels. "Yikes. Are you sticking with jeans and T-shirts?"

"If I can, but my mom took me shopping. She wants me to look more ladylike, but I'm going to hold out as long as possible."

I laugh. "Good luck with that."

"I'll need it. So, what's up with you? Spending more time at the old-folks' home?"

"I can't visit anymore. They banned me."

"They can do that?"

"It's bullshit. I'm not a family member. I didn't think it was a problem because Dr. Hughes asked me about it the other day."

"But something changed," says Tara.

I slam my closet door shut. "It's probably that bitch Helga. I'm a little worried about her, but I don't want to get into it right now."

"What happened?"

I nibble on my fingernail. "Did you destroy the things from that day like you said you would?"

"Absolutely. Destroyed. Never to be found again."

"Good. Just erase that day from your mind. You've never seen or heard anything about it."

"Is somebody asking questions?" she asks.

I plop down on my bed. "Not really, but it's better if we never speak of it again. Ever."

"I'll take it to the grave."

"Promise?"

"Cross my heart and hope to die," Tara says.

"Thanks," I say. "It's late. I should probably let you go."

"So I can get my beauty sleep?"

I smile. "Talk again soon, okay?"

"You know we will."

I end the call and curl into the fetal position on my left side. I place my other pillow over my head to block out any light or sound. What am I going to do? Helga found the glove. She has the other vial. They found a witness at the cemetery. I'm banned from Oak Bluff. How in the world am I going to get the vial to Dr. Oliver?

Chapter
29

On Wednesday morning, I arrive at the clinic a little late. During my ride to work, I review the story in my head a dozen times. If Dr. Hughes asks me about the security video, the only time I've been inside her house was that Saturday during the storm.

When I enter the reception area, two dogs and their owners wait for their appointments. Christina is busy on the phone. I give Opal a pat on the head before going to the back. Dr. Hughes stops me in the hall.

"I only have a minute," she says. "I need to talk to you in my office."

Here it comes. She's going to ask me about the video.

We enter the office and Dr. Hughes turns around to face me. "Overall, you've been a good worker, but I have to let you go."

"Let me go?" I ask.

"You're fired," she says.

My heart drops like a rock into my stomach. "Why?"

"You lied on the visitation form at the nursing home. You're not Doctor Oliver's granddaughter, and there's no school club. I can't have a liar working here."

"But that was the only way I could talk to him," I say.

She crosses her arms over her chest. "It's a lie."

"Can I at least tell Doctor Oliver goodbye?"

She shakes her head. "I don't need you bothering him, and I don't need dishonest people working here."

"Sorry." I bow my head and take a deep breath. "I should have asked for permission."

"But you didn't."

I keep my chin pointed down, but look up. "I thought I was doing something good."

Dr. Hughes stares at me with cold, hard eyes. "You don't know what's good for him."

I swallow the bile in my throat and press my lips together, focusing on the wall behind her while she continues.

"He's incompetent and doesn't know any better."

"But he seems fine," I say.

"He's not fine. I'm his conservator, and I decide on his behalf. You're not permitted to visit."

I hang my head and look at the floor. The familiar tug of tears emerges, and I bite my tongue to force them back. "I thought it would brighten the spirits of a lonely old man."

"You were wrong. Meeting him was a waste of time."

I look up and her face freezes in a frown, her arms clamped across her chest. Nothing I say will change her mind.

"Get your things and leave."

Her words cut through me like a whip, and I break down, releasing a flood of tears. They slide down my face, and I wipe them away with my fingers. I want to crawl under the desk and hide. Without another word, she opens the door to her office and I scoot down the hall to the bathroom. I try to compose myself by splashing cold water on my face, but my eyes are red and swollen.

On my way out, I stop by the reception desk.

"Bye," I say to Christina, choking back my humiliation.

"You're going?" she asks.

"I got fired."

"Oh, Penn, I'm so sorry." She stands to give me a hug. "What happened?"

"It's a long story." Where would I even begin?

"It's going to be all right." She tightens her hug and rubs my back.

I nod. If I try to speak, I'll start crying again.

"I'll miss you," says Christina.

I drag myself out the door to my bicycle, and don't even look for the *280zx*. I just want to go home. When I get there, it's quiet.

Thank god I don't have to face my mom right now. I close my bedroom door and bury myself under the covers. In the semi-darkness, I text Mel.

I got fired. Typing the words makes me remember Sasha's voice and my stomach churns.

No way, he texts. In a few seconds, my phone vibrates.

"Hey," I say.

"Are you okay?" Mel asks.

"I guess." I pull the covers off my head.

"What happened?"

As I tell him, my tears return, and my face burns with shame.

"That's brutal."

"I feel like a total shit. I tried to apologize and say it was just a volunteer gig, but she was too pissed off to care."

"It was a credible story."

I sniffle and find a tissue to blow my nose. "I can't visit Doctor Oliver anymore."

"She contacted them already?"

"Yesterday. I'm banned from the building."

"Damn. We knew it was a risk."

"But it's such a bummer. My visits were going so well."

"You learned a lot from him."

I roll over onto my stomach. "I know, but not enough. I really want to know if TR-97 can help my dad."

"You may never find out," he says.

"But I don't want to give up."

"Maybe it's for the best."

"That's easy for you to say. It's not *your* dad."

"What are you going to do with the serum?" he asks.

"I don't know yet."

"But you can't bring it to him."

I pause for a moment, my mind spinning. "I have some ideas."

"Maybe you should destroy it. Just get rid of it so nobody finds it."

"But then it can't help anyone."

"Think about it, Penn. It's been nothing but trouble."

I rest my forehead on the bed. "At least I got to meet Doctor O."

"And it pushed you to get a job."

"And now I'm jobless again."

"I'll be home on Saturday. Wait for me, and we can decide what to do then."

I sigh. "Okay, Mel. See you Saturday."

About ten minutes later, my phone vibrates again, and I glance at the screen. It's an unknown number from a strange area code. I usually ignore those calls, but something compels me to answer this one.

"Hello," I say.

"Is this Penelope Heavnor?" the caller asks. I freeze. It sounds like the same female that left me the voicemail.

"She's not here," I squeak, attempting to disguise my voice. "Do you want to leave a message?"

"Tell her to return this call before nine o'clock tonight. It's a matter of life and death."

I gasp. "Whose life?"

"Just tell her. She'll know what I mean."

The line goes silent and I stare at the phone in my hand. Whose life does she mean? Dr. Oliver's? Mine? I roll over onto my side and hug my pillow. Thank god it's still morning. I have time to come up with a plan.

———

At eight-thirty that evening, I call the unknown number and wait. My heart pounds like the hooves of a thoroughbred.

"Is this Penelope?" the voice on the other end asks without a greeting.

"Yes," I say.

"You have something of mine, and I want it back."

"What are you talking about?"

"It's too late for games. Hand it over, or I'll call the police."

"Hand what over?"

"Don't play dumb. I know you have it. Bring it in the backpack, or I'll turn your fingerprints and all my evidence over to the police."

Oh shit. The glove. The video. The backpack. "What if I don't have it?"

"Like I said, don't play games with me."

It's Helga, but she's trying to disguise her voice.

"Okay," I say. "I don't want trouble. I'll bring it to you on Friday."

"Bring it to me tomorrow."

My voice drops an octave. "If you want it, you have to wait until Friday."

I hear static on the line. Did she hang up?

"Nine o'clock Friday morning, at Sandwich Buddies on Monroe Street. If you're not there, I'm going to report you to the police."

The line goes dead before I can reply, and I'm left holding the phone against my ear. My hand shakes, and my shirt has stains under the armpits. I have one day to figure this out.

Chapter
30

The next morning, my mom knocks on my bedroom door. It startles me awake, but at least I'm not trapped in the running dream.

"Penn? Are you up? It's almost nine. You'll be late for work."

"I don't work today. I'm playing golf with Dad."

"Sorry, honey, I didn't know. I'm leaving."

"See you later," I say.

"Sorry to wake you. Bye."

I lie in bed for a while, staring at the ceiling. Maybe I should call Mel and tell him what's going on. He'll be furious with me, but he'll just have to get over it. I find his name on my recent call list and hit SEND. He picks up after two rings.

"Hey there. What's up?" he asks.

"I'm going to get rid of the serum," I say.

"You're not going to wait for me?"

I sit up in bed. "I need to do it right away."

"Did something happen?"

I scratch a bug bite on the back of my neck. "Not really. I'll explain later."

"How are you going to do it?"

"I haven't decided yet. What do you think?"

"Make sure you do it in several steps, mostly away from your house."

"Where?" I ask.

"Take it somewhere you've never been before, like a fast-food restaurant bathroom. Open the bottle and pour the contents into the toilet, then flush a couple of times."

"Then what?"

"Wipe your fingerprints from the lid and throw it into the trash can at a different restaurant."

"Not the vial?"

"Wipe the vial and put it inside several small plastic bags. Find someplace to break the glass with a hammer."

I get out of bed and open my closet. "Can I do that at home?"

"Yeah, but don't let anyone see you. Crush the vial until the glass is like a powder."

"Then dump the bag?"

"No. Take it to the lake. Wade out into the water with the plastic bag and release the pulverized glass."

I nearly drop the phone. "I have to get in the lake?"

"Yes. Swirl the bag around so the glass disappears. Then throw the bag away in one of the trash cans."

"Are you sure I need to do all that?"

"If you don't want it traced back to you," he says.

"Got it."

"Can I call you later? We're supposed to go sailing."

"Later," I say.

Around noon, I change into golf shorts and a clean T-shirt. My dad will be here soon. I make a ham and cheese sandwich and sit at the table with a bag of Fritos and a root beer. I skim through the newspaper, looking for any mention of the cemetery vandalism incident. Nothing. I forgot to tell Mel about the report of a witness, but it can wait until Saturday.

Underneath the newspaper, a stack of mail begs for attention. Most of the letters are addressed to my mom, but one has my dad's name on it. It's from the Mendota Fire Department. A bold red stamp covers part of the envelope. URGENT. IMMEDIATE RESPONSE REQUIRED. I put it in my pocket. I'll give it to him when he picks me up.

I flip through the others. My mom already opened the one from Community Mortgage Company. I peek inside at the letter: "Mortgage Billing Statement: Past Due. You are notified that unless you pay the amount stated by August 15, we have the right to begin foreclosure on the property." Foreclosure? I look at my phone. Today is the sixteenth.

A large white envelope from Dominic & Dorrey, Attorneys at Law, captures my attention. Lawyers? This can't be good. I shouldn't look, but it's also open, so I pull out the papers. I only have to read the top line to know what this means: "Petition for Divorce."

I cram the papers back into the envelope and glance at my phone. Twelve-thirty. My dad should be here any minute. I rinse my plate and leave it in the sink, then grab a water bottle. I notice the red blinking light on the answering machine next to the phone. Almost nobody calls the land line. I press the PLAY button and listen.

"I'm calling for Jason Heavnor. This is Sheila Jacobsen from the City of Mendota, employment development department. We've been trying to reach you. Please contact our office right away."

I better tell him about that, too.

At twelve forty-five, my dad isn't here. I pace around the kitchen and consider putting my plate in the dishwasher. Did he forget again? I text him, then call. He doesn't answer, and my call goes directly to voicemail.

"Hey, it's Penn. Are you on your way? Call me."

At one o'clock, I'm angry, and I stomp around the kitchen. Dammit. Where is he? I call him again and leave another message.

"We're supposed to play golf today. Where are you?"

I try one more time at one-fifteen. "What's up, Dad? We're late for our tee time. Call me."

At one-twenty, I call my mom. She picks up right away. "Hi, honey. Is it urgent? I'm in a meeting."

"Have you heard from Dad?"

"No, and I can't talk right now."

"He was supposed to be here."

"You know your father. Call him. Sometimes he forgets."

I continue pacing. "I tried calling. He didn't answer."

"He's probably out for a run or something. I have to go."

"Where does he live? Do you know?"

"The address is on the notepad by the phone. We'll talk later."

"Bye," I say, but she has already ended the call. I find the address: 3102 Nautilus Drive. That's less than a mile from here.

I shove my phone into my back pocket and retrieve my bike from the garage. If he's going to ignore my calls, I'm going to track him down and give him a piece of my mind. I'm going to tell him how fucking angry I am about the divorce. And I'm going to tell him he needs to get his shit together. I pedal fast, as rage and adrenaline pump my legs up and down. When I get to the house, I throw my bike onto the grass and rush to the front door. I ring the doorbell and wait. Nobody answers, so I bang on the door. Nothing. None of his neighbors are outside, so I pound on the door again, then try the doorknob. It's unlocked, and I step inside.

"Dad? It's Penn. Are you here?"

The living room is empty, except for a cushioned loveseat and a wooden coffee table piled with empty beer cans and fast food bags. I walk into the kitchen and see dishes piled in the sink. My dad's cell phone rests on the counter.

"Dad?" I turn and proceed down a short hallway. Maybe he's in the bedroom. I glance to my right into the bathroom. The light is on and the floor is littered with plastic pill bottles and white lids. All of them are empty.

"DAD? WHERE ARE YOU?"

I lunge toward the bedroom and find my dad face down on the bed in a puddle of vomit. I drop to his side and prod his shoulder.

"Dad? Are you okay? Wake up!"

He doesn't respond, and the stench makes me retch. I pull my phone from my pocket and dial 911. Shit, shit, shit. Please don't be dead.

"Nine-one-one, what's your emergency?" says a female voice.

"My dad passed out. I think he took a bunch of pills."

"Is he alive? Can you find a pulse?"

I put my fingers on his neck and press down. "I don't know. His skin is warm."

"Is there a pulse?"

"I can't find one."

"Try the inside of his wrist."

My throat tightens and tears spill from my eyes. "I don't feel anything," I say.

"Remain calm. Put your hand in front of his nose and mouth. Can you feel his breath?"

"He's on his stomach. There's vomit everywhere. I don't know what to do."

"What's the address? We'll send an ambulance right away."

I give her the address and start sobbing. Oh my god, please be alive. You can't die.

"Stay on the phone with me. It's going to be okay. What's your name?"

"Penelope Heavnor."

"What's your dad's name?"

"Jason."

"Do you know what pills he took?"

I wipe my eyes with the back of my hand. "I saw some bottles in the bathroom."

"Get them and tell me what they say."

I sprint to the bathroom and grab the four bottles. I bring them back to the bedroom and read the labels to her.

"Do you know if the bottles were full?"

"I don't know. I've never been to my dad's house before. He just moved here a few months ago."

"That's okay. The ambulance is close by. Is the front door unlocked?"

"Yeah, the door is open."

"The paramedics will be there in two minutes."

"I hear the siren."

"Go meet them at the door," says the woman. I run to the front door and out into the yard.

Chapter
31

That night, after waiting at the hospital for hours, I can't sleep. Even though the doctors told me my dad will survive, he must stay in the mental health ward until he's stable. That could be four or five days. When I undressed for bed, the letter from the Mendota Fire Department fell out of my pocket. I opened it and learned my dad failed the psychological evaluation and they demoted him.

I curl myself into a ball, pulling the covers up around my neck. He could have died. Why would he do that to himself? Why would he do that to us? Is life really that bad? Tears dampen my pillow. I doze off a few times but wake up with the image of him motionless on the bed, the stench of vomit in the room.

In the morning, my mom paces around the kitchen cradling her coffee mug. She has dark circles under her eyes. Her hair is a tangled mess. "Did you get any sleep last night?" she asks. "I couldn't sleep at all, but I didn't want to bother you."

"I'm okay," I say.

"I'm so sorry, honey. I didn't realize he was so bad, that he was that depressed."

I stare at the mound of Cheerios in the bowl in front of me, knowing I won't eat them. He was pretending to be okay, putting on an act. We didn't know he was so close to the edge.

My mom rests her hands on my shoulders and bends down to kiss the top of my head. "I'm so glad you went over there. I hate to think what would have happened if you hadn't."

"I have to go to work," I say, standing and taking my bowl to the sink.

"Maybe you should take the day off."

"I can't." I lift my chin and clench my jaw, meeting her eyes.

"But we need to talk about this."

"Later," I say, leaving the house without another word. I can't talk right now. My dad is alive. The universe has spoken. There's still a chance.

The fresh air clears my head as I pedal to the bus stop on Whitney Way. I lock my bike to a signpost and wait for the bus to Oak Bluff. I had planned to destroy the serum, but I can't do that. And I'm not turning it over to Helga. The best chance to help my dad is Dr. Oliver's treatment. If Helga reports me to the police, at least I won't have the vial anymore.

When I reach the nursing home, I look at my phone. 9:45 A.M., right about the time some employees take a break and several deliveries arrive. I'm dressed in scrubs that match the color of their uniforms. We look identical, except my top doesn't have the Oak Bluff logo or a name tag. The vial rests in the left front pocket of my pants. I take a deep breath to calm myself.

My heart hammers as I peek around the corner of the building. Two workers exit their cars and move toward the entrance. This is my chance. Without a key card to unlock the door, I need to enter when someone else goes in or comes out. If I act like I work there, no one will question it. Oversize sunglasses shield my eyes and I hang back a little to make sure I'm the last one. I don't recognize either employee, which is good. I don't want to get anyone else in trouble. When I nod hello to a young woman, she holds the door for me. "Thanks," I say, and step into the service area.

I glance around and see doors leading to the kitchen, laundry, and pharmacy. Dr. Oliver's room is to the right, so I turn in that direction and stop. Every door needs a key card. While I consider my options, the door to the hall pops open, and a woman I recognize walks through. I can't remember her name. Bethany? I stare at the floor and reach for the door, grabbing it just in time. "Thanks," I mumble, proceeding into the hallway, letting the door close and lock behind me.

An employee down the hall looks in my direction, but turns to enter a resident's room. I hurry to room 103 and peer inside. Dr.

Oliver rests in his recliner. When I enter and close the door, he hears the click and looks up.

"Penelope," he says.

"This is probably the last time I'll see you," I say.

"I hope not," he says with a smile. "Thank you for the book." It rests in his lap.

"You're welcome." I reach into my pocket and grasp the vial. "I brought you the other half of the puzzle."

"Let me see it." Dr. Oliver extends his pale hand. I place the vial in his palm, and his fingers curl around it. He kisses his hand, then opens his fist. "Thank you." He closes his eyes and inhales a deep, wheezing breath.

"Helga's probably going to call the police."

"Why would she do that?" he asks.

"Because I was supposed to meet her and give her the vial. She said if I didn't, she'd notify the police."

"I doubt she'll do that. They'd have a lot of questions for her."

"You think she's bluffing?"

"Definitely. The last thing she wants is to involve the police."

I sit down in my chair. "That's a relief."

"You did the right thing bringing it here," he says, still gripping the vial.

"What are you going to do with it?"

"Change the world."

"Can you really do that?" I ask.

"Not by myself, but others will help, just as you have helped."

Dr. Hughes's words pop into my head. *He is delusional.* It's just a serum. It's not magic. But part of me wants to believe in miracles.

"Can I ask you a question?"

"Of course," says Dr. Oliver.

"Is hypnotism part of the treatment?"

He nods. "An important part."

"So it's real?"

"Hypnotherapy is real. You seem skeptical."

"It just sounds hokey."

"But it works if you have the right person leading that part of the treatment."

I cross my arms over my chest. "Like Helga?"

"You read the Treatment Protocol."

I nod.

"I'd appreciate it if you kept that confidential."

"Sure," I say, knowing I have a copy of the file at home.

"If you saved any of it, please shred or burn it."

He studies my face, and I nod again.

"So, how does it all work?" I ask.

"The TR-97 treatment?"

"Yeah."

Dr. Oliver inhales deeply and his chest rumbles. We stare at each other for a few moments before he speaks.

"A psychologist works with a patient for an extended period to uncover the source of their trauma. Then together, they discuss and create a new memory to replace that trauma. It can take years to prepare for the treatment. When the patient is ready, I inject the TR-97. A therapist hypnotizes the patient, inducing a tranquil state, then guiding him to the traumatic event. During that heightened emotional state, the drug acts on the amygdala. That part of the brain activates in response to fear and memories of traumatic events. While under hypnosis, the suggestion and repetition of the rehearsed positive outcome replaces the old memory with a new one."

"That sounds complicated," I say.

He nods. "Plenty of things can go wrong during the procedure."

"What went wrong with Harold Foster?"

"I'm not sure I'm the right person to ask about that."

I lean forward in my chair. "But he was your patient. It was your treatment."

"True, but in his case, I failed to follow protocol and left the room during his treatment. That's the main reason I pled guilty to the charge of criminal negligence."

"You left your patient?"

"I believed Francine and Helga could handle the situation. I was wrong."

"So, you don't know what happened?"

"Months later, when Harold took his life, Francine and Helga told very different stories about what happened. Everyone believed Helga."

I frown. "Do you believe Helga?"

He shakes his head. "I'm pretty certain she was the problem and blindsided Francine with her story. I couldn't help Francine because I had no first-hand knowledge, only what she told me. So, when I packed my office, I vowed to protect any sensitive files, hoping there was something that might save Francine."

"But she went to prison."

"She did, but some of the information may clear her name if she ever has the chance."

I nod, pretending to understand what he's talking about, but I'm lost. I think of my dad in the hospital and wonder if I should tell Dr. Oliver.

"Do you know anything about dreams?" I ask.

"Dreams?"

"What they mean."

He shakes his head. "Not much."

"I have the same dream a lot. I want to know why."

"A recurring dream? Tell me about it."

I sit back in my chair. "I'm alone, running, but it feels like slow motion. My arms and legs are heavy. I think someone is chasing me because I look over my shoulder and fall. I always wake up before my face hits the pavement."

"Running is a classic theme in dreams, especially ones where you feel you're not getting anywhere."

"Really?"

He folds his hands in his lap. "A psychologist might ask you what you're running away from."

"But that's just it. I don't know. I never remember how the dream starts."

"It's not what you're running from in the dream, it's what feelings or emotions you're trying to escape in real life."

I look at the floor.

"So, Penelope, what feelings are you trying to get away from?"

A jumble of thoughts flood my brain. I turn my head to the window and stare into the parking lot.

"It's okay to take your time," he says, "but typically, it's the first thing that pops into your head."

I close my eyes and swallow, then look at Dr. Oliver. "It's my dad. He's in the hospital. He tried to commit suicide yesterday."

"I'm sorry to hear that."

I bite my lip and look down at my lap.

"How does that make you feel?" he asks.

"Awful," I say.

"How so? Can you be more specific?"

"I'm angry that he would even think about doing that to me and my mom. Isn't divorce bad enough?"

"What else?" he asks.

"I'm sad because he almost died." I press my fingers on the inside corners of my eyes. I don't want to cry.

"And?"

"I feel helpless, like there's nothing I can do to make him better." Tears run down my cheeks and I wipe them away.

Dr. Oliver's voice is calm and caring. "We only know another's feelings if they reveal them to us."

"Something has been wrong for months, and I can't help him."

"That's a lot for a young person to handle. No wonder you're running in your dreams."

I nod my head and take a deep breath.

"It might help for you to talk with someone too, a professional. They can help you sort out your feelings and understand that nothing your dad does is your fault."

"Okay." I swallow the lump of emotions in my throat and blink back the tears. It feels good to speak the words out loud and share the burden.

When we hear someone talking in the hall, it snaps me back to the present.

"I should go," I say. "I'm not supposed to be here."

"Jesse told me," he says.

"If someone finds me here, I'll be in big trouble, and you, too, probably."

"I can handle whatever comes my way, but your journey isn't over."

I stare at Dr. Oliver. "It's not?"

"It's time to pass the puzzle along to the right people."

"What do you mean?"

Dr. Oliver glances outside. "Someone is waiting for you in the parking lot."

"Who?" I ask.

"You'll know the car."

"The *280zx*?"

"That sounds right." He pulls the envelope from the pocket of his chair and slips the vial inside it. "Take this now, before it's too late."

When I grasp the package, we hear commotion in the hall and my heart skips a beat.

"Get out of my way before I knock you down!"

Oh shit. I know that voice, and I'm already standing when Helga bursts through the door. She stops, placing her hands on her hips, elbows out, blocking the exit.

Jesse appears beside her, attempting to calm her down. "Ma'am, you must wait for an attendant." When he sees me, his eyes widen, and his mouth drops open.

"I don't wait for anyone," she says, turning away from Jesse to face Dr. Oliver and me. "Sasha was right. She said I'd find you here."

"What do you want?" asks Dr. Oliver.

"I'm here to take back something of mine," she says.

"Over my dead body," says Dr. Oliver.

"Suit yourself." Helga pulls the small gun from her purse and points it at Dr. Oliver.

How did she get that past the receptionist?

"Ma'am, you can't have that in here," says Jesse, stepping forward into the room.

For a split second, Helga shifts her focus to Jesse. Dr. Oliver rises from his chair, grabs the Nancy Drew book, and throws it at Helga, shouting, "GET OUT OF HERE!" As the book flies across the room, a small gap opens between Helga and Jesse. Dr. Oliver wobbles on his swollen feet, and Jesse leaps to support him. I grip the envelope in my sweaty fingers and lower my shoulder, checking Helga like a hockey player. She yelps in pain as she hits the floor, and I sprint out the door. Without a pass key, I turn right toward the lobby, racing for the exit, ignoring the voice behind me yelling, "CALL SECURITY!"

My focus remains on the main entrance until I pass Agnes Gerhardt's room. She lingers in her doorway, leaning on a walker. As I run by, she points a bony finger at me and screams, "THIEF! The witch is a thief!"

When her words reach my eardrums, I hear footsteps behind me. As I approach the lobby, I glance over my shoulder and stumble, kicking a CAUTION: WET FLOOR sign. I fall headfirst, just like in my dream, but my hands hit the tile first and I avoid smacking my face. I'm still clutching the envelope as I scramble to my feet, racing out the door into the parking lot.

I search to the left for the silver Datsun, but don't see it. Dammit. Where is the car? When I turn to my right, Sasha hurries toward me. Her eyes narrowed, her mouth pinched.

"What are *you* doing here?" she demands.

I glance around her into the parking lot, then at the envelope in my hand. "Delivering a message," I say, squeezing the package tighter.

"To whom?"

"A friend."

Sasha scrutinizes me, staring at the envelope.

I pull it behind my back, hiding it with my legs.

"You went to see my father," she says.

I swallow hard and feel the blood drain from my face.

"And, that's mine." She points to the package. "Give it to me!"

"It's for my dad," I say.

"That belongs to me."

I take a step backward, scanning the lot for the silver car.

"Don't move," she says. "Give me it to me, or I'm calling the police." She unzips her purse, but instead of grabbing a cell phone, she lunges for the envelope.

I yank it away just in time, then turn and run.

"Get back here! That's mine!"

I dash down the side of the building, not daring to look back. Where is the car? Dr. Oliver said it would be here. As I round the corner near the employee entrance, the silver car streaks into view. The windows are down, and an older woman is at the wheel.

"I'm here!" I shout.

"Get in!" says the woman.

I fling open the door and jump inside the car. She steps on the accelerator, squealing the tires as we leave the parking lot behind.

Chapter
32

The car races around a corner, and I grab my seatbelt, clicking the buckle into position. "Oh my god," I say. "She almost had me."

"Who did? What happened?" she asks.

"Helga showed up in Doctor Oliver's room with a gun, and then Sasha was waiting for me outside."

"Oh, goodness. I hope Helga didn't shoot anyone."

I shake my head. "I didn't hear any gunshots."

"Well, we can't go back to find out," she says, looking over her shoulder.

"And Sasha was furious."

"I'm just glad you got out of there."

"Who are you?" I ask, after catching my breath.

"Francine Baker."

"Francine? You're not in prison?"

"Not anymore," she says, speeding through a yellow stoplight. As we drive, she tells me she married and changed her name to Susan Wilcox. The car belongs to her son-in-law Roger.

I'm still grasping the envelope when I notice the wet stain on the side. No! Tell me I didn't break the vial when I fell. My throat constricts, and the familiar sting of tears nudges my eyes.

"Are you all right?" she asks. "You're awfully pale."

"The vial broke," I say, holding up the envelope for her to see. "I fell in the hallway on the way out."

"Are you hurt?"

I shake my head. "I panicked because someone was chasing me."

"Don't worry about it, dear. The papers are the most important part."

"Are you sure? Doctor Oliver said the serum was the other half of the puzzle."

"It's going to be all right. Hopefully, James is safe too."

After I've had a few more minutes to calm down, my brain whirs back to life. "How did you know to meet me in the parking lot today?"

"James, I mean Doctor Oliver, told me."

"But how did he get in touch with you? He doesn't have a telephone, and his daughter doesn't allow visitors."

"I could ask you the same question, but I already know the answer. My niece Kathryn works at the reception desk."

"Kat? She let me visit the first time."

Susan nods. "When you showed up, she called me. We thought it was better to approve you as a guest first and see what you wanted."

"But then you changed your mind?"

She shakes her head. "Sasha banned you."

"I figured," I say with a frown. "She was pretty upset when she found out I was visiting Doctor Oliver."

"I bet she was."

"Did Kat get a job at Oak Bluff to watch Doctor Oliver?"

"No. Kat's been working there for several years. She agreed to monitor my sister, who is a resident, since I didn't live in town. It was a lucky coincidence that Sasha moved Doctor Oliver to Oak Bluff."

"Who is your sister?" I ask.

"Agnes Gerhardt."

My mouth drops open. "Agnes is your sister?"

"Yes."

"You're Frankie?" I ask.

"Agnes has called me that since we were little girls."

"But now your name is Susan."

"I wanted to change it and leave Francine in the past, but my sister has dementia. She doesn't understand."

I nod. "So you visited Doctor Oliver. That's how you planned today."

"I saw him yesterday, and he told me to be ready."

"Is your son-in-law a private investigator?"

Susan grips the steering wheel and speeds around another corner. "Yes."

"Why was he following me?" I ask.

"He had been following Helga ever since she reappeared in Mendota, but then you appeared, and he had to follow both of you."

I let the information sink into my brain as we merge onto the interstate. "Did he send me the text messages telling me to stay away from Doctor Oliver?"

"Yes. And he let the air out of your bike tires. Sorry about that."

"That was you?"

"We wanted to see who you would call for help, and determine whether you were working with Helga or Sasha."

I sigh and stare at the envelope in my hands. "I knew someone was following me. I'm just glad it wasn't Paulson."

"Ted Paulson?"

"You know him?"

"No," she says, "but Doctor Oliver told me about him."

"So, you know he works for Feester, and has been trying to buy the TR-97 documents from Sasha."

"Doctor Oliver didn't want to do that. He's convinced that Paulson was only interested in the money and a promotion."

"He's right. Paulson doesn't seem like the generous, compassionate type."

"He'll be disappointed when he learns Sasha doesn't have the documents," Susan says with a smirk. "But, that's life."

I shudder and slouch down in my seat. "He won't be angry?"

Susan glances at me. "If he is, he'll get over it. He's a glorified salesman. They have thick skin."

"I never want to see him again," I say, crossing my arms over my chest.

"You're safe now, especially since you no longer have the file or the serum."

The truth gnaws at my gut as I nod my head and look out the window. I need to burn my copy of the file before anyone discovers it.

"Where are we going?" I ask.

"The University of Chicago."

"That's a long drive."

"About two hours. Is that a problem?"

I shrug. "My mom might worry."

"You can call her."

I nod.

"For the next few hours," she says, "it's probably best for you to be with me than at work or home."

I turn and look at Susan. "Am I in danger?"

"I'm not sure, but Sasha can be unpredictable."

"Well, I don't have a job. She fired me."

"When was that?"

"Wednesday," I say.

Susan looks over her right shoulder to change lanes, but glances at me. "It's for the best. Sasha is toxic."

I sigh. "I thought she was nice at first, but she has a mean streak."

"Sounds like you met the real Sasha."

"I guess she's not very nice to her dad, either."

"No, she's not."

I shift in my seat and scratch my head. "But Helga seems like the mean one."

"Actually, Helga turned out to be helpful."

"No way."

"She turned over the other vial of TR-97 yesterday."

"You're kidding?" I say.

"She agreed to give it up in exchange for us not reporting her to the police."

"Why would she do that?"

"To avoid questioning about the cemetery vandalism. Somebody reported seeing her car in the area that night."

I sit up straight and turn toward Susan. "They reported seeing *her* car?"

"I guess so. She was worried if they found her with the serum, they'd accuse her."

"What a relief," I say, running my hand through my hair. "I was worried someone had seen my friend Mel's car."

Susan gives me a puzzled look.

I take a deep breath. "I knew Helga had something to do with digging up the grave. My friends and I heard her in the cemetery that night talking to a guy. They were looking for the vial."

"You were there?"

I nod. "On Friday the thirteenth. I found a vial earlier in the day when I was looking for my golf ball. We went back to check out the hole that night."

Susan laughs. "And Helga didn't think anyone knew.

"I recognized her voice."

"Helga didn't confess. She actually blamed Sasha, but Helga was the one with the vial."

"Why would she just hand it over?"

"Helga told me she was following Sasha's orders to dig up the grave and get the vials. They planned to gather the information and sell it, sharing the profits. But when Sasha couldn't find the right file, she accused Helga of stealing it. Since Helga didn't have the file, she gave me the vial to avoid having any incriminating evidence."

I massage my temples with my fingertips. "But Helga called me and wanted to meet this morning. She wanted me to give her the other vial."

"You planned to meet at the nursing home?" asks Susan.

I shake my head. "At Sandwich Buddies."

"Are you sure you were going to meet Helga?"

"Not one hundred percent," I say, "but I thought it was Helga."

"It was probably Sasha impersonating Helga, and I bet she wanted the files."

"She didn't want the serum?"

"I don't think so," says Susan. "Her focus was on finding the files."

I rest my head in my hands. "I stole the file. Will the police come after me?"

Susan shakes her head. "Not if they can't identify you on the video, and you don't have any of the evidence."

Acid burns my stomach and I envision the documents nestled between my mattress and box spring. I need to destroy those as soon as possible.

"Without your help," says Susan, "we would never have been able to accomplish our goal."

"Which is?"

"To allow the University of Chicago to develop Doctor Oliver's treatment for PTSD."

I lean my head back against the seat, watching the rows of cornstalks flip past. We cross a small river, and a raft of ducks floats on the placid water. Maybe Dr. Oliver can change the world. I close my eyes for a moment, feeling the vibration of the vehicle on the road.

"Do you think Doctor Oliver is crazy?" I ask.

"What?" Susan asks.

"He was in a mental hospital for two years."

Susan doesn't respond right away, and an image of my dad pops into my head. He's in the hospital. Is he crazy? Should they lock him up? The hum of the tires fills the void and my eyelids grow heavy.

"He's not crazy," says Susan. "Obsessed? Passionate? Broken? All of those things, but not crazy."

"Is it true that Sasha had him locked in there?"

"He told you."

I nod. "Who locks up their dad?"

She sighs. "We're all a little crazy, but at least he's out."

"But living in that prison."

"He'll be okay," she says. "He hasn't lost his focus. TR-97 is still important to him. It was his life's work."

I ponder this, Dr. Oliver's life and his work, and how intertwined they were. I guess it's not uncommon. It suits Susan, Sasha, my mom, and at one time, my dad, too. Maybe that's what happens when you grow up.

I surprise Susan with another question. "What happened during Harold Foster's treatment?"

Susan looks at me and grimaces.

"I asked Doctor Oliver," I say, "but he said he wasn't the right person to ask."

"It's difficult for me to talk about," she says.

"I understand if you don't want to."

She nods. "Maybe it's good to talk about it. I've kept it inside for so long."

For the next hour, Susan tells me about Harold Foster and the two years they prepared for his TR-97 treatment. They had agreed on a positive memory to replace the traumatic one, but when Helga hypnotized him, she also hypnotized Susan. Once Helga realized Susan was in a trance and unable to guide Mr. Foster through the details of his positive memory, Helga reinforced the traumatic memory instead. At the end of the treatment, when Susan regained consciousness, Helga acted like everything had gone well. Susan had doubts because she couldn't remember the encounter. Both of their reports stated the treatment was a success, but after Mr. Foster committed suicide, Helga presented an alternate report that claimed Susan screwed up. Since Susan couldn't recall the details from that day, she relied on her own report of success. The jury found her guilty.

I shake my head. "Why would Helga do that?"

"She was jealous of me and Doctor Oliver, and our relationship. He and I were close, and he confided in me after his wife died. We often shared dinner at the office, discussing patients and the research. Helga tried to be a surrogate mother to Sasha, hoping Doctor Oliver would notice and include her in his life. I think Helga even thought she might be his next wife. When that didn't pan out, Helga spread rumors around the office that Doctor Oliver and

I were having an affair, which wasn't true. Our relationship was strictly professional."

"So, Helga wanted revenge?"

Susan nods. "She wanted to hurt Doctor Oliver and me, which she did, but she ignored the damage she inflicted on Harold Foster and his family."

I scrunch up my face like I'm in pain. "You must be furious with Helga."

"I think my anger has faded."

"I would be raging," I say, balling my fingers into fists. "You had to go to prison, change your name, and start life over, and Helga got away with no punishment."

"I suppose I'm still a little bitter, but she didn't win this round."

I nod and relax my hands. "I guess she went to a lot of trouble for nothing."

"And her trouble will end up benefitting Doctor Oliver and me." Susan points to the envelope. "We have the Treatment Protocol and the key to the safe-deposit box."

"Is that what the key is for?" I ask.

Susan smiles. "The future looks bright."

"But Helga still has her career and her reputation. You have neither."

"We'll see about that," she says. "Revenge is a dish best served cold."

I stare at Susan for a moment, then gaze out the window. Is that from Shakespeare? What does she mean? Maybe I don't want to know.

Chapter
33

Several days later, I visit my dad in the hospital. His physical condition has stabilized, but he plans to spend another week in a mental health facility. He smiles and gives me a giant hug when I walk into the room. I bury my face in his chest, feeling his arms wrap around me. The warmth of his body and the tightness of his embrace make me feel like a little girl again. I cling to him and he surrenders. When I'm ready, I let go and take a step backward. He sits on the twin bed and I take a seat on the chair.

"How are you doing?" I ask. "You look good."

"Better. I'm going to get better," he says, bobbing his head up and down.

"I know you will."

"You look good too," he says. "How are you?"

"Okay. It's been hard. I'm just trying to understand."

"Understand?"

I glance at my hands and then at my dad. "Why you took the pills?"

His face, ears and neck flush, and he drops his head, closing his eyes.

"I'm sorry if it's too soon," I say, shaking my head. But we almost lost you, and I don't want it to happen again.

He opens his mouth to speak, but stops, lifting his head, then lowering it again. I don't fill the silence. I wait and let him find the words he's looking for.

"I hope I can talk to you about it someday," he says, "but I'm not ready."

"Okay."

"Maybe we can play golf again soon," he says.

"Or just hang out," I say.

"I'd like that." He gives me a weak smile and we stare at each other. He shifts his position on the bed and I gnaw on my thumbnail.

"It's okay to ask for help," I say.

"You were trying to tell me that weeks ago."

"We all need help sometimes."

He bows his head and studies his hands. "Thanks for giving me a chance to get some help."

My throat tightens. "I need you, Dad."

A few tears slide down his unshaven face.

I clench my teeth to keep from crying, but it doesn't work. I can't believe I have any tears left.

"I need you too," he says.

We both stand and hug again.

"Maybe someday you can meet Doctor Oliver," I say.

"I would like that."

"I'll see you tomorrow," I say, and join my mom, who has been pacing in the waiting room. She tries to smile, but I can tell by her downcast eyes and hunched shoulders she's feeling anxious. I'm anxious too, but hopeful. My dad has a long way to go, but he wants to get better. We can help him, and maybe we can be a family again.

Later that day, I get a text from Susan Wilcox. *Dr. Oliver is fine. He thanks you again and hopes you are well.*

When I knocked Helga down on my way out of the room, the gun fell to the floor, and Jesse retrieved it. Helga didn't shoot anyone. They arrested her and charged her with aggravated assault. I smile when Susan tells me Helga could go to prison.

———

By mid-October, frost blankets the ground in the mornings, and colorful leaves parachute from the tree branches. My life as a high school junior keeps me busy with classes, homework, and weekends with friends. I've talked to a psychologist, and my subconscious no longer drags me through the running dream. I also got involved at school. To honor Dr. Oliver, I started an actual club called Meeting with History. Mel and Madison both joined, and with the help of our U.S. History teacher, we spend time with local veterans, listening to their stories and learning about their experiences.

Although Sasha made it impossible for me to visit Dr. Oliver, he occupies my thoughts. Susan sends me occasional updates, and I wrote Dr. Oliver a letter about the history club. She plans to work with an attorney who will petition the court to dissolve the conservatorship. Dr. Oliver would like to regain control of his life, and I hope he does so I can visit him again.

But, on this Saturday night, we're celebrating. Mel and I are going to the homecoming dance together since neither of us has a date. We finished taking photos at my house and hang out in the kitchen with my parents. Dad hasn't moved back home, but he looks healthy and seems a lot happier. He attends regular therapy sessions, and we play golf on the weekends when the weather cooperates. He came over tonight because he wants to see me wearing a dress.

While we talk and joke around, sharing some of our favorite photos on Instagram with Tara, the television news drones in the background. Mel and I pivot toward the screen when we hear a familiar name.

"Earlier today, the Mendota police arrested psychologist and bestselling author Helga Thorstad. She's already under investigation for assault charges stemming from an incident in August, but has now been charged with manslaughter in the death of Harold Foster, a former patient. Foster, a Gulf War veteran, committed suicide after receiving the controversial PTSD treatment, TR-97. This reporter learned Susan Wilcox brought the additional evidence to the attention of authorities.

"Wilcox, formerly known as Francine Baker, was a psychologist at Wisconsin State University, and worked alongside Thorstad. Ms. Baker changed her name after serving three years of a five-year prison sentence for manslaughter. Although a jury found her guilty, Baker has maintained her innocence. We understand the additional evidence she provided led police to seek a warrant for Thorstad's arrest, and Wilcox claims the same evidence will prove she was wrongly convicted."

We stare at the television, our mouths agape. "Holy crap," I say.

"That's nuts," says Mel.

"What?" my mom asks, turning to face me.

"I know the woman they arrested," I say, pointing at the television.

"You do?" asks my dad, turning to look.

"She was friends with Doctor Hughes."

"The veterinarian?"

I nod. "I can't believe it," I say. "Susan provided the additional evidence."

"Do you think it was in the file all along?" asks Mel.

"At least part of it."

"What file?" asks my mom, and Mel and I glance at each other.

When Mel returned from Florida, he and I burned my backpack and the copy of the TR-97 file in a barbeque pit at the park.

"It's a long story," I say.

"Forget about that for now," says my dad with a clap of his hands. "You two should focus on tonight's festivities. It's homecoming. The news can wait."

"That's right," says my mom, patting my shoulder. "Tell me about it later. You two need to get moving if you're going to eat dinner before the dance."

Even though the broadcast has shifted to the weather forecast, Mel and I linger a few minutes longer, shaking our heads and staring at the screen.

"Okay," I say. "See you later, Mom. Bye, Dad."

"What time will you be home?" asks my mom.

"Late," I say. "Madison is having a party after the dance."

"Mel, will you please get her home by midnight?"

"Yes, Mrs. Heavnor," he says.

We drive toward Central High School in Mel's Volvo, our heads buzzing with the news of Helga's arrest.

My spirits lift to the sky like a balloon filled with helium. "I really can't believe it," I say with a smile. "Helga will finally get what she deserves."

"And you helped catch the criminal," says Mel.

"Correction, *we* helped catch the criminal."

"Okay, *we*, but you did most of the work."

"Thanks," I say, with a grin. In my heart, I know justice will be served. I stare out the car window at the houses decorated for Halloween, knowing all is right in the universe.

www.ingramcontent.com/pod-product-compliance
Lightning Source LLC
Chambersburg PA
CBHW030657260626
47157CB00007B/2688